ANCIENT TIDE

GW00808267

This is an IndieMosh book

brought to you by MoshPit Publishing
an imprint of Mosher's Business Support Pty Ltd

PO Box 147
Hazelbrook NSW 2779

indiemosh.com.au

Copyright © Simon Harding 2016   simon-harding.com

The moral right of the author has been asserted in accordance
with the *Copyright Amendment (Moral Rights) Act* 2000.

All rights reserved. Except as permitted under the Australian
Copyright Act 1968 (for example, fair dealing for the purposes of
study, research, criticism or review) no part of this publication
may be reproduced, stored in a retrieval system, or transmitted
in any form or by any means, electronic, mechanical,
photocopying, recording or otherwise, without the written
permission of the publisher.

Cataloguing-in-Publication entry is available from the National
Library of Australia: http://catalogue.nla.gov.au/

Title:	Ancient Tide
Author:	Harding, Simon
ISBNs:	978-1-925595-67-3 (paperback)
	978-1-925595-29-1 (ebook – epub)
	978-1-925595-30-7 (ebook – mobi)

Cover layout by Ally Mosher   allymosher.com

Cover images from Adobe Stock.

This story is entirely a work of fiction. No character in this story
is taken from real life. Any resemblance to any person or persons
living or dead is accidental and unintentional. The author, their
agents and publishers cannot be held responsible for any claim
otherwise and take no responsibility for any such coincidence.

ANCIENT TIDE

Simon Harding

This book is dedicated to Tanya,
For whom the moon is always smiling

1

NONE OF THEM had seen it coming. Fate had lured them in. It had baited them with promises and then suckered each and every one of them. They had thought they were chasing destiny, thought that they could succeed where others had failed. None of them had been able to focus on anything else, such was the seductiveness of what was on offer. Even when it was too late, they had still clung to their hope, determined to the bitter and tragic end.

And now it was Lauren's turn. The memories she had inherited were intimidating in the extreme and she wanted none of the despair that oozed from the ghosts of those who had gone before her. Their histories were haunting and violent, their demises confronting. Their lives fizzed inside Lauren like soda bubbles, jostling to make it to the surface and share the misery they contained. As they did so, her intense green eyes welled with tears.

Along the way, each memory revealed snippets of what they had all been seeking. Now that fate was dangling the prize in front of Lauren, she began to understand why they had all pursued what was on offer against such daunting and impossible odds. That elusive prize was everything. The more she thought about it, the more she wanted it. It mattered not that death was almost certain, what was awaiting her if she succeeded was just so alluring. All she had to do was roll the dice, though fate had clearly loaded them.

Destiny had revealed itself to Lauren Kennedy at the end of a bleak October day in 1990. One of those where the lazy English sun had called in sick again and left the country shrouded in shadow. She had been at the beach. Evenings at the waterfront were always her time, a time when nothing else mattered, a total, sandy solitude, during which she reflected on what might have been, had her twenty-two years worked out differently and had she been able to pursue her dream. There was much for her to be grateful about, not least that she lived in a part of the world that she adored. There were so many special memories tied up in this south-eastern tip of England. The nearby marshes were the first place she had ever seen sheep, and she remembered the sound of the newborn lambs calling to their mothers in a pneumatic chorus across acre upon acre of lush grass. And she had loved the joyous springtime drives along the course of the River Rother, as it writhed through the wetlands.

Life was different now. The innocence of her childhood had been ripped away from her when she lost her father seven years earlier. From that point on, she had made an unfortunate choice and there wasn't a day that passed in which she didn't regret making it.

Folkestone's one sandy bay was usually quiet during the winter anyway, but that night it was barren. The beach was pale and smooth, and any trace of humanity had been wiped like a shaken etch-a-sketch by the cleansing tide. The glow of the full moon had removed all colour. Even the swampy hue of the water was gone and its blackness seemed like a mourning outfit as it grieved for its fallen foot-soldiers, who continued to die on the beaches. One by one.

Usually Lauren found peace on the beach. It was an escape from the fearful reality in which she existed, but not on this particular day. There seemed to be an overwhelming sense of purpose all around her. The wind was whispering secrets as it toyed with her long liquorice locks, and the hairs at her nape prickled with excitement. A sense of the surreal surrounded her and it gnawed away at her like a determined rodent. Never before had she ever encountered such electricity in the air. She was fully alert. Wired. All of her senses seemed super, tuned up to the maximum. The pebbles that the sea tossed gently onto the sand thudded in her ears like cannonballs as they landed. Occasional clouds darkened the vivid moon and threw spectral shadows across the empty beach. She flinched as her eyes registered their presence.

The ambience was oppressive as it continued to

invade her thoughts. There was a sense of urgency. Imminence. The more she tried to dismiss it, the more forceful it became until, in the end, it was screaming at her to listen. But to what? There was no-one. Nothing. The beach was deserted and silent, save the remorseless murmur of breaking waves that spat malevolently as they impaled themselves on the sand.

Lauren felt the need to move. In itself, that was nothing different. She was, after all, a constant fidget and had been since the day she was born. Her parents had often reminded her just how difficult it had been to keep her swaddled as a baby. Just as they thought they had finished, a random arm or hand would poke out of the wrap. The trait had continued throughout her childhood and adolescence. Toe tapping, finger drumming, and constant repositioning—that was Lauren. She might have been a little taller than her five feet nothing if she hadn't wasted so much energy fidgeting.

This need to move was a little different though. It wasn't an unconscious urge for habitual movement, it was an absolute, conscious call to action, one that was growing rapidly inside her mind, the kind that can be suppressed for a while, but never forever. Lauren succumbed quickly and began to walk slowly along the beach. As she did so, she began to feel certain that the waves were whispering to her.

Help.

Now.

Must.

They seemed to hiss the words as they raced to shore. She dismissed it as a trick of her vigilant mind, grateful that she still had a firm grasp on reality. All the while, the pressure on her to take some kind of action seemed to grow. It was becoming urgent. Insistent.

Ahead of her, a dark shape lay at the shoreline. The rhythmic waves prodded and poked it, pushing it forward, trying to remove an unwanted invader. She started towards it.

Help me!

Was that the sea? She wasn't sure, but instantly she recognised the shape at the water's edge. It was a body, a person. Her heart thrashed inside her as she sprinted across the sand at full tilt towards it. All the while, the moon's ghostly beams lit the way. Lauren gasped as she felt the presence of death in the area. It was dark. Sinister. Ready to pounce on the form ahead, whose faint and occasional chest movements gave the only indication that death had yet to claim it.

As Lauren approached, it became evident that the figure was a woman. She lay there, face down and naked, her raven hair matted by the clumps of moist mud that surrounded her. Occasional patches of pale skin were outnumbered by the clammy granules that clung to her body. Without slowing her pace, Lauren tore over the last

few metres. Within moments she was at the shoreline and
instinctively placed her hands on the failing female form in
front of her. As she did so, fear rippled through her mind.
Awful memories of her father's death flooded her head.
Here she was again, she thought, confronted with death.
Although six years had passed, she was suddenly placed
right back there, distraught, clinging to his cold and lifeless
hand.

She reached forward, then hesitated. The inner
turmoil that had been unlocked was running rampant
through her mind, but she suppressed it courageously.
Whoever this was needed her help. With strength that
belied her petite frame, Lauren rolled the girl into the
recovery position and instantly recoiled in shock. It was
uncanny. There was just no mistaking those vivid green
eyes, even though their polish was gone. Her facial
features. Her hair. Everything. She was identical to Lauren
in every way.

As Lauren began to inspect her more closely, she
could see that the girl was older. Perhaps middle-aged,
though she could have been in her early thirties, it was
difficult to tell. Lauren knew that age was deceptive at the
time of reckoning. Everyone looked older as their life
drained away, and this woman was no different. She was
also covered in scars. Old ones that had healed but stayed
around to bear witness to a violent past. The last of the
light was draining from those misting eyes and it was clear

that the girl was beyond saving. There wasn't much more that could be done other than try to comfort her, and so Lauren reached for her hand. As their fingers touched, it was like a mast to an overhead power cable. A tsunami of power surged through their connection. Wave upon wave of memories. Thousands of them. Each just a mere snapshot in time, but together a tide that roared into Lauren's mind with irresistible force. Three names flew into her head.

Sabine.

Diego.

Isabel.

The torrent inside her raged. Lauren's consciousness was bailing manically to try to remain afloat. It was a losing battle. Before she slipped into unconsciousness, she was filled with a bewildering range of emotions. A profound sorrow. Desperation. Hope. Above all, love. Tears exploded down her pale cheeks as she felt her double's life slip away. Blackness began to set in as her mind shut down, but not before a smile burst across her lips. Everything was now clear. Lauren knew exactly who she had to find, and what she had to do.

2

AS HE WATCHED the relentless breakers surge to shore, for the first time, James could see how they exposed mankind's very existence for the sham it was. Somewhere out there in the distance they began their journey and then roared through a raucous adolescence. At their glorious adult peak, they waged war against the sand before dwindling to a trickling end. Life was just like that, he thought. People weren't free. Perhaps they chose how to reach their destination like the occasional wave that veered sideways, but in the end the outcome was always the same. Death.

He knew that he should have been happier, given it was his twenty-first birthday, the day he should have received the key to the door in celebration of his coming of age. The trouble was he'd received the key a year earlier, when cancer had taken his mum. Ever since, James Jordan had been reeling. He was lost. He felt cheated. Where he had once been full of hope and expectation, there was now nothing but anger and regret. Like everyone who had lost someone, he anguished over the many missed opportunities to tell his mum he loved her and cringed at the thought of the hugs he'd hidden from. He felt he had taken her for granted. Right at that moment he would have given anything to hold her, to tell her he loved her. He missed her with all his being.

'I love you mum!' he screamed across the desolate English sand, but the words were plucked from his lips by a thieving coastal gale.

James gagged on the scorching liquid that he swigged from what was becoming an indispensable hipflask. It turned out vodka was a liar. It had promised him relief from his lonely suffering but all it had brought him was despair. Tears slithered down his cheeks like saline snakes and the wind seized them as they pooled at his youthful and wispy chin. He wasn't even sure why he was there, on the beach. His birthday celebrations had finished several hours earlier and throughout the party his brave face had served him well until the guests left, and then his real emotions surfaced. He knew he needed to talk about his feelings but he had no idea how, or who to. Instead, he kept a lid on the grief and it churned inside him. He was lonely in his misery and wondered if he would ever be truly happy again. The real James seemed to have disappeared. These days, doubt and fear ruled inside him where spontaneity and confidence had once been king.

He found the waves truly mesmerising. One after another they threw themselves to martyrdom on the sandy cemetery. James felt his head begin to loll in time to the beat of their demise. He fought the burning tiredness in his blue-green eyes, though their lids became heavier with every blink. His body was warning him to set off home, but he ignored its signals and, before long, his vodka'd brain succumbed to drunken slumber. While he slept, the wind battered his shirt-sleeved body and whipped his short, chestnut hair to soft peaks. He felt no cold; alcohol was a great insulator.

James woke to the drizzly nuzzling of an inquisitive labrador on its morning run. Its tongue was like a mildewed flannel across his icy skin. He was freezing. The alcohol had abandoned him to the cold and left him with little more than a pounding head.

'Are you alright?' said a middle-aged woman, presumably the dog's owner. Anyone would have been concerned at James' dishevelled appearance. He had clearly slept on the beach all night and that would have been unwise in the summer, let alone in January.

'I'm so cold,' he groaned. She reached for his hand and flinched at its glacial greeting.

'My God, you're freezing! Take this.' she removed her thick Puffa jacket and wrapped it around his shoulders. 'We need to get you to a hospital.'

'I'm fine,' James protested. 'Just a little cold.'

'Don't be silly. You're verging on hypothermia! We need to get you checked out.'

'No, please! I'm okay. Honestly. Please. I'll be fine,'

James begged. The woman relented, much to his relief.

'Well you're lucky you didn't die of exposure. Fancy sleeping on a beach in the winter! What on earth were you thinking?'

There was no answer to that. James knew he had been lucky. Overnight the temperature had fallen close to zero and he had been oblivious. If death had wanted him, he would have been there for the taking.

'Well I'm not just going to leave you like this. Look, stay here, wrapped up. I'm going to buy you a coffee to warm you up.'

'Thank you, you're so kind,' said James. He meant it too. He really was grateful. As she left, he felt reassured that maybe the world did care about him after all.

The events of the night before were somewhat foggy. James was unsure how he had ended up on the beach. Only one thing was clear in his memory. The murky waves. There had been something inevitable in their rhythmic pulse. Their unerring focus screamed of a wider purpose and it troubled him, though it was a challenge for him to think more deeply than that. He cursed his inability to switch off the alcohol tap once it had been opened, and vowed, not for the first time, that a drop would never cross his lips again. The return of the Samaritan with a steaming coffee was a welcome distraction.

'Thank you again,' said James. 'I don't think I've ever needed coffee as much as I need this one.'

'You're welcome,' she responded. 'Just promise me you won't make a habit of this?'

'I won't. Don't you worry!' with that he returned her jacket and staggered to his feet while thawing his hands on the polystyrene cup. It wasn't just the coffee that warmed him inside, it was the selfless act of this stranger. It filled him with an esteem that seemed to have been missing for a while.

The last of his childhood had left him when circumstances had snatched his mother away. Now, he was rudderless. He had begun what he expected to be a long and solitary journey through life, learning as he went. He had never cooked nor cleaned until his mum first became sick; in fact, until that point he'd had no responsibility at all, had not even paid a bill for God's sake. Since then, in some respects James had come so far but inside he felt abandoned. With a tell-tale tickling, his eyes threatened to tear and it was all he could do to hold back his emotions.

It was a short walk up the cliff steps to his home. James was frustrated that he had failed to make it all the way, considering how close it was. He lived in the East End of Folkestone, a small town in south-east England, so small that it was possible to walk from one side to the other in less than an hour. It was one of those towns that had a habit of under selling its features. Decades of neglect and poor planning had taken what was once a beautiful seaside town, off the map, and the holidaying masses no longer cared about what it had to offer. Anywhere else in the world, people would have come from miles around to stare in awe at the arches of the town's glorious viaduct, but Folkestone had somehow managed to ignore its masterpiece, which spanned high over the roofs of the nineteenth-century houses below, camouflaged from view like a brick chameleon. It was only from the distant hills that an observer really achieved the right perspective to wonder at its construction.

Even though he was unable to recall the details of the night before, James felt a faint glimmer of hope inside him. It was a sensation that had been absent for a while. He wondered whether, somehow, he had found meaning in those incessant waves. He was certainly fixated on the idea of life having purpose, and wondered if perhaps his future might be orchestrated in the same way as that irrepressible swell. If it was, then all that was left was to work out what tune he would be playing.

Once home, he made his way to the shower and dodged a few days' clothes that still lay where they fell. Living at home was something that James didn't yet have a grip on. It was too soon. The walls still echoed with his mum's voice, and part of him hoped she would be there in the kitchen each morning. The steaming water dispersed the lingering remnants of his exposure, tantalising his skin like the dance of a thousand heated spiders. A hot shower made everything feel better, he thought. It blew the cobwebs away.

He dried himself to Simon Mayo's meaningless warbling on the breakfast radio show. It was the nation's favourite and occasionally his antics made James laugh out loud. Really though, the radio's role was nothing more than to fill the emptiness that surrounded the morning household, and he was grateful for any help on that front.

He wiped a hand across the clouded mirror, and protesting bags chastised him for the lack of recovery time that the poor night had given his eyes. James was attractive in a whimsical way. His eyes seemed to smile even if his face chose not to, and his adolescent beard teased around his face in auburn wisps, adding what he felt was an important two or three years to his age. Without it he would have had one of those baby faces that meant he was challenged for ID wherever he went.

After the usual dreary breakfast, he downed his coffee and left the house, squinting despite the gloom of the day. It didn't seem to matter how dull the weather was, it was always brighter than the place he called home. Outside, it was a cold day, and a sneaky wind whipped around corners, seizing on any opportunity it could find to make contact with skin. It was the usual gale, the one that always seemed to be blowing during a Folkestone winter, as if that was the trade-off for beautiful coastal summers.

It was approaching eleven o'clock on Saturday

morning, and the plethora of pubs were beginning to open their doors for the day. Through the quartered windows of each, James could see the vanguard of patrons perched in position and taking the first public sip of the day's consumption. He felt for them, he really did. Like so much of society they were struggling. Millions had lost their jobs as the country moved away from manufacturing and, for many, alcohol had seized the opportunity to take control of their lives as soon as the work dried up. In the space of a few short Thatcher years, 'Made in Britain' had disappeared. In the beginning, that change had brought prosperity to the masses, but by 1991 the nation was on its knees. At that point even Margaret Thatcher had lost her job, ousted by those closest to her as soon as they felt the Iron Lady had begun to rust. There had been jubilance across the nation at her departure as John Major promised to bring harmony back to the economy but, so far, he had failed to strike a chord with the British public.

With everything going on, James felt grateful that he had a job. He worked in a call centre. It wasn't the hardest job in the world, but it was a means to an end. He had a grand plan to be running the company one day and, though the events of the last year had diverted his focus, he still believed it. He was young and had natural ability as a leader. People gravitated towards him, even those older than he, like his two best friends, Adam Jeffreys and Nick Draper for example. They were such a combustible mix that they needed his level head and his ability to disarm with a smirk or a quip, to prevent them from coming to blows every so often. Adam was four years older than James but eight years wiser. He was quick-witted, bold, and brash, and he dominated conversations. He had the confidence of a man who knew that women found him attractive, and he made the most of it. Nick was older still, and had been made the team leader. The whole team moved heaven and earth for him because they knew how much he cared about them. James didn't know anyone more loyal. Nick had even invited him to his house for that first awkward Christmas after his mum had died. At the time, it had blown him away. That one gesture of kindness and compassion had meant so much to him. Nick was exactly the kind of leader that James wanted to be, although rather randomly he had no concept of time. His constant lateness was infuriating, but what he brought to those around him more than made up for it.

James enjoyed talking to people all day. The conversations meant he could escape from the darkness that overshadowed his personal life. At work, he was able to just be himself; there was no time to dwell on the sadness that surrounded him – too much was happening. If he wasn't talking to customers, he was right in the thick of his team, swapping friendly banter throughout the day.

Although he had left the house, James was unsure where he was headed, just conscious of the need to be outside. There was nothing worse than lying in that dark and empty house with a hangover – there were too many emotions there, too much sadness. He found that fresh air always lifted his mood. It blew new life into him. As he wandered aimlessly, his thoughts turned once more towards the sense of purpose that he felt. It tantalised him but, just as he felt he was on the verge of something insightful, it slipped through his fingers. He was desperate to put it all together but, try as he might, the important pieces always seemed to be missing.

After a few blocks, he realised that the feeling seemed to be growing. Around him the atmosphere was brimming with promise and he began to feel as though every step was bringing him closer to a revelation that would change his life forever. Before long, every part of his body was on an expectant alert. He felt alive and responsive for the first time in over a year. For once everything seemed right. The darkness had gone, and in its place, was a blistering excitement. James was certain that something incredible was about to happen.

At the corner, he stopped dead in his tracks. His jaw hit the floor like a discarded medicine ball at the end of an exhausting work-out. Across the narrow street, a girl seemed singled out by a spotlight as she spoke to a friend. Even at what must have been fifteen yards, James was dazzled by her earthy emerald eyes as they sparkled in the light. Her raven hair framed her flawless face and fell across it like an unclipped satin curtain. She seemed to be performing just for him, a leading lady on a street-corner stage, playing to a silent and enthralled audience of one. He hung on every movement of those sweet, pink lips as they spoke unknown and unimportant words, and he greeted every flick of that shoulder-length hair with rapturous applause. She was enchanting. Bewitching. Around her there seemed to be an aura that held him willingly captive. It enticed him with a warmth and passion that James had never known.

This was a sign alright, of that he was certain. There was an ethereal radiance to her. In that moment, she was like a sun. She had locked him in a helpless orbit, one he would have willingly stayed in forever.

Then she walked away, unaware of his presence and oblivious to the encore that his ovation craved. In that instant, James knew he had found purpose, even though he didn't know how to embrace it. How long he stood there, he wasn't sure. The theatre lasted mere moments but it was a show that would remain eternal in his mind.

For the rest of the day he could think of nothing else. He found himself longing to see her again and just couldn't get her out of his head. His mind tormented him with thoughts that she would be around every corner, or in every recess. That night it was no better. Even when his eyes were closed, she was there, beckoning him towards her.

The need to see her again consumed the next few weeks of his life. Every day he lived for the thrill that it might happen. As each passed and he played that scene again, he became more and more convinced that they were destined for each other. James knew that jumping to such a conclusion was irrational, but his mind was all over the place. He had only seen her once. Once! Yet for some reason his heart leapt every time the phone rang. It was absurd. Not only did she not have his number or know who he was, she hadn't even noticed him that day on the street corner. It symbolised just how desperate he was to see her again.

On nights out, he entered every bar with the hope of seeing her. Anticipation sat expectantly on his shoulders like a meerkat sentinel that jumped at the shadow of every passing brunette. No matter where he was, he was unable to concentrate, he just couldn't keep his thoughts away from her for long enough. She was becoming an obsession, and he knew it. He could feel the boundaries of rationality shifting in order to provide him with some kind of hope as he forlornly tried to re-establish contact, like a transmission line that had been severed and was flailing after a storm. Such helplessness was a new feeling for James. Until recently, he had always considered himself to be an agent for change. If something wasn't working, he was always the one who suggested an alternative. He had little time for bureaucracy and broke rules regularly at work if he thought that it was the right thing to do, and his judgement was rarely wrong. His moral compass seemed to be perfect for the work he did and the relationships he kept.

With each passing day, he became more and more frustrated. If his desperation to see her again wasn't tearing him apart, the idea that there was nothing he could do to engineer a meeting, was driving him crazy.

All that changed the day she smiled at him for the first time. He would never forget it. There was something special about the way the sun sparkled across the snow that day in early February. His primitive sixth sense registered her presence and he sensed an awakening inside him in the moments before she appeared. Elation spread through his body and every pore of his skin tingled until the hairs danced a pulsating polka across his forearms. Then he saw her. He inhaled her beauty with his gaze. The soft angles of that delicate face were so perfectly framed by the liquorice locks that curled across her breast, and her lips were even more alluring than he remembered. This time he felt them beckoning him to come forward and touch them with his own, to seal a collective destiny. Her vulnerability and inner passion screamed from those cabochon eyes as they anchored his stare. He wanted to sweep her up in his arms and declare that she was now safe. The first time he had seen her, she had been oblivious to his attention, but this time she responded with a smile so radiant that it ignited the kindling passion inside him.

James had promised himself that the next time he saw her, he would seize the moment and talk to her. Despite his impetuous nature, he had practised what he would say and do for hours on end, such had been his focus. He wanted to leave nothing to chance, even though he was convinced that they were destined to be together. But, in the heat of the moment, he found himself rooted to the spot. Unable to move. Unable to act. That smile just mesmerised him. Captured him. And then she was gone. Again.

Since the day he first saw her, he had emerged from a bottomless blackness, ready to clutch destiny with both hands. She had been the one thing that had jolted him out of his depression. He wanted her, needed her, yet once more he found himself in little more than a state of limbo, wondering whether this was what purgatory was like.

Despite his desperation to see her again, James was troubled. He was convinced that both times he had seen her, he had felt her presence beforehand. She seemed to exude electricity and it charged the air around him. Her pull had been gravitational. But how was that possible? It was a question that haunted his mind. He needed to understand why he was able to feel her radiance like that. It was exhilarating, yet unnatural, almost spiritual. He needed answers but had no-one to ask. All he knew was that he felt a joy he had never experienced before. He dreamed of spending the rest of his life with her in exaltation; it wasn't a question of whether they would be together, it was a question of when. And, once that happened, he knew that only death would tear them apart.

*

A third pair of eyes witnessed that smile. They were set deep in the watcher's head, so deep that they would have seemed black to any observer. He made sure there were none, keeping himself hidden in the shadows as always. He too knew that there was purpose in their meeting. It had happened before and, if he didn't do something about it, it would happen again. The clock had started ticking once more, and his stomach knotted inside him at the thought.

This was all part of her game. It was the way that she enticed them, drew them in. That first glimpse on the street corner had been no accident. His fingers scratched the yin of his thick, black moustache and the yang of his whitening goatee as he began developing yet another plan to deal with her. He watched that smile from behind the filthy arches where he had sucked in the stench of the morning's catch. There was no mistaking it. He had seen it before, too many times, but never once aimed at him.

The rage inside him tightened his jaw and pursed his cheated lips. The hatred from his charcoal eyes could have melted the snow in front of him. With fists formed he struck the fetid brickwork that obscured him from view. He imagined that its unrelenting resistance was the bones on the face of whoever the fuck that was who had captured her attention. A wry smile crossed his surly lips as he imagined them crack under his repeated pounding. And he would make sure she would be watching, mortified at the punishment she had triggered. Acute pain burned across his knuckles as they smashed those arches repeatedly. It didn't hurt. Jealousy was the perfect anaesthetic and quickly numbed them each time.

He was tired of this. Exasperated. He wondered how many more times he would have to endure this misery. When would he finally be free of seeing her lock those beguiling green eyes onto someone else? That flirtatious curl of her lips was like the twist of a knife stabbed inside him and each wound unleashed a bitter fury.

Yet still he followed her. He shadowed her every step. He had known it would only be a matter of time before she showed her true colours again, and here they were, raised to the finial for all to see. Did it count for nothing that she was still his wife? Despite loving her all these years he seemed destined to sneak behind her in shadowy surveillance. How was that fair? She was his, was she not? She had given herself to him.

Except she hadn't, and she had yet to cast those verdant gems longingly at him. Perhaps his torment might have been less had she ever looked at him like that but the fact that she hadn't infuriated him. It made him feel worthless. A nobody. He was used to getting what he wanted, as was anyone in his position. The fact that she was withholding the affection that he longed for made him all the more determined.

One thing was for certain. If he was unable to have it, then no-one else would either. He would take great delight in ensuring that the only way these two would be together would be in death.

3

ON 16 MARCH, at the end of the evening, James felt drawn to the nightclub. It was usually the last stop on a Saturday evening out with Nick and Adam anyway, but on this particular occasion he felt a real need to be there. It was the day before St Patrick's Day, and the bars were decked out in shamrock green. The Guinness was flowing and the young people of the town were out in force to rejoice in all things Irish. James didn't feel much like celebrating, even though he was half-Irish himself. His mum had been raised in Dublin and she had hated her upbringing. Since hearing her stories, James had purposely distanced himself from his Irish heritage. Besides, the ubiquitous green with which every bar was decorated served only to remind him of those electrifying eyes that he pined for. It had been six weeks since that smile, six long weeks during which he had hardly slept. He just couldn't. Resting his head on the pillow was like a starter's pistol to his brain. Lying in the bed with no distractions at all, meant that his mind was free to relive those two special moments over and over again.

The dance hits floated through the frosty night from the warmth of Folkestone's premiere club, a pinnacle it had reached mostly through the ineptitude of the competition. As a consequence, the queues were quick to build and that was something the three friends wanted to minimise as much as they could. There was nothing else in the vicinity, no bars to ease the wait, just the exposed seafront where the channel wind brought tidings of animosity from Portugal. The incumbent south-westerly whipped along the English Channel and straight into those in the queue. Despite the wait, entry to the joint was by no means guaranteed. To a certain extent, it was in the lap of the tuxedoed gods, who openly abused their power. They were bilingual, fluent in the languages of money and sex, and prioritised the rich and flirtatious customers, whose offerings they accepted readily. That meant the queue moved slowly for everyone else, inching its way inside like saline through a regulated drip. The friends knew that too many men in the queue together spelled trouble, one of the few words that the neo-Neanderthals on the door knew how to spell. With that in mind James, Adam and Nick made sure they joined the queue between two sets of girls. As usual, Nick had them all hanging off his every word. To the outside world, he was a minor celebrity, full of bravado and basking in attention. It helped that he was the stereotype of handsome too, tall, dark and rugged. His looks and charm regularly swept women off their feet.

The prices always increased at eleven and even the

untrained eye couldn't help but be cynical when the pretence of number control vanished after this time. For each entry after eleven, they made double the entrance fee. This was a version of supply and demand where, if customers chose not to buy, their only option was to go home. If the owners had thought they could get away with it, they would have trebled the price.

Once inside, Nick led the way to the raised walkway that surrounded the oval dancefloor. They stood there like sentries, watching as waves of dance were driven on by a lunar beat, so seductive that even they had the impulse to abandon their watch. None of them would have claimed to be able to dance if asked, but once alcohol had suppressed inhibitions, and if the moons aligned, the beat was beguiling.

James' favourite part of the club was the upper bar. The glass screens that surrounded it dimmed the music sufficiently to enable conversation. He was well known and at home there, surrounded by familiar faces. Adam loved it too, it was a place where he could hold court and that was a role he relished. Occasionally Nick would breeze through, chasing particular girls he had singled out, in the knowledge that he would have a limited opportunity to strike before alcohol removed his celebrity and left him a drunken fool who would go home alone.

The music was so loud that it bypassed James' eardrums and thudded through his veins, to the point where he was convinced that his heart was controlled by the DJ. His senses were on fire too, but he wasn't sure it was just the music. A feeling began to creep over him, one that he'd had twice before. Each time it had been the precursor to something magical. He became distracted and nervous. Expectant. Was he about to see her again? Heart in mouth, he decided to lap the nightclub several times, certain that he would see the mysterious girl there, but the light was dim and there were too many people. He gave up and headed back to the upper bar. Adam was already in full flow up there, talking to some lads from work, who both boys knew but wouldn't quite classify as friends. Tom Fairbrother, the dour accountant from Yorkshire who was always good for a loan if the evening became too expensive; Pete Campbell, long-haired, slightly overweight and extremely short, though he hid both with a combination of loose clothing and platform soles; and Robert Harvey, a serial maker-upper of stories, to the point where nobody believed anything he said any more.

Adam was espousing his informed view on the war in the Gulf, which was drawing to conclusion now that Kuwait had been liberated two weeks earlier. The group were struggling to argue with him. Even when his opinion seemed wrong, few people had the tools to take him on. It was like turning up to a gunfight with a vial of poison.

'… and what does it achieve? My guess would be that most of these people were either innocent or serving their country because of the same misguided loyalty that we show to ours. Is it right that we should celebrate their death? And do you think the kids are going to grow up happy that America and Britain bombed their families from the sky? I'll tell you the answer. They're going to grow up hating us and all we stand for, and we'll be fighting them for generations to come.'

'Jeez Adam, where did that come from?' James finally found a break in which to join the conversation.

'Can't you see how they're manipulating you?'

'Who?' responded James.

'Major and the rest of the government.'

'No?'

'They want you to feel proud of what we're doing. They want you to rally behind our war effort. They want you to celebrate every victory. The more success they have, the better it is. You know why, James?'

'Because they want us to feel good?' James was hoping that the rest of the group might take the focus off him at some point, but they remained silent. He felt under the spotlight even though he had only just joined the conversation.

'Because they want you to forget about all the shit at home. Forget you've lost your job, your house, your health. Surest way to turn opinion polls around in your favour is to win a war.'

'Have we ever lost one?' James interjected, trying to

gain a footing in the conversation.

'My point exactly. These days we wouldn't even go to war unless we were almost certain of winning. Did you see us intervene against Ceausescu in Romania?'

'No …'

'Because even though he was slaughtering his citizens he was an ally of Russia. Were we horrified about what happened at Tiananmen Square?'

'Yes.'

'And did we do anything about it?'

'No …'

'Because the Chinese are just too damn powerful and would wipe the floor with us. I call it selective morality. We're prepared to join in and give the class wimp a good kicking if he does something wrong but we won't help anyone out against the class bully. We don't have the balls.'

James began to tune out Adam's diatribe. His thoughts turned once more to the desire that was smouldering inside him. He could feel her near him. The hairs on his arms were beginning to rehearse their moves. He could almost hear the whisper of fate. This was the time, his time. The void of the last six weeks had been unbearable and he wasn't going to go through six more. His heart was on pause as his eyes scanned the bar once again. If he was honest, it concerned James a little that he could feel her presence, like a cat sensing the onset of a storm, but he dismissed those thoughts immediately. His desire to see her was such that nothing else mattered.

His eyes darted from left to right and returned nothing. He was snatched from his disappointment by a touch, as her hand slipped silently and sensuously into his, where it hung loose at his side. There was no question it was her. Her touch was electric, like no other feeling on earth. What felt like waves of current inundated his nerve endings. Every cell of his body was on fire, as though molten steel had replaced his blood and was scorching through his veins. The connection was nothing short of extraordinary. In her palm, she had the power to seal the deal before any had even been discussed. It was a grip of permanence, not the touch of a one-night stand. With it, James knew he was holding his future.

He turned in sensory ecstasy and looked down at his new and much shorter companion, expecting those stunning eyes to be looking longingly up at him. He thought she would be preparing to cement their newfound togetherness with a kiss, but he was wrong. He was greeted instead by the back of her head. She wasn't even looking at him. There was no question at all that it was her, but bizarrely she was engrossed in conversation with her friends. All the time she was maintaining a dynamite connection behind her back.

James was powerless to move. Speechless and confused. He wanted to interrupt her, to seize the moment as he had promised himself that he would, but he knew he wasn't supposed to. He didn't know the rules of the game they were playing but the energy that flowed through that connection was asking him to hold his ground. She had so much control that he felt he needed to play it her way, as if by taking the initiative, he would lose the game. So he waited, trying to look part of the conversation around him, yet mindful not to break that exciting link.

'… bomb … ground troops … propaganda …' James had no idea what Adam was talking about. He caught the odd word, but in truth he was merely witnessing lip movements. He could think of nothing other than the awakened desire at his fingertips, willing her to turn, to engage with him. It was all he could concentrate on.

After what would have been no more than minutes but seemed like the combined lifetimes of his entire ancestry, James felt her turn towards him. He knew that was his cue to follow suit and he noticed that she was now alone. Without words, she led him to a corner of the bar and they sat next to each other at an empty table. All the while that explosive grip remained intact. She was even more beautiful this close up than he had ever imagined. Those eyes that had sparkled from a distance, blinded him at close range. They beckoned him forward and he complied. Their lips touched and he could feel the warmth and longing in them as they parted. Their tongues tangoed together. James reached up to grasp the left side of that perfect face with his right hand and it was rewarded with the smoothness of her pale skin and the silk of her hair, as his fingers furrowed to their resting point.

This was a kiss he knew he would remember for a lifetime. James was so excited about where it would lead. While he would welcome it, he had no desire for just one night with this girl; he wanted to spend all his nights with her. He would settle for nothing less. But he knew nothing about her, not even her name. As that thought broke to the surface of his floundering mind, she broke off the kiss.

'I'm Lauren,' she half-spoke, half-whispered, in a voice that James longed to hear more of yet knew it would keep him from kissing her further. She offered no follow-up question, and silenced him with a kiss when he went to speak. He had no idea why, but at that moment James was convinced that she already knew who he was.

*

A swarthy stare surveyed them in the distance. He watched them through the tottering horde that swayed rhythmically to the pounding drum and bass. He didn't call it music. To him it was just noise. He hated being there. It was the last place that he wanted to be on earth, but she had left him with no choice. Where she went, he went. He had to watch her every transgression.

He sneered as revellers teetered from the bar, slopping their drinks indiscriminately. They were all so vulnerable in this state, especially to people like him. He knew he could overpower any of them if he wanted to. It would be simple. Their defences had been left behind with their inhibitions, long ago, and that made them easy prey. But he had no interest in them, save for the occasional shove that he gave to the ones who obscured his view, or lurched drunkenly into him. None of them retaliated. He exuded such dominance. He intimidated. They kept their distance and they were wise to do so. A man like him commanded respect. His worldly face attested to his power and experience. And his eyes. Even in the poor light, their darkness stood out.

His only interest was in those two, who he thought of as adulterers. He saw it all. The way she sidled up to his youthful replacement and sneakily held the boy's hand, even though she was pretending she wasn't. He knew that she was the one making all the moves. The young boy was just the willing slave, held captive by her touch. Soon, he would understand the ramification of his actions but at the moment he was oblivious.

Through jealous eyes, he saw James lost in the moment, mesmerised by her beauty, just as he himself had once been. His wife was younger than him but that didn't make what she was doing right. He felt like he could no longer compete for her attention, and watching that poisonous contact between them made his stomach wretch.

He saw as she led the usurper to the table. He hoped the two of them could feel the hatred of his stare, but they showed no sign of it; they were lost in what he knew was an electric clinch. All he was doing was torturing himself and he knew it. This had been on the cards since that street corner and there was no going back. He would make her pay the next time they were together, that was for sure.

Knowing it would happen and being able to watch it, were two different things. Seeing them sitting together was like a thump to his stomach, and he felt the taste of bile rise inside his bitter mouth. Jealousy ate away inside him and its ferocity was nauseating. Not for the first time he felt inadequate. His possession was being stolen from him, and he didn't like it. He was a law maker, not somebody's victim. He would see to it that their end was poignant and painful. Their journey would be an ordeal. That would teach them.

Jealousy barrelled upwards from its acidic depths. He knew that seeing them canoodling in the corner was consuming him, but he had to watch. It was all too much for him when their lips touched. Their fornication made him sick. He clapped a meaty hand to his goateed mouth and bolted for the toilets. In his haste, he barged the wobbling fools around him out of the way, and locked himself in what he considered to be vile and stinking

toilets. He found it repulsive how modern society had
deteriorated to this level. This was no better than pissing
over the battlements in the Middle Ages. At least back then
there had been the pleasure of ruining someone's day as
the excrement fell on their unsuspecting head. To avoid
the pooling urine, he doubled over the toilet and vomited
his vitriol, as he cursed her betrayal.

★

James felt as though the final jigsaw piece was hovering in
place. For the first time, he could see the full picture of
what life had in store for him, and he liked it, even though
it was so different to what he'd always imagined. The
beautiful house, the fast car, the high-powered executive
job, all these had been important to him before. They
were what had motivated him through every day, yet now
he realised how artificial all that was. What was really
important to him was there, right in front of him. The
trouble was that, not long after she had whispered those
beautiful words, announcing who she was, Lauren broke
away. She leaned forward to pick up her handbag and in
doing so she offered him a peeper's panorama, as her
singlet temporarily neglected its duty. It revealed a
tantalising insight into what James hoped to explore
further, nestled cosily in a simple, yet sensuous, white lace
bra. She stood. Her petite frame meant her standing head

was only a foot or so above him as he sat. It was glorious looking up at her like that.

'I have to go.'

'No! You can't!' James stood awkwardly, mindful that the combination of that momentary glimpse and the passionate embrace meant his legs weren't the only thing attempting to stand.

'I have to, it's late. I need to go home.'

James distracted her with another kiss and it delayed her departure significantly as she responded to his advance. If it hadn't been for the fact that he had already stolen this extra time it would have felt as though time was standing still, such was the magnitude of the moment. He couldn't quite relax though, he knew the clock was ticking in the background, and that, sooner rather than later, Lauren would make another move to leave. Despite that, James felt a little more in control, even though he knew that at some point she would still take the ball home with her, and that would be the end of the game for the time being. He felt his main goal now was to make certain he would see her again, but it was difficult to think clearly through the fog of random thoughts that were clouding his judgement.

'Hey. Go if you need to,' James whispered. 'How about we meet up for lunch tomorrow? We could take a drive out to the marshes?'

'Sounds lovely but I can't, I'm sorry.' Lauren was

playing with her hair nervously, bunching it together into a pony tail and then seductively letting it fall back again.

'Er, okay, er, what, what about dinner?' James was struggling now and even stammering. 'Drinks? Your, your choice. As long as I'm with you I, I don't really care where we go!' What was he doing? He was so flustered that he wasn't even waiting for an answer.

'That's sweet. But I can't think at the moment.'

'Okay, well, well give me your number then. I'll, I'll call you. We can work it out later.'

'No!' She surprised him with her assertive tone. It seemed she was clearly unwilling to relinquish the control that James was so desperately seeking to take.

'Why not? You clearly like me.' His nerves had disappearing now, replaced with abject frustration.

'It's complicated.' She started moving away towards the door and he followed her.

'Then let me walk you home.' By this point, James was running out of options.

'No. I don't want you to.'

'Well I'll give you my number.' He was exasperated. That was it. He had fired his last salvo. It was a reluctant shot too, because it came with hours, days, sometimes weeks of praying that the phone would ring. In his experience, if a girl said she was going to call you, she rarely did. But what other choice did he have? He checked his pockets for a pen and cursed his hands when they came up empty. He had nothing more than the remnants of old receipts that had disintegrated during the wash. James began to feel the pressure. Lauren was nearly out of the exit and he had yet to secure any hope of a follow-up. He knew he couldn't let her go without leaving some opening for the future. He was desperate for a semblance of control, but he knew that he had none.

As they reached the door, his eyes scanned around for something, anything that would do the job. He had to give her his number. He cursed his luck. Why did this have to be so complicated? He felt he was gambling the treasured last moments with her in what was becoming the forlorn hope of winning more time. Out of the corner of his eye he spotted a pen at the empty reception desk. In desperation, he grabbed it without a second thought. As soon as he'd done it, he knew it was a mistake. Almost immediately he felt the plod of a nearby doorman who, having witnessed James' grand larceny, was intent on punishment. The rush was on now. It would only be a matter of time before the bouncer separated them for the evening and then any chance to give Lauren his number would be gone.

As they set foot outside, the chill reminded them of its presence. The icy breeze scalded the sides of their faces and chastised them for the evening of refuge they had sought. At that point, sensing the impending intervention, Lauren interrupted James' panicked thought process with a kiss. It was a goodbye kiss this time, and distinctly different from those that had come before. It brought with it a finality that made it clear any thoughts he had of begging her to stay, would fall on deaf ears.

'Hold on!' he demanded, his impetuousness breaking free from the frustration. He was tired of the helplessness that was increasing with every second. 'I really don't know what's going on here, and I don't get what game we're playing. You started this. I'm glad you did, but you started it. Now you're ...' Lauren placed her finger to his lips and that silenced him immediately.

'We'll see each other again soon, trust me. We'll have lifetimes together James, you and me.' With that she turned, climbed into a cab and was gone. James had no time to even contemplate her departure. Immediately, he found himself facing the muscled one-man court, who handed out the sentence of a hefty blow to the stomach. James doubled over, sinking breathlessly to his knees as the bouncer snatched back the eleven-pence biro, ripping the skin from his fingers as a parting insult.

That was how he recalled the end of the evening, and James had no reason to believe that his mind embellished or erased any of the content. It was as clear in his memory as it had been at the time. Aside from the obvious question of when the hell they would see each other again now, there were a number of things that piqued his curiosity.

The first thing that puzzled him was how Lauren had known his name. He was positive that he hadn't told her and, while he felt that they had communicated bountifully on an emotional level, the actual conversation had been extraordinarily arid. There had not been a scrap of fertile ground that he could nurture in subsequent meetings. Other than their parting dialogue, James realised he had not spoken to her at all. Indeed, until that point, the only words she had spoken were in telling him her name. He was sure of it. He recalled every other aspect of their meeting and all the occasions he had seen her before. This was definitely the first time that they had talked. He guessed it was possible that she had asked someone his name—James had, after all, been in his favourite part of the club, and frequency brought familiarity—it just didn't seem likely.

The rest of her words were more curious.

'We'll have lifetimes together James, you and me.' James was certain she had said lifetimes. No matter how many times he played it over in his head, the words remained the same. The idea of spending a single lifetime with the mysterious Lauren would be beyond exciting; it would be a dream. But how could they spend more than one lifetime together? It made no sense. All it did was raise an awful lot of questions, to which James had no answers. At least, not until he was able to discuss them with her anyway. Sadly, that was a conversation whose likelihood seemed to diminish with each passing day.

For the first few days, James had at least felt that while he had no idea when he would see her again, fate would find a way to make it happen. But with the passing of time he began to question whether his feelings were reciprocated. It was true that absence made the heart grow fonder, but it also seemed to bring anguish and self-doubt. As the weeks passed, he found a miserable comfort in convincing himself that, despite her words, she couldn't possibly have shared his sense of a permanent bond between them. Had she done so, surely she would have found a way to contact him? Had James held any cards, he would have played them by now. He would have seized the day. If they were truly meant to be together then why wait? Why delay destiny? Why talk about lifetimes, and yet allow a single moment to be frittered away in frustrated isolation?

In the end, James kept coming back to those words. Offering a single lifetime together was certainly not an expected platitude at the end of a first meeting, and Lauren had offered even more. *Lifetimes* was a lifeline to which he clung tenuously.

Of course, he discussed the events of that evening with Adam and Nick, to the point where they began to sigh at the mere mention of the subject. James avoided disclosure on a number of key points, naturally and most notably those intriguing parting words. He had no intention of sharing something that they would consider absurd, and open himself up to the kind of abuse that would trigger. James also worried that divulging the detail would somehow reduce the heated intensity that was forging his future and melting his mind. Despite the omissions, his story was still met with a mixture of condescension and ridicule.

'Okay, Willow,' chortled Adam, using the derogatory nickname he had invented for just such occasions. It was one that James hated, and worse still it was beginning to catch on across the whole company. Random strangers were now referring to him as Willow, even though they had no idea why. They might suspect it was because he was tall and wiry, but they would be wrong. It was a reference to the bum-fluff that disguised his youthful looks. Willow the Wisp. That's what it was short for. 'So what you're saying is that you've fancied a girl for ages, you finally pulled her and then forgot to get her number. You'll forgive me if that sounds vaguely familiar?'

'It's not like that!'

'Sounds like it to me.'

'Gee, thanks for your support Adam—it's not like I didn't try to get her number.'

'Look Willow, when was the last time you saw me moping about some girl?' Adam continued. James had relatively low expectations that what was to follow would be of any use. 'Like an idiot, you've let her leave you without getting a number. Now move on and next time make sure you get one.'

'I'd like to have seen you get one Ads. She was off in a flash. She was like Cinderella!'

'More like one of her ugly sisters, I expect,' said Adam, triggering a multitude of guffaws between he and Nick.

'You should've tried to slip 'er one!' Adam wouldn't let it drop. He was stretching the friendship.

'Cut it out mate, you might think it's funny but I can assure you that I don't.'

'Want my opinion, JJ?' Nick added.

'If it's sensible, yes.'

'Look, if it's meant to be then you'll see her again.' Somehow this was worse than the ridicule. It was a platitude. Nick had no experience of falling for someone. He had no need of, or desire for, companionship. His was a carnal thirst and it was one that he had no problem quenching. His words were telling James what he thought he needed to hear, but Nick's eyes were screaming at him to move on and get a life. James couldn't bear it. Not from Nick. Deep down, James knew he was right, too. The trouble was he couldn't get her out of his head. It was like the obsession was snowballing in his psyche, hurtling through his consciousness.

4

M OST OF THE TIME, Lauren felt like a prisoner in her own home. The events at the beach six months earlier had helped somewhat though. At least she now had a plan and was working towards its implementation. The knowledge that the end was in sight made the pain and fear worthwhile, and though she still tiptoed around her home, she did so with a purposeful step.

It hadn't always been that way. Her childhood had been somewhat idyllic, growing up in Newchurch, on the Romney Marshes. It was no more than fifteen miles away from Folkestone, yet it could have been in an entirely different continent. English villages were so tranquil, so green. Each had its own charm and Newchurch was no exception. Its claim to fame was the crooked tower on the church of St Peter and St Paul, and the hospitality that flowed in the adjacent Black Bull Inn was legendary. A solitary, single-lane road passed through the village, separating the comfortable symbiosis that the two congregations had shared for hundreds of years. Indeed, some questioned whether the pub's presence on the other side of the road was the true reason why the church tower stood at such a strange angle. But those who believed that were denying the church its three-hundred-year advantage.

Lauren's parents, John and Maggie, had leased the pub when she was four. It became her home and she loved the atmosphere that the low seventeenth-century beams gave the place. Each was made from the timbers of ships that had been wrecked along the coast. She was fascinated with the tales of how smugglers had been rife in the village at the turn of the eighteenth century. Her mind ran riot at the thought of their sneering and surly plotting amongst those blackened beams, and she shivered at their callous disregard for the lives of those whose ships they had wrecked. It was astonishing to think that just three hundred years earlier the tide had been close enough to support their illicit activities. Now it was five miles away at the taupe sands of St Mary's Bay.

She had been happy there, popular at the local school and with the children whose parents frequented the pub at the weekends. She developed a love for animals and always befriended the dogs tied up outside while their owners drank the afternoon's away. She fetched water and sneaked food from the kitchen for them, and was overjoyed when they recognised her the next time they came. It was in those years that she decided she wanted to be a vet. There could be nothing more exciting for her to work towards than a life with animals, and as a result she worked hard at school, committed to fulfilling her plan. The idea that she might have to euthanise really sick animals troubled her greatly, but she determined to deal with that when the situation arose.

Unfortunately, the magic of her childhood disappeared for good on 10 June 1983. That was the day she found her father dead, a day she would never forget. The pub had been open later than usual so that the regulars could follow the result of the general election on the radio. Being a staunch Liberal, John, or Jack as the locals called him, didn't hold out much hope for the result as the electoral system just seemed stacked against them. The drinking had gone on late into the night and Lauren had fallen asleep to her father's voice booming its opinions downstairs.

The next morning, she came down to find her father slouched across one of the sticky tables. The nightcap he had poured was still in front of him untouched. He looked so grey and absent, and when she touched his icy hand it was nothing more than a lifeless limb. Whenever she thought of her father now, that was the vision that she saw. Not the happy times that they had spent together, nor the embraces they had shared. Just the vacant body of her beloved father, who had moved out of it during the night.

There had been nowhere better than the Black Bull itself to hold the wake. Family, friends and regulars had turned out in force to drink to Jack's memory, while

Lauren and Maggie had hidden in the kitchens, too distraught to join in. As they consoled each other among the idle hobs, they knew that from now on life would be different. From a practical point of view there was far too much work for Maggie to do alone, but at a deep and personal level there would be too many painful memories each day to make a continued life in the pub bearable. Each night at eleven, in their minds, they knew they would hear him ring the bell and call 'Time!' and that would just be too raw a reminder of what they had lost. The next day, the pub was put on the market and, two miserable months later, as soon as the lease had been transferred, they moved out.

The rest of Lauren's teenage years were a far cry from those that had gone before. Money was tight and Maggie had to make many sacrifices for the sake of her daughter. The biggest of all was a move to dreary Dover. They were forced to swap their rural lifestyle for little more than a bedsit in the dirty and inhospitable world of the transit town. Day and night, they were surrounded by the unemployable. It was an unpleasant existence and a difficult environment for a teenage girl to grow up in. No parent wanted their son or daughter surrounded by drugs, alcohol and prostitution, but Maggie had had no other choice. The nights were the worst. The bleating of lambs became the bleating of sirens as police responded to the latest incident. Late-night knocks on the door were common-place, either from the police requesting information, or worse still from addicts who had the wrong address for their score.

The days weren't all that much better. Youths with nothing to occupy them, gathered in shadowed corners of the estate and there was a constant stream of muggings and burglaries. On more than one occasion, Maggie's flat was broken into. Until the first time, Lauren had never thought their house could be burgled; after all, they had little. It was only when someone actually did so that reality dawned on her. She returned home from school one day to find that she couldn't open the front door. That, she discovered, was one of their tricks. They bolted the door from the inside in case the homeowner came back early. It gave them more time to escape. Inside the apartment, Lauren found every drawer in the house had been emptied. Her father's watch and wedding ring were taken. They had been all she had to remind her of him and were presumably sold for a pittance in order to subsidise an addiction. Those things were irreplaceable. They were gone forever.

It was a wonder that Lauren had grown up as unscathed as she did. Much of that was thanks to her resilience. It seemed that, no matter what life threw at her, she was able to bounce back somehow. It was never easy, but each time she picked herself up off the floor and started anew. All the while, her dream of working with animals

burned brightly, though there was less to love about the
aggressive pitbulls who snarled at all who passed, than the
salivating labradors she had grown up with.

At fifteen, she developed a crush on one of the
policemen, Sean Kennedy. He looked incredibly handsome in his uniform and so virile with his neatly trimmed
goatee. He was ten years older than Lauren and took a
shine to her. His attention kept her safe from the daytime
muggers and, even when he wasn't around, they left her
alone. Everything about him screamed security, sanctuary
and safety. It was something Lauren craved but hadn't felt
since Newchurch. As soon as she hit sixteen they began
dating and by eighteen they were married. Lauren was
delighted to finally be free from the estate and on the verge
of her veterinary dream, until she discovered very quickly
that she had merely jumped out of the frying pan and into
the fire. Such was Sean's controlling nature once they
were together, that he beat the resistance, the resilience,
and the dreams out of her, with his words and fists. He
even tried to beat the fidgeting out of her, such was his
annoyance at her near-constant movement. Over time,
Lauren grew into the role of victim.

And then everything had changed when the surge of
memories flooded through her at the beach. At first, Lauren
had been overwhelmed by the sheer volume of information
that seemed to be bursting out of her. Then, after a while,
she began to learn more about the lives of those who had

gone before her. The courage and bravery that she witnessed as she relived their thoughts, regenerated her own. Her resilience returned, and with it some of her self-esteem, though she was careful to hide it from her husband, lest he beat it away. Then she began to learn of the prize, that tantalising destiny which she now understood, and began to plan her escape. It would only be a matter of time before she was rid of her miserable existence.

Lauren knew she had to be patient. She longed for the moment that she would share the truth with James. She had played him, and for that she felt guilty, but there had been no alternative. The memories she had inherited were littered with the consequences of failure at this first step. In order for her to have half a chance of success, she needed to know that James was ready to hear the truth, that he was able to handle it. So many had failed at this point and the repercussions of doing so were dire. This was by no means the hardest challenge they would face, but it was certainly their first.

The plan had worked well so far. James had taken the bait and she reeled him in slowly and surely. This next part was trickier though. Lauren had to do something she had never done before, something she had witnessed only once in her own lifetime. It wasn't the kind of thing she could practise either. This was a one-off, make-it-work kind of moment. The pressure to perform was intense. She had to succeed.

As soon as she could, she made her way to the beach. It seemed the perfect location for what she needed to do. When she arrived, she was surprised and relieved to find it empty. Even though it was a clear, crisp spring day the wind roared across the sand, buffeting her every move. The tide was almost completely out, and that meant the shoreline was a fair way out from the path. She walked two-thirds of the way and sat on the cool, smooth sand, staring out to sea. The waves hit the beach with a mesmerising rhythm as she watched them. There was something wholly appropriate about the way the sea replenished them. It renewed them. It resurrected them and set them to their task once more. Each wave was being driven forward to its own demise. As individuals, they were bold yet brief and their power lasted just moments, but they were part of something much, much larger. A force that over the centuries had battered down the toughest of enemies. Alone, the waves were mighty yet insignificant but, together, they were an ancient tide.

Her thoughts turned to the task at hand. She concentrated. Focussed all her energy. That familiar prickle skipped across her skin. It was time, and her fingers tingled as they tapped absently on her thighs.

★

There was something different about Monday 22 April. James could feel it. He just couldn't quite put his finger on what it was. It started in much the same way as any other Monday, with every bone in his body wanting to stay under the warm duvet and protesting against all of his attempts to move. After several coffees, James began his usual walk to work. The sun was shining and it illuminated the petals of the hundreds of daffodils that lined every front garden in the street. Their trumpets heralded the arrival of warmer weather and he breathed in the sweet smell of spring with each stride.

The seagulls screamed their tawdry tune and it sliced through his brain like a massacring chainsaw. As always, they called each other to share newly found tasty treasure they had unearthed, and then fought ferociously for the slim pickings. James hated the seagulls. They were a kilogram of crap that rendered alleys impassable by excreting indiscriminately from their lofty perches, like castle owners in the Middle Ages. They tore open bins with their yellow daggers and strewed decaying debris randomly across roads, then they gathered fleetingly to guzzle on the catch of the day, before leaving it to whatever rodents lusted after the leftovers.

He made sure that the walk took him past the place where Lauren had first smiled at him. It seemed so long ago now. Since that moment, the days without her had dragged so much that he felt he had lived every day twice.

A huge grin flashed across his impassive face as he recalled her gaze once more. It drew a flicker of flame off the roasting embers inside him that lay poised, ready to engulf the slightest fuel that might touch them. It reminded him that hope, while fading fast, still smouldered inside him. Those joyous kisses were now almost a month ago, yet it might easily have been a decade. Time was ticking away and, while he knew the image of their embrace would forever remain fresh in his memory, the fact was that in four weeks he had heard nothing. The prospect of spending lifetimes together with Lauren seemed more and more remote with every passing second.

Many times a day he replayed the scene at the nightclub. Aside from the desire he felt for her, whenever he conjured her image, James was full of frustration. He wished he had played it differently and found a way to stay in control, but he couldn't work out what he had done wrong. Whenever he had gone to say something, Lauren had silenced him with a kiss. It was as though she didn't want him to ask any questions. He regretted not finding a way to give her his number. She had no way to contact him now and whether or not he saw her again was now down to fate. That wasn't something that sat well alongside his usually wide circle of influence.

There was a mysterious wind blowing, one that teased the hairs on his arms into a frenzy, whispering words at him that he couldn't quite understand. The day certainly felt like it had something promising to offer and James was intrigued about what it might be. He hoped, no begged, that it was something to do with Lauren. That familiar purpose hovered around him, the one he had felt three times before and longed to feel again, though it lacked the intensity of what he had felt when she was near. With every step, it seemed to grow, and the air crackled with possibilities. His senses were on fire, teased by the slightest disturbance. His eyes saw shadows where there could be none, his ears seemed to hear voices in the rustling of the trees, in the squeal of the seagulls, in the rush of passing cars.

Come.

It is time.

James shuddered in dismissal and shook the thought out of his head. Since his mum had passed away, he had suspected that he needed counselling, but in the last three months, since— since Lauren— he'd felt alive again. Now, for a brief moment he questioned his mind once more, wondering if he might be ready for the psychiatrist's couch after all. He was hearing cars talking to him? He allowed himself a smirk at the thought of explaining this to a professional.

'Cars you say. And what exactly are these cars saying Mr, er,' he'd look down at his notes, 'Jordan?'

The truth of the matter was that the cars weren't the only things that seemed to be calling to him. Everything was. A peculiar chant was whistling through the air.

By now James was at the top of the Old High Street,
where the cobbles merged into Rendezvous Street, the
start of the paved central precinct. It was dirty and
dilapidated. Every time he passed through, he noticed
more and more boarded shop-fronts. It was now little
more than a sequence of betting shops, bars and pawn
brokers. In a few hundred yards, he would be at work. He
could even see the office looming ahead. It towered over
the centre, like a cathedral to working worshippers whose
diligent homage was rewarded weekly or monthly, but
who were preyed on annually by shareholder greed. As he
walked, the calling was everywhere, from everything. His
senses were nearing overload and nausea began to dizzy
him. James was grateful for a nearby bench and sat, lest he
should fall. He placed his hands on his ears as though that
would stop the whispering, but it didn't. It amplified it,
clarified it. A familiar wave of excitement broke over him.
The words had changed. They were meant for him. He
was certain.

Beach. Come to the beach.

He felt the need to move. Underneath him, the bench
was nudging him away, like a numbing leg shooing a
sleeping cat. Even the wind seemed to have changed
direction and was trying to buffet him away. Tired of
fighting his growing psychosis, James decided it would
cost him nothing to go there. He would be late for work
of course, but right now he was in no state to perform.

Come to think of it, it had been a while since he had done anything spontaneous. He had been too absorbed by the frustration of his pining for Lauren.

So, he retraced his steps back down towards the harbour, and all the way the omnipresent orchestra played its seaside symphony, encouraging him forward. He was compelled onwards. On, under the fishy arches and through to the promenade above the sea defence. Despite the tide being out, James could hear the familiar rolling of the sea as it breathed in and out in a comforting rhythm, welcoming him. It looked so calm. Like a snoring bear, calling to be cuddled, yet whose anger once awakened, was ferocious. He could taste the coastal air on his tongue. It fizzed slightly as it penetrated his gently panting lips.

James marvelled at the fifty or so arches that curled around in front of him, supporting the fragile chalk foundations of the town above. He was so familiar with them, that for years he had passed them without really noticing them. Today he was on alert, however, and noticed everything. Beyond the dull and rusting metal railings of the sea defence lay a pure page of golden sand. It was as yet unmarked after the tide's recent retreat. On this stretch of beach there were none of the encroaching pebbles that defined the town's western coast. The sweeping arm of the harbour protected it. Here there was nothing but castle-making sand. Not the flimsy and dusty Mediterranean sand that basked in perennial sunshine and ran through fingers like caster sugar. This beach received a daily drowning from the high tide and, on this particular day, it was still damp.

The pristine sand called as it always did to be defaced like freshly fallen snow, and James felt duty-bound to do so. He had lost track of how long it had been since he'd last felt its coarseness on his fingers and toes. A childish excitement that had been absent for a while paid him a fleeting visit. It wouldn't hurt, would it? He sat on the slippery seaweed that clung for dear life to the arched seawall and removed his shoes and socks. The seaweed released its bottled smell of the sea as he stepped past it onto the sand. He was excited about the blank canvas that lay before him. Except on closer inspection it wasn't completely blank. Large swathes lay untouched and awaited a master painter's first strokes, but they were divided by a set of footprints that led out towards the dozing sea. He followed their line and in the distance sat a slight, but indistinguishable figure, staring out across the channel towards the distant French Coast.

James wanted to be alone. He started to walk along the sand, away from the existing marks. Instantly he heard the sea begin to call out to him. It was urging him out towards the distant shoreline. He suddenly felt glad it was pushing him that way too. For some reason, every part of his instinct wanted to join the figure at the water's edge. He began the long walk out towards the sea and felt the give of the sand push his feet sideways with each step. He fumbled his way across the beach, and at the midpoint he felt a familiar warmth. It was a feeling he had craved like a withdrawing addict. He broke into a run. As he closed in he felt a pervading gravity reach out to him. Sucking him in. He complied without hesitation.

By now, the figure had turned towards him and was smiling at his puppy-like arrival. It was a face that James had studied so many times in his dreams, yet had seen all too briefly in reality. Its beauty was everything that he recalled and more.

Lauren smiled as James pulled her towards him and held her close. He took a month's comfort from a momentary embrace. Once more James could feel the overwhelming togetherness that he had felt that night in the club. The simmering embers inside him were now aflame, and Lauren's gaze just kept on fanning them. His stomach filled with excited butterflies. A million questions flew through his mind like bubbles on the wind, bursting as he clutched them. He was speechless. The more he struggled to form words, the more useless and inappropriate they seemed. He was simply wrapped in a comforting silence.

James guessed that all his questions would be answered in time, at least that was if he could ever actually articulate them. More pressingly, an unnerving realisation began to develop inside his mind. He was unsure where it

was coming from but it was growing rapidly. He wasn't
scared but his instinct was in overdrive. Primal warnings
sounded throughout his body. What he was thinking
wasn't normal. It wasn't possible. Yet the more he thought
about it the more he was convinced. He knew what
Lauren was going to say.

'You came,' she whispered gently, and enchanted him
with a kiss like no other.

Right then there was nothing other than Lauren and
he, and it felt magical. Yes. Magical, that was the word.
Her presence bewitched him. Her gaze left him
spellbound. It really was extraordinary. James still felt
trapped inside his body. Unable to move and unable to
speak. He was helpless, and he loved every minute of it.
Such was the power of his obsession with Lauren. After
several failed attempts and what felt like an eternity of
scrabbling for sentences, he managed to say something.

'H-how did you know I was coming?'

'You tell me? What do you think brought you here?'

In all honesty, James felt a little reluctant to explain the
events of the last half hour. He really wanted to make sure
that he made the most of this opportunity with Lauren.
She had an uncanny knack of slipping through his fingers
and the last thing on earth that he wanted now was to say
anything that might ruin his chances with her. Under the
circumstances, talk of whispering cars, prodding winds
and a shrugging bench that had forced him here hardly

seemed a sensible opening gambit.

'I'm not sure I know.'

'So, it's just a coincidence that you turned away from work at the last minute and found your way to me at the beach, is it?'

James was dumbfounded. He had longed for this moment since that night at the club. He'd cursed himself every day since for allowing her to leave without any means for follow-up. Despite his hopes, he had all but resigned himself to never laying eyes on her again. It had suited him to accept that this was all a convenient coincidence, even if it was way beyond anything he had experienced before. Of course, the idea that there was a deal of orchestration to this meeting had occurred to him; it was just too uncomfortable to consider, so he had buried it in his excitement at seeing Lauren. Unfortunately, it had now wormed its way to the surface again and was wriggling itself in front of him. He couldn't ignore it any longer. Something otherworldly was at work here. Something he didn't understand.

'Come on James. We've got lots to talk about, but we can't talk about anything until you can accept how you got here.'

'W-what?'

'How did you end up here? Tell me!' Lauren's insistent tone left James in no doubt that it was she who had made him come here. That meant it was okay to talk. It didn't make the subject any more comfortable though.

'Y-you?'

'I what?'

'You made me, somehow?'

There. He'd said it. Now perhaps they could fast-forward to 'look, it was nice to meet you, and of course I'll call you,' spoken with a pleasant tone that would conceal the fact that he was clearly a weirdo.

'There. That wasn't so hard, was it?'

'You have no idea …'

'What, of the way that everything calls to you and overwhelms your senses?'

'Yes …'

'… the fear that you were going completely mad?'

'Ye …'

'… Trying to work out what to do? Do you go with it, into the unknown? Give yourself up to what you suspect may be a psychotic episode?'

'Okay! Perhaps you do know!'

'Of course I do! How do you think I found out I could do it?' Lauren announced. At a basic level, James was relieved that at least he'd not ruined his chances with her, but at every other level he was all over the place. Lauren seemed to be telling him that she could control him, make him do whatever she wanted. That was not an attractive quality!

Lauren sensed James' unease and gently took his hand.

Pulses of that familiar power leapt through the connection. She looked at him longingly, desperate for him to understand, and nestled her warm, soft cheek against his.

'That was me calling you. And you came!' she whispered. With that she nibbled his ear gently and excitement exploded through his body. At that moment, he felt he would gladly surrender himself to her control, such was her magic.

'But how can you do that?' James said after a time, temporarily breaking her hold. 'This is freaking me out Lauren. Most people pick up the phone if they want to see people?'

'I know, James.' Her voice was smooth as silk. Her tone soothed his fears like a mother settling a newborn. 'But I had to show you.'

'I'm not so sure. I think I probably could have coped without knowing any of this to be honest.'

'On the contrary, you needed to believe.'

'Believe what exactly?'

'Who we are and what we can do.'

'I think you mean what *you* can do.' James was scornful.

'No, you can do it too.'

'Oh, come on. You think I can make people do things with my mind?'

'No.'

'Isn't that what you just did to me?'

'It is.'

In an entirely new twist James began to feel Lauren's voice inside his head. She began to talk straight into his consciousness and demand attention.

I can transmit my thoughts to you and you alone. I can share your mind and you can share mine.

James could feel her inside his head. She was there. She could see his thoughts. He flushed with embarrassment as some of the many thoughts of making love to her immediately popped in. He sheepishly looked away as the prized stolen image down Lauren's singlet that night presented itself. There were a million things that he could have been thinking, and he cringed at the idea that his sleazy mind had sold itself out so quickly.

It didn't matter though. Lauren shot him an arresting gaze that screamed togetherness. To defuse some of his discomfort and equalise the balance of power, she shared some of her own intimate thoughts with James. He was astonished at how clearly he could see them. It struck him that if this was the way they could communicate with each other there would never be misunderstandings, there would be no confusion, and certainly no secrets. Considering their exciting content, James held on to the images for as long as he could. Meanwhile, Lauren pushed ahead with her explanation.

Let me share the story with you.

James braced himself to focus on her message but he needn't have done. It reverberated so powerfully through his head that it would have been impossible to ignore. Within seconds it had slain its erotic predecessor. In telling the story Lauren occasionally spoke words, but they were mostly for effect. The details were in the images that she shared with James and they needed no comment or clarification. Watching them was like watching a movie, only clearer and in more dimensions. It was real. It felt like James was there. He was living through her eyes. He could feel everything she felt. Whatever she touched, he did too. It was incredible.

In her images, Lauren took James backwards through recent events. It was truly bizarre. James saw situations that he remembered, but through someone else's eyes. She started with their previous meetings and James had to confess that he preferred his own image of their passion that night at the club. He screwed up his face and tried to look away as he watched his own lips pucker. There was something very disconcerting about watching himself come in for a kiss. Lauren chuckled at his discomfort and replayed the scene again and again, just to remind James that she was in control. It was her story and she wanted to be able to tell it without interruption. After a number of repeats she playfully threw in a seductive image that captured James' attention immediately. Briefly they swapped erotic thoughts like teenagers 'sexting' from their bedrooms while their parents assumed they were busy doing their homework.

Lauren picked up her story again and continued to take him backwards. James stopped her when that first encounter on the street corner came into view. He was surprised to see it. All this time, he had assumed that Lauren was oblivious to his captivated stare. Clearly, he had been wrong. Even then, she had known he was there, but had chosen not to acknowledge him.

'Of course I knew you were there, I told you, I can feel your thoughts and emotions,' she spoke this time, and the change in channel offered a welcome relief from what was an awesome, yet slightly nauseating experience. 'You could have come and spoken to me.'

'Oh come on, that's not fair. You were talking to someone else and, besides, you obviously must have known that we were supposed to be together.'

'You're right, I did.'

'So why didn't you talk to me? It would have saved me a whole load of anguish over the last few months!'

'Haven't you heard the saying that a man chases a woman until she's caught him? Don't you like the thrill of the chase?'

'Well yes, but I'd all but given up, if I'm honest. If it had been me there's no way I would have been able to keep away from you!'

'I was desperate to see you too, James. But you have

to understand that we needed to do it this way. I had to show you what we were capable of, how much power we share, before we could talk about it. Otherwise you'd have thought I was mad!'

'Look, I take your point. That doesn't take away from the pain of the last few months though. You made me feel helpless and out of control.' Any churlishness in James' response evaporated immediately with Lauren's responding embrace.

Her lips tasted salty. It was a present from the seaborne breeze that wrapped up an occasional spray and thrust it into their arms with thanks. James immersed himself in Lauren, and she in he. They responded to each other's counter with increasing frenzy, though Lauren deftly fended off any unwelcome advances before James had any opportunity to enact them. Such was the betrayal of his mind.

'I need to tell you the rest.' Lauren deliberately chose voice over vision to break the contact between their lips. Straightaway, James felt her inside his head again and the images seized his attention as she shared the story of the day she found the body on the beach. Throughout it all, he felt as though everything was happening to him. He registered Lauren's discomfort at the thought of taking the girl's hand. He jumped when he registered that she was identical to Lauren in every way. He felt the charge fire through his body when the two girls connected.

Sabine.

He too felt aware of Lauren's consciousness bailing manically against the tide that had flown through her, trying her best to stay afloat. At the same time, he felt an overwhelming sorrow as the life force of Lauren's double extinguished.

'Bloody hell!' was all James could muster as he forced Lauren out of his head in an act of self-preservation.

'It's okay James,' said Lauren, reassuring him with her touch.

'Is it? It doesn't feel okay! What on earth just happened? Who was that woman? Why did she …' Lauren silenced him with a finger to his lips, as she seemed to be doing quite regularly.

'I'm still trying to make sense of it myself. All I can tell you is that you've only seen a tiny part of it.'

'A tiny part of what? What do you mean?'

'Well, all you've seen are *my* memories.'

'You mean there's more?'

'Yes. The surge that sent me unconscious. It was a surge of memories.'

'Whose?'

'People like us, James.'

'What do you mean by people like us? Until just now I'd thought I was the same as everyone else. Is that not the case?'

'No, people *exactly* like us. Identical in every way.'

'W-what?'

'You'll see. Are you ready?'

With that she clasped James' hand tightly and immediately he felt more visions seep into his consciousness. They trickled through the connection at first, without the urgency this time. Lauren seemed to be holding back the deluge, though the rapidly increasing speed made James wonder how long she would be able to hold it back. Memories began to tear into him in waves. Each molecule of water a recollection, each wave a lifetime. The sheer volume of information was swamping him. He couldn't process it. Whenever he tried to concentrate on one memory it was quickly engulfed by a million more. He was drowning.

In his brief gasps for air above the almighty swell of information, James clutched at snippets. In each there was some brief record of a time long gone. And Lauren had been right. There were constants in every one that astonished him. Lauren. James. Individually. Together. These seemed to be chronicles of their lives over many centuries. Lives that were inextricably intertwined. An unbroken line that spanned almost a millennium, in which people identical to James and Lauren had met and loved each other. In what must have been hundreds of individual lifetimes, the two of them had managed to find one another and had fallen in love. It didn't seem to matter where, or what century. The love they shared was fierce and ferocious. They had history, James and Lauren. Of that there was no doubt. They'd been together in wars. They had found each other across continents at times when travel within a single country took weeks. James could feel the love that he already knew he felt for Lauren reinforced over and over again by a passionate history. With each episode, its intensity grew.

He could only gather brief insights before the weight of their collective made concentration impossible. It was like he was trying to keep his eyes on a single drop of water across an expansive ocean. Despite the brevity of each experience, James was in each life vicariously. He could feel what they were feeling. The love, the terror, the sadness, the euphoria. Generation after generation they had found, loved and lost each other. Tragically.

That was a less welcome theme. Wherever James located an ending, it was always wretched. Despite the supremacy of the love that bonded each of those lives together, the lilies of death were never far from the joyous roses. There was an undercurrent of abject sorrow and from what he could tell the love that was handed down was, without exception, unrequited. Every time, circumstance and fate conspired to keep the lovers apart.

By now, Lauren was struggling to hold back the flow. Entire lives flew through James' consciousness like files transferred from an external hard drive. The speed at which they began to pass was phenomenal. Initially, they had been viewing the images at the speed of a dial-up connection, but now they were positively fibre optic in comparison.

Absorbing any information became impossible. The waves were coming so fast. James felt his brain swelling with its new load. He was struggling to stay in control. The inputs were enormous. Eventually the strain was too much. All he could grasp were two names.

Diego. Isabel.

Without warning, the tempestuous torrent ceased as if the power cable had been severed and James and Lauren both hit the sand, rendered unconscious by overloaded senses that had shut down with the enormity of content.

5

THE SEARING ARAGONIAN sun continued its lifetime of branding on Diego's fast-weathering skin. Its relentless power had long since banished any semblance of water from the dusty, barren soil that cracked under his feet. An occasional warm breeze whipped up an onslaught of dusty earth that invaded his eyes and infiltrated every fold of his tunic. Heat had painted over nature's colour and left a sandy and featureless canvas. Even Diego's clothes were monochrome. They camouflaged him seamlessly against the arid thirteenth-century landscape.

Only one person could afford vivid colours and fine linens, and that was Don Pedro de Azagra, the dreaded Lord of Albarracín. He flaunted the most recent arrivals from the rest of the continent and this year, 1212, it was blue. But his was far from an assured azure authority that commanded respect from the generic fawn; he was a tyrant. He ruled on a whim and by the sword. With a tell-tale stroke of his blanching stubble, he sentenced those who had wronged him to horrific deaths. He had no legitimacy, but his wealth and the fear that he instilled in the masses, kept him on his beloved pedestal. He was the richest man in Teruel and he made sure that everyone knew it.

The toiling serfs scratched out a living as they fought to regain what they had lost when the locust plague had hit four years earlier. Those infernal insects had pillaged the peasants' crops like a million marauding Vikings. So total was the devastation, that even Diego's family, the House of Marcilla, had been all but ruined. All they had now was their family name, one that Diego's father had built up in his short period dispensing justice to the people of the town. Nowadays, Don Martin was merely a barren baron with a wife and three children to support. Diego and his brothers, Sancho and Domingo, were reduced to working the fields day in and day out, and only now were the shoots of new crops beginning to sprout.

Life was hard. No doubt about it. Only one thing made life worth living for Diego and that was the occasional glimpse of his childhood sweetheart Isabel de Segura. They had grown up together at a time when their families had been equals. Back then they had been free and each day had been a gift. Throughout it all they had been watched over by the mighty Muela de San Juan. It stood guard, supported by the rest of the Universal Mountains, which shadowed the meandering Guadalaviar as it swept all before it to distant Valencia and on to the mysterious Mediterranean.

Diego and Isabel chased each other throughout the rolling lands of Teruel. And as they grew so the game turned from one of escape, to one of joy at capture as each chase ended in a scorching embrace. Inevitably Isabel would be the chaser and Diego would half-heartedly evade her until he would succumb in feigned reluctance to her glorious entrapment. He would revel in those eyes of dusky jade as they glistened through the raven curtains that so often concealed them. Then he would part them with his hands and open the window to that sweet, delicate face. They were meant for each other, Isabel and he. They felt a profound destiny in their togetherness. It was as if a divine will had ignited their passion for each other.

'We'll be together forever, my sweet Diego,' she had whispered, the last time they embraced, and those words branded themselves into Diego's memory.

'I adore you Isabel,' he countered, not for the first time. What Diego felt for her was way beyond anything that could be called love. A single word was not enough to describe it. Nothing would be sufficient to convey how he felt about her at that moment, at every moment. He longed for Isabel. He needed her.

Isabel had held him closer as she absorbed those words. Diego felt her passion erupt through their clasped hands. When they touched, it was like a bolt of lightning. The incandescence of her response engulfed Diego as it tore through her every physical connection with him. The flare of her feelings somehow communicated what they both felt for each other, in a way that words could never emulate. It was an unstoppable love that would destroy everything that blocked its path.

The locusts changed all that when their ubiquitous onslaught hit the Sierra de Albarracín that fateful summer. In a matter of days, the generations of wealth that had propped up the prosperity of the Marcilla were gone. Those insects ingested their inheritance. The army routed their root vegetables and slaughtered their corn. Overnight the Marcilla lost parity with the Segura family. This was an age in which alliances between families were the key to unlocking power and wealth in the Kingdom of Aragon. Unlike Diego's family, who were left counting the cost of the swarming plague, the wealth of the merchant Segura remained intact. They continued to ply their trade, untouched by the onslaught. Almost immediately, Rafael de Segura cut Diego's family adrift. In his eyes, they no longer had the status that friends of his should possess, and he distanced himself from them in favour of loftier ambitions. The Marcilla didn't mourn for his superficial friendship—they had troubles enough of their own to overcome. But Diego was disconsolate. Rafael removed the beautiful Isabel and her sister, Maria, from temptation. He surrounded them with servants whose role appeared to be to assist, though who had clearly been instructed that their true purpose was to keep Isabel away from Diego. What had once been just a handful of doorways that stood between Isabel and Diego as they grew up, turned into an arid ravine. At the foot of it, Diego could do nothing but stare upwards in the forlorn hope of some assistance from above.

For the four long years that followed, Diego and his brothers pounded their picks against the unforgiving earth. Day after day their skin pruned in the scalding heat as they tried to rekindle a fortune from the ashes of disaster. At first, their noble hands bled from the blistering work they had previously been sheltered from. In no time, where once there had been soft pads on their palms, calluses began to grow. Diego's upper body lamented his labour. At the end of each day it screamed its agony. Over time, the sun bleached his youthful beard and cemented the look of determination on his face. Where once his eyes had smiled, they now seemed to rue his very existence.

Despite the pain, Diego worked ferociously. Each day he made the soil pay for his miserable separation from Isabel. He smashed it as if it were those who kept her away from him, and he punished it for its unwitting role in severing the indestructible bond that the two of them shared. For fourteen hundred and sixty-one consecutive days, he worked the ground. He ignored the convenient ailments that seemed to target Sancho and Domingo during that time and, on those occasions, he ploughed a lone furrow. His brothers had managed to accept the family's plummet from prosperity in a way that sometimes Diego envied, but more often despised. They had not lost what he had. Their one true purpose had not been wrenched from them as Diego's had. Unlike them, Diego had no choice but to dedicate his existence to regaining the family's riches. The quest for a return to loftier status consumed him. He never rested, such was his determination. He stopped for sustenance only when the sun withdrew its last tentacles of light from the twilight horizon.

On the fourteen hundred and sixty-second day, something distracted Diego from his resolve. He had been raking his retribution with his usual vengeful vigour when, for once, he felt the need to down tools. Not because he had lost any of his desire to drag the House of Marcilla back to its rightful position and reclaim his most beautiful Isabel, or because, for once, he could see beyond the futility of his perpetual labour, though it was clear that his near-constant toil was bringing him no closer to his goal. Something strange was happening. The soil seemed to be calling to him. The clink of his mattock echoed its words. He felt peculiar. Normally he would have assumed that the heat had got to him, but it was too early for his daily duel with the sun, especially in winter. He tried to distract himself by working even harder, but the less attention he paid to it, the louder the soil whispered. All around him, nature seemed to pick up the chant. Birds sang it, flies hummed it. Always the same sound, the same rhythm. It was torturous and Diego doubled over the worn shaft that had become an almost permanent extension of his right arm, trying to block out the sound. He clasped his hands to his ears, as if that would somehow shut it out, but it did nothing other than magnify the effect. A river of sweat squirmed along the canal of his unclothed back as he felt the bewildered stare of his brothers. For once they had failed to find an unlikely injury to keep them at home, and they were astonished when they saw him start to walk away.

Something about walking seemed to harmonise with the whispering and he felt as though the sounds were spiriting him away, like the haunting sounds of a piper. He was unsure of his destination but clear on the direction. Everything was leading him the same way. He felt his senses heightened. For the first time in many years he registered the serenity of the Sierra. It was spoiled only by the squealing of silhouetted griffon vultures that circled it before returning to their lofty mountain perches.

Diego felt pulled towards the cool of the murmuring Guadalaviar, as if it were keen to share some frosty fable with him, and after a while he reached the lapping edge. His rippling reflection kept him company as he cupped the cooling water to his lips and over his sun-withered face. His determined blue-green eyes sparkled back at him from a face that was far older than its twenty years. His baby-face had gone, and the sun had leathered his skin. He wondered what Isabel would have made of its coarseness and the wearied auburn whiskers that had usurped the smooth and well-born countenance that she had grown to love. Diego lost himself slightly in the joyous memory of Isabel's last touch as he splashed his fatigued face with the wintry gift from the Muela. He smiled in recollection and it was returned by occasional swirling eddies that distorted his features into a grotesque and misshapen monster that resembled the turmoil of his inner emotions.

You're no monster.

Diego felt Isabel's words in his head. They bored straight into his tortured mind. He could sense that she was somewhere near. It was a feeling he'd felt countless times since his childhood, a magnetism that drew him towards her, an awakening inside him whenever she was near. His heart leapt with rampant anticipation. He scoured the shimmering banks for the source and saw a shadow on the shore, rendered featureless in the brilliance of the day. But he knew it was Isabel, and her fiery desire was urging him to cross the river.

Without hesitation, he threw himself into the icy flow. His skin flinched as its freezing fingers tightened their grip around him. Still he could hear Isabel in his mind. Calling him forward. Urging him on. She was stoking the furnace inside him and it roared into life. With it came the power he knew he would need if he were to overcome the penetrating flow. Time and time again he was ripped off-course by the water's deceptive flow. It was all he could do to hold his position before finding that extra effort that set him back on course. All the while he felt Isabel at his side. In those darkest moments as the flow snatched in seconds what he had gained in what seemed hours, it was Isabel that kept Diego going. He used her warmth to battle the bitter hold that the water had on him. He felt her fingers soothing his burning muscles. Above all, he felt fate driving him forward.

Eventually Diego broke the mighty river's hold and staggered into the shallows, where he collapsed on the riparian silt and it enveloped him in a sodden squelch. Immediately he felt Isabel's electric touch as she clawed at his sandy shoulders and helped him to crawl to the safety of the bank. She held him for what seemed an eternity, and then the two lovers kissed with a boundless desire that had once been shackled but now roamed free and wild. Diego had longed for this day. He had dreamed of once more gazing on that exquisite visage and to kiss those sweet lips. Four years of repressed rapture inundated the backs of his adoring eyes, and salty tears of joy weaved their way slowly down Diego's smiling cheeks, merging with Isabel's.

They spoke little at first. There were no words that could describe how they had missed each other. Instead they allowed their love to speak. When Diego finally uttered words he did so with a courage and determination that had been the only positive to emerge from those desolate fields. They were words that he knew by heart.

Words that he had memorised as he had split the dusty earth in the withering sun. It was a moment that he had prepared for. He would not falter. It was his destiny.

'Isabel, for four years I have tasted life without you and it is not a dish that I would ever sample again. It is for you that I exist and without you I am nothing. These have been the hardest years of my life. I have been separated from you by a wretched distance, yet still it is you that I have woken up to in the mornings. You have been my first and last thought of the day and every thought between. It is true that I can no longer give you riches or titles. I can no longer bring power to your family. But what I have for you is an eternal love that is blind to such boundaries. I know you share it. Isabel, will you marry me?'

'Diego, I have loved you for as long as life itself. Even though we have been apart for four years I have felt our love simmering in the distance, waiting for the heat that your presence brings. I have felt empty and void of purpose without you. The world has become a joyless chasm with depths that I will never return to again. I have longed for the day that we would meet again. Of course I will marry you.'

The embrace that followed was like no other. The heat of their love formed an alloy of passion that sealed them together in a perpetual bond. Diego and Isabel lay there on the river bank shaded by the broad and gnarly span of a giant Portuguese oak, which cast an ever-growing shadow as the sun retreated for a hard-earned rest and lit up the clear Spanish sky in a celebration of umber.

As the light faded, they made their way to Isabel's father as quickly as possible. They skipped through the familiar streets of the town, their hands and minds locked together in a sensory embrace. The stars seemed to twinkle their joy, and the waning moon tipped them an occasional wink of support through the evening's cloud. Being with Isabel once again was everything Diego had imagined and more. He was in ecstasy.

The town had changed in the four years since Diego had been there. It had grown threefold since Alfonso had liberated it from the Moors forty years earlier. In part, that was because people had returned, now the Reconquista had brought a newfound security to the region, but the largest influx of people had come to help build the cathedral of Saint Mary. It was going up little by little, just a block away from the street where the lovers had grown up. Even in the darkness, the chiselling of the masons chirruped through the town, and that day it was like a chorus of wedding bells that announced Diego and Isabel's arrival.

At last they reached the door of the Segura. It was one through which Diego had come and gone with greater and greater frequency as his love for Isabel had blossomed through their early teens. Though it was familiar, it had been closed to him for the past four years. Diego knew that Rafael would not welcome him, and he began to feel a little nervous as he pounded for attention. Isabel shared his trepidation and squeezed his hand a little tighter in support as the two of them waited for the door to open.

Rafael de Segura answered it himself and his displeasure at seeing Diego and Isabel together after all his efforts to keep them apart was noticeable. He had not spoken to Diego for some years, such was the distance that had grown between their neighbouring families and, if he was at all pleased to see him, he hid it well. Deep down he knew why the lovers were there, and the blood drained from his cheeks as though the arrival of a plague had been announced.

'What is the meaning of this?' he demanded of Diego. 'Did I not make it clear that you were to keep away from my daughter?'

'Father ...' Isabel attempted to interrupt.

'Don't *father* me! This boy is unworthy and unwelcome. Get out!' He waved his hand at Diego in dismissal.

'I will not,' Diego declared.

'Then you leave me with no choice but to throw you out!' He grasped the front of Diego's worn and dusty tunic and began pushing him back towards the door. Diego sensed at that moment that it wasn't just the door to the house that might close on him; he was sure that if he allowed it to slam shut it would also signify the end of his dream of a life with Isabel. The same determination that had willed him across the mighty Guadalaviar began to course through his body, and he could feel Isabel willing him on too, like bellows coaxing a fire.

'Stop!' Diego commanded, in a voice so assertive that Rafael instinctively paused. 'Rafael. You have made your point. It is clear that I am unwelcome in your house, a house that I once roamed freely as a child. In those days, you treated me as if I were your son. You taught me to hunt, to fight. It is you who encouraged Isabel and I to spend time together. Well I am still the same person, Rafael. All that has changed is my status. A status that was ripped away by circumstance, and one that I have worked tirelessly to regain for these last four years.'

'It was indeed unfortunate. But nonetheless, it happened.' Rafael continued to march Diego to the door.

'Rafael! Isabel and I have loved each other for many years. Keeping us apart has done nothing other than make that love more intense. I can no longer be apart from Isabel, nor she from I. Today, I ask you for her hand.'

To his credit, he did pretend to consider the idea for a while, deliberating long enough for Diego to foster a glimmer of hope. He knew that Rafael could see the love that Isabel and he shared—it was obvious to all. And, if he had any regard at all for Isabel's happiness, he would agree. Up to the point where those damned locusts had wreaked such havoc on the Marcilla name, he would have shaken Diego's hand and welcomed him into the family in a heartbeat.

'Diego, I have long known of your love for each other, but I simply cannot grant you permission to marry my Isabel.'

There it was. Rafael didn't care one iota for his daughter's happiness. It was all about money and status to him; nothing else mattered. There was little to gain from marrying his eldest daughter to a fallen family. The fact was Rafael wanted more for her than Diego was able to give.

'Father. That is unfair!'

'Isabel, your wishes are irrelevant. It is your duty to help to advance the Segura name and you are to be married to Don Pedro de Azagra, the Lord of Albarracín.'

'He is a tyrant! Do you have no care at all for me? Would you expose me to his cruelty just to feed your love of money?'

'Enough!' Rafael commanded. 'For the last year, he has been looking to take you, and it is just a question of agreeing the right deal.'

'You disgust me!' Isabel stared at her father, defiant and forlorn. His mind had been made up long ago and Isabel knew that it would be impossible to defy his wishes. Diego felt her overwhelming sadness rip the joy from his body and replace it with a black and empty hole that echoed her melancholy.

He knew he had to do something. He couldn't just

walk away from her. But what? He had no hope of proving himself worthy of her hand to a man who knew full well the true state of his family's decline. He had to buy some time. He knew her father had chosen status over love, but he also knew Rafael had to be aware how painful his decision was to both of them. Even if he wasn't prepared to admit it.

'Rafael, I understand your desire to marry Isabel to someone worthy, especially as she is your eldest daughter. But you know the kind of man that Don Pedro is. You've seen his cruelty on a daily basis. You can't surely expect that he will treat Isabel well?'

'Diego. I have grave concerns over Isabel marrying the Lord. But I have no choice. When they are married, the Segura will want for nothing.'

'But the deal is not yet done?'

'No.'

'Then let me propose an alternative.'

'Go on.'

'The only thing that stands in the way of us marrying is that I have no fortune.'

'Yes.'

'Then let me go and make one. Give me some time!'

'That is preposterous!'

'Why? All I ask is that you refrain from marrying Isabel to a heartless bastard who will beat her, and any children they might have. Is that so hard?'

'And how long do you propose, exactly?' Diego could feel Rafael warming to the idea.

'Five years.'

'Five years? You want me to keep the Wolf of Albarracín at bay for five years, while you supposedly earn enough status to return?'

'Yes.'

'And what is your plan?'

'I don't have one. All I can tell you is that with the love of Isabel driving me forward, I have no doubt that I will succeed.'

'Oh father. Do it! Let him try! Please? If Diego isn't able to do it, I will happily marry Don Pedro de Azagra.' Isabel's words were well chosen. Diego saw a tear beginning to well in Rafael's left eye. He was hopelessly caught between ruthless ambition and protecting his daughter. He knew how much she loved Diego. He pounded the wall a few times in exasperation at the choice he was presented with, pacing the room and loitering at the hearth, searching for inspiration among the dancing flames. After a time, he spoke.

'Go, Diego. Make your fortune. I will promise you that Isabel will marry no-one for five years, but if you do not return or are not of sufficient status when you do, then she will be married to the Lord of Albarracín five years from today.'

Diego fell silent. He had snatched a stay of execution

from Isabel's father, yet the prospect of making a fortune in five years, when he had achieved nothing in the previous four, seemed remote. He couldn't bear the idea that Isabel would marry someone else, let alone the black-hearted Lord. He also knew that he would be apart from her for that whole time, as he would have to seek his fortune outside Teruel, since there was none to be made locally. That meant he would once more be sentenced to being apart from his beloved Isabel, and that was the most painful thing of all.

Diego gathered a sobbing Isabel in his arms and embraced her as if it was the last time he would see her. He held her for as long as he dared, mindful both of the watching Rafael, and that the longer he held her the less he wanted to leave. At that point he reaffirmed his total commitment to her and gazed one last time on her beauty. He painted an image of her with his eyes. It was an image that he would take with him throughout his quest, to remind him of his worthy cause. As he left the house Diego heard Isabel's voice inside his head.

Stay safe Diego. My love will follow you to the end of the earth.

Across the street, Diego bade a tearful farewell to his family. They tried to make him stay, on a promise that the fruits of his labour were about to ripen. That once more the name of Marcilla would be worthy of the Segura. He wished he could believe them, dearly he did. The fact was that they had worked the field for four years and had little return. He couldn't gamble idly on being successful.

Diego travelled the length and breadth of the Kingdoms that would one day unite as Spain. He fought in battles alongside kings and lords and reaped the rewards of that fearless determination that Isabel had unlocked, which masqueraded as bravery. His reputation grew and, with it, his status. He marched with King Pedro the Second's force across the Pyrenees, and on to Muret. It felt incredible to be one of forty thousand Aragonese who were marching to liberate Toulouse from Simon de Montfort. There was camaraderie. Jubilance. Many had fought at the Battle of Las Navas de Tolosa where the Moors had been routed. The men were boisterous. Fearless. They relished the idea of further bloodshed as they swept over the mountains.

De Montfort's army was a tenth the size, and the Aragonese smelled victory. So overwhelming were their numbers that they chose to engage the enemy in battle rather than lay siege to the town. King Pedro himself led the vanguard dressed as a common soldier, so desperate was he to deliver victory from the front. It was an act of complacency that would cost them the battle, and Pedro his life.

The enemy's knights were far more disciplined and superior in every way, and crushed the first line of the Aragonese. In that first wave, King Pedro was killed.

Seeing their ruler fall so quickly, the remainder of the army lost their nerve and fled the scene. The battle was lost.

Diego ran for his life, and hid in the woods from the marauding aggressors, who pursued the fleeing thousands. Once they had passed, he returned to the battle scene and located the dead King, who had been passed over as just another corpse by the advancing victors. Diego felt that the King deserved better. He leant over King Pedro's filthy and bloody body, and strained as he hoisted it onto his shoulders and staggered away.

For weeks, Diego battled the elements as he carried the King across the Pyrenees. He was alone. Exhausted. Scared. The conviction that even in death the King deserved to be treated like one, drove him on across those icy Pyrenean paths. Many times he lowered the body to the floor as fatigue overcame him. Each time his determination to once more feel the love of Isabel forced him to his feet. All the while he counted each day that passed as if it were a golden maravedi that he had plucked from his treasure chest and discarded. Time was that precious.

Battered, frail and frozen, he arrived at Monzón near Huesca, with the festering remains of King Pedro. There he handed the now putrid body to the Knights Templar, who were caring for the boy-King Jaime, while his Uncle Sancho single-handedly looted the country over which he was Regent. They saw to it that King Pedro's body was buried fitfully and thanked Diego for his actions. Their hospitality kept him alive, but their gratitude alone wasn't enough. He knew that the pleasantries of a group of foreign knights would no more help him than the pointless earth pounding that he could have done in Teruel.

The days turned to months, and months to years. With the passing of time, the pressure on Diego to succeed grew exponentially. He travelled up and down the long road between wintry Huesca and Zaragoza, looking for opportunities where there were none. The Kingdom was in such disarray. Alliances and fortunes were hard to come by in such a lawless and ruthless society. Diego proved himself a determined worker and was paid well for his services but, while the money he had earned would make a huge difference to the Marcilla family, it was nowhere near enough to be seen as an equal of the Segura.

He always slept rough. It was a small hardship in his pursuit of a higher destiny. It kept him grounded, and it meant he wasn't paying the swindling inn-keepers and making merry. At night, he would sleep beneath the broad canopy of a Portuguese oak and stare longingly at the clear night skies. He was desperate for the moon to wink at him once more, as it had in that brief moment of ecstasy with Isabel. As always, his final thoughts of the day were of her. Each night as he closed his eyes, he could see that portrait of Isabel that he had painted in his memory. Even with time, those eyes lost none of their rich green hue and her lips were as pink and moist as they had been for that last, desperate kiss.

In early 1217, just weeks from the impending deadline that loomed ever larger on the horizon, King Jaime was brought to Zaragoza to be crowned. He was aware of the monumental effort Diego had made to bring back the body of his father, and one of his first acts as the new King was to summon him to his court. Diego went willingly and hopefully, and knelt before the new King.

'Diego de Marcilla, you performed a great service to my father in life and in death. I would have you rewarded. How can I repay the great service that you gave to the King of Aragon?'

'You are most gracious, Your Majesty. I did what I felt was right. I need only one thing. That is to be deemed worthy enough to marry my true love, Isabel de Segura.'

'Don Diego, you are most certainly worthy in the eyes of the King, and I will reward you handsomely. I will also decree that you are to marry Isabel at my court in Zaragoza.'

Diego wept tears of joy as he thanked the King. Finally, fortune seemed to be favouring him. He pictured the delight on Isabel's face as he imagined her opening the door to him, throwing her arms around him. And to be married at the King's court! Rafael de Segura had wanted status and it didn't come better than that.

He bolted the one hundred miles to Teruel. Rode

through the blackest of nights and the brightest of days. All the time he was mindful that the end of five years was fast approaching. He did not rest, did not eat. He needed nothing for himself other than the love of Isabel. His only stops were at the insistence of his poor exhausted horse.

As the sun began to set on the last day left of his five years, Diego caught the first glimpse of the walls of his hometown. In his absence, it had changed significantly again. He spurred his ailing horse forward and rode through the gates. He had made the deadline, and his elation kept his physical frailty at bay. All he wanted was to see his beloved Isabel. It would be just one more day before they were married.

Belying his fatigue, Diego thumped on the Segura house with an air of invincibility. This time he had none of the nerves that had betrayed his knock five years earlier. Confidence oozed from the King's decree that lined his pocket.

The door opened and Rafael's face fell as he opened the door. The man seemed to have a knack of sucking the joy from Diego's heart with the merest glance.

'Diego! I'm surprised to see you! I assumed you were dead! Come in.'

'No thank you, Rafael. I want nothing other than to see the light of my life and prepare for our wedding tomorrow.'

'Why, my boy. You are a day too late!' The last three words impaled Diego like daggers in his heart that twisted to ensure their damage was complete.

'I am not a day too late!' His fury at Rafael's greeting was fuelled by a lustrum of lament, and Diego spat his words as he dangled the parchment in front of his bulbous face. 'I have marked the passing of every one of the one thousand eight hundred and twenty-five days that I have been away and I can assure you that I am not late! Not a morning or night has passed where I haven't remembered my sweet Isabel. My desire to be her husband has driven me from great lows to great highs. I have fought for the Kingdom and earned the gratitude of King Jaime of Aragon. It has been decreed by his majesty himself that I am to marry Isabel at his court in Zaragoza. Would you defy your King?'

'Diego, you don't understand! It is too late! Isabel was married to the Lord of Albarracín this morning. Even a King cannot annul a marriage!'

For a moment, the words bounced around in the air as Diego's ears refused to allow them access. When they finally made their way in, he fell to the floor in shock. Once more a remorseless fate had whipped him. What had he done to upset the natural order so? Why did it continue to take vengeance on him?

The sheer force of will, the torch that had lit Diego's way for these last five years and the four before, exploded out of his body. His inner fire extinguished. Destiny lay steaming in front of him like a dog's fresh excrement.

Strength evaporated from his body. Five years of running on adrenalin and love alone had taken their toll on him. Now that determination had vanished, he was just an empty and brittle shell.

A guilty and devastated Rafael helped Diego to his feet. He was mortified. Not only had he sacrificed his daughter to a life of cruelty in order to further his status, he had also missed the opportunity to give her away in the King's court at Zaragoza. He muttered mild platitudes and apologies at Diego as he led him to his horse, but they fell on deaf ears, as Diego didn't even have the energy to respond. He slumped in the saddle, and with enormous effort spurred the horse forward and on, on to the fortified mountain residence of Don Pedro de Azagra, Lord of Albarracín.

Night had fallen when Diego arrived, and the moon, friendly until now, seemed to laugh at him through its waxing crescent, as even it conspired against him. With what remained of his energy, he stole into the castle through an underground passage that he had known of since childhood, when he and his friends had dared each other to go further and further into the evil Lord's lair. He sought out Isabel's chambers, letting his senses guide him as he stumbled through the fortress, while the flickering torchlight danced a devil's jig on the maze of walls. When finally he located her room, Diego knocked at her door.

'Who is it?'

It had been so long since Diego had heard that sweet voice and the thought of the embrace that awaited him on the other side gave him new life.

'Diego de Marcilla, servant of King Jaime and eternal companion of Isabel de Segura.'

The door flew open and there stood Isabel. His heart leapt at the thrill of seeing her and for a brief moment it replaced the betrayal at her failure to wait for him. Isabel's inner guilt burst through her smile, and in that instant his sense of betrayal returned.

'Isabel what have you done? You promised to wait for me. I have counted every day that has passed until today, the third day of January. The fifth anniversary of my vow to return. In each, you have been the first, last and only thought on my mind. Has it not been the same for you? After all my efforts, I have returned to find that you married that evil wolf this morning. Did you not count the days as I did? Were you so desperate for a title that you jumped at the opportunity?'

'Oh Diego I didn't just count the days, I counted the mornings, the afternoons and the nights. One thousand eight hundred and twenty-five days that passed without a single word from you! I rejected numerous advances from the Lord of Albarracín during those five years in the hope that you would return. Finally, I agreed that I would marry him today, the fourth day of January, after much pressure from my father. You hadn't returned and I thought you were dead!'

'Were it not for you I surely would be dead by now, Isabel. It is you alone that has spurred me on every day since I left. But how could you have mixed up the dates so? This is your fault!'

'How dare you blame me! I have not mixed up the dates!' Isabel was indignant. 'With all my heart I wish you had returned yesterday, so that we could be together. But you did not! You left me with no choice. I had given my father my word.'

'But your dates cannot be right! Only nine days ago, I watched, alone and miserable, as the court of King Jaime celebrated Christmas.'

'You have made a terrible mistake Diego. That is just not possible. We celebrated Christmas ten days ago. Somehow you have lost a day somewhere on the journey.'

Diego was adamant that he had not miscounted, knowing that his singular focus on returning to his beloved made it inconceivable that he would miss a day. But was he really saying that the whole town of Teruel had celebrated Christmas a day early? It was an argument he could never win. He felt deflated, punctured by yet another blow that fate had aimed at him. All he had left was his love for Isabel. He knew she felt the same.

'Isabel, after all this time apart, let us not argue about dates. My love for you burns as brightly now as the stars on my happiest night.'

'When the moon was winking at us.'

'Now, I'm afraid it does nothing but laugh. I cannot live without you Isabel. Come away with me, my horse is outside. Let us go before the King and seek his help!'

Tears filled Isabel's eyes. They were a cocktail of joy and sorrow that reflected her hopeless position. With every beat of her heart, she wanted to leave with Diego. The fire that burned for him was raging once more, but she knew that Don Pedro would retaliate if she did so. He had already made it clear to her that, if she ever left him, he would have her father killed and do unspeakable things to her sister.

'Diego I am overjoyed to see you after all these years and my love for you surges through my veins. But it's too late for us. I am a married woman and wedded to my word. I will not break the vow that I made to Don Pedro this morning and bring shame on myself and pain to my family.'

Diego winced as this second dagger seemed to stab his already bleeding heart. His chest began to heave and he felt himself explode inside. The colour drained from his face as he thrust both hands to the source of the pain. He was struggling for breath. His chest was heavy. The agony was intense. He knew that fate was about to take the ultimate revenge on him. The punishment that he had put his body through in the name of love had been too much, and he knew that in a matter of moments he would be dead.

'Isabel … kiss … me …' Diego gasped with what was almost the last of his breath.

Right now, he welcomed death. There could be no life without Isabel. He could never have forsaken her as she had, him. Her back was turned away from him, oblivious to his condition. Diego sank to his knees. He gasped for an elusive breath and tried to hold back the extraordinary pain in his chest. He fought it fiercely but to no avail. With all his remaining strength, he forced his thoughts into Isabel's head.

Isabel I am dying! Kiss me.

He could feel the turmoil inside her. He could sense the futile war that love was waging. It was hopelessly outnumbered by fear and a domineering sense of duty. With a symbolic finality, Diego felt Isabel slam her mind shut to his intrusion and with that their love was forever to be unrequited. It was a final, mortal wound and, with it, Diego fell to the floor. As he did so, Isabel came rushing over and clasped his clawing outstretched hand. Fireworks scorched through that final clench. In his final seconds, the memory of everything that Diego had ever experienced, exploded into Isabel's mind.

6

THE TIDE TICKLED James' toes as it inched forward, like a child sneaking in to do something mischievous and then running off before being caught, only to return emboldened. Its cold tongue licked him from a dreamy slumber, and it was several seconds before he realised that he was still lying on the beach. The tide was coming in.

The last thing he recalled was a tsunami of senses submerging his mind in sensations. And names. Diego and Isabel. He had felt centuries of touch laying claim to every inch of his body as he surfed a clawing crowd. He had heard the echoes of eons exploding in his inner ear, and seen glimpses of the world through the eyes of others, each desperate to tell their story. As a collective, their deluge had dragged him downward and he had fought the relentless swell of their suffocating surge until it overwhelmed him completely.

James cleared the remnants of the onslaught from his head and turned to Lauren, who was stirring next to him. She had been luckier than he, in that the childish waves had only just begun their game with her, whereas they had seized the opportunity to slip under most of his body in those bleary seconds as he awoke, and beneath him he could feel the squelch of freshly washed sand.

He rose to kneel and felt the unpleasant chill of wringing wet clothes as they fell away from his skin. He leaned over to Lauren and gently placed his lips to hers, then watched the fog subside from her clearing jewels as she woke.

'What the hell just happened?' he whispered.

'Sensory overload. I think it must happen every time. These are the entire recollections of hundreds of real lives. In minutes, we've felt everything that every one of them experienced over nearly a thousand years.'

'I had the strangest dream!'

'It wasn't a dream, James. That was the memory of Diego de Marcilla.'

'You had it too?'

'Yes. It's the earliest and strongest memory.'

'It was incredible! I was there! I felt it all! The love, the determination, the pain, the betrayal, the abject misery. I *was* Diego de Marcilla. I felt … him … die.' James' voice cracked unexpectedly as the sadness temporarily took control, and Lauren embraced him until the grief subsided. 'Why is this happening Lauren?'

'I wish I could tell you, but I really don't know. There are hundreds of these lifetimes. I feel an extraordinary privilege to be able to feel and share this love that has been nurtured over centuries. It's like the Olympic flame being passed from one identical lover to another. I just wish it didn't come with such abject sadness.' Lauren was welling up herself now and James could feel precursory spasms fire uncontrollably across her shoulders. They hinted at the tears that were to follow and, as the salty sorrow sculpted its way across her exquisite cheeks, she continued. 'I felt my heart blacken.'

'What happened to you—I mean—Isabel?'

By now they were walking back up the beach and away from the childish tide. James' sodden clothes squeaked a melody with every step, and the chill reminder and responding flinch beat out an unwelcome rhythm, as the two of them strode hand in hand across the sand.

With the sea far behind them in the distance, they perched on the pebbled concrete of the sea defence and huddled together, bracing themselves for the next instalment. Lauren grasped James' hand firmly and teased out the memories from Isabel. Within seconds they were back there. Back in that dreaded room. Immersed, once more, in the misery of the moment.

'Don Pedro! Don Pedro come quickly!' Isabel was out of control and hysterical. She could hear the misery in her own piercing screams, as the castle walls returned them with interest. 'Something terrible has happened!'

The flagon that Don Pedro de Azagra had just depleted clattered to a faraway floor. Isabel heard a distant curse that bemoaned the interruption. His steps were slow at first but his pace quickened as adrenalin vanquished the last of his stupor. In no time at all he was at the door. He seemed to pause briefly and steel himself for whatever unwelcome twist of fate had dared to interrupt him. This, after all, was the night in which he hoped to finally lay claim to Isabel after being made to wait by that meddling merchant. It hadn't gone well so far, and now this. What the hell was it now? He burst into her quarters with his sword raised, and parried the platoons of shadows that the candlelight commanded towards him.

Isabel was wailing uncontrollably, distraught at the fate of her sweet Diego, and still shocked by the consequences of a decision she had thought she would never need to make. She saw Don Pedro glance around the cool stone walls of her chamber, still coiled and ready to spring at any adversary. For a brief moment, she saw fear in the eyes of a man who instilled it in others, but in seconds it was gone. He spotted poor Diego's limp frame and leapt into action, ramming his shimmering blade through his lifeless throat. A smile crept across his lips as he withdrew, then thrust again. And again. With each blow, he disfigured and dishonoured Isabel's beloved Diego. Desperate for him to stop, she ran to Don Pedro and clung to his sword arm, holding it back with all her strength.

'No! Stop!'

Don Pedro turned his head and stared at Isabel with blackened eyes that seemed to be revelling in her misery from their murky depths.

'Get your hands off me woman. How dare you touch me without my permission.' He twisted his upper torso to gather momentum and smashed his free hand into Isabel's face. Pain seared across her cheek from the sickly crack she had heard. She slumped to her knees and clutched her trembling hands to its source.

He stormed towards her. In that moment, Isabel felt more vulnerable than she had ever been. This was a man who fed on the fear of others. A man who would stop at nothing to achieve his lofty ambitions. She braced herself for death.

Don Pedro pressed the cold steel against her pulsing throat. It felt wet and warm from Diego's blood, which dripped from the end and ran across Isabel's clavicle, down to the sanctuary of her breast.

'Do you want some too? Do you?' He demanded a response.

'Do it! You will spare me a lifetime of despair.' By now she had no fear. There was no life without Diego. Isabel knew she could not carry the burden of his death through the rest of her years.

She felt the seconds tick as Don Pedro callously contemplated action. While he did so, he ran a bloody hand through his unkempt, ebony waves and stroked that bushy, whitening goatee.

'And then who would carry my children? No. Now is not your time. You will watch while I take my revenge for the five years that I have had to wait for you. Nobody keeps the Lord of Albarracín waiting.'

With that he returned to his maniacal butchery. Isabel watched his savagery through rivers of helpless tears. This was the man whom she had spurned Diego for. She had known he was cruel, but taking revenge on a corpse like this was demonic. What had she done? What on earth had possessed her? Why had she not run away with her dear Diego? Now he was dead, and she was powerless to stop this torturous mutilation.

The longer it went on, the more considered his surgery became. The frenzied blitz had passed, and now his incisions were designed to punish rather than to satisfy his blood lust. Isabel felt the agony of each slice and each gouge. Though her pain was far from acute, it was the chronic torture of betrayal.

Tired of his gruesome artwork, Don Pedro turned to Isabel once more. His default snarl had become a macabre smile.

'Do you like my masterpiece?'

'You disgust me!'

'I own you.' Once more he raised his sword, this time to her shuddering breast. In an act of closure, he wiped his sword across her flimsy gown as if he were buttering bread. With a self-satisfied laugh, he picked up Diego's corpse and threw it over his shoulder.

'The pigs will be pleased.' He swung his fist again and connected with Isabel's temple, sending everything to darkness.

She woke some time later from a mix of unconsciousness and sleep. During that time, her mind had been exploring the memories of Diego. She shivered with pride at the thought of his actions in Muret. He had truly been a hero. She had shared his solitude as he watched all around him celebrate Christmas, while he waited to see the King. And she felt his triumph the following day at the court of King Jaime, a euphoria that drove him on for what was clearly eight nights on his journey to Teruel.

She gasped in horror. Diego had been right. He had only celebrated Christmas nine days earlier at the Court of King Jaime. By rights they should now be looking forward to a long-awaited wedding, but instead she was married to a monster, and Diego, poor Diego, was dead. Isabel couldn't understand where the missing day had gone. How could a whole town celebrate Christmas on the wrong day? The thought whirled around in her spinning mind, but she couldn't concentrate on it. All she could focus on were the fateful five minutes in which she had denied him. It played over and over in her head. Her mind began to torture her for taking that decision, even though she had done so to protect her family. All she could see when she closed her eyes was the defeat etched across that familiar face, and the accusation in his eyes that stung her like a scorpion.

Worse still, Isabel could see Diego welcome that painful last breath, as he embraced the finality of death, rather than live a life without the woman that he craved. A woman who worshipped the ground on which he walked, yet couldn't bring herself to break a vow that she had made to a man she despised.

There was only one thing for it, she needed to right the wrong she had done. Despite the chill of the night and the reverberating throb in her forehead, Isabel reached for a flaming torch and slipped quietly through the corridors. Her bare feet burned each time they touched the cool earth floor. She had to find out where that bastard had taken Diego's body. She had to give him the kiss in death that she had refused him in life.

Isabel heard Don Pedro return, and watched from the window as his squire helped him from his horse. She heard him say that he had strapped poor Diego to his own horse and ridden to the gravediggers, where he had cast the body onto the earth, ready to be dug the next day. Isabel thanked God for the small mercy that her beloved had been spared the piggery.

She flattened herself into a shadowed recess as Don Pedro passed her. The wall was so cold it felt moist through her gown, but its icy touch was nothing compared to the glacier that had replaced her heart. She heard him head towards the great hall, chortling about how pleased he was with himself as he filled his flagon and guzzled to his glory. Standing in the shadows, Isabel thought about how much she loathed him. It was a hate deep enough for her to kill him. She contemplated running that filthy sword through his throat, as he had done to her Diego. The thought of taking his life satisfied a primal need for revenge within Isabel and she revelled in it as she waited for drink to incapacitate him again. There was no doubt that she would kill him, but not until she had found Diego. However, if Don Pedro was still sleeping when she returned, then there would be a second death that evening.

Darkness was Isabel's friend as she ran across the courtyard and scurried silently towards the stables. She mounted the chestnut riding horse that her odious husband had given her when her father agreed to let him marry her, and galloped across the countryside to the town of Teruel, past fields in which Diego's tapered torso had once toiled. Isabel remembered the meaningless journeys that she had undertaken just to catch sight of him pounding away in the breaking sun. He would never know how she had watched him from afar, admiring his determination, his fight. She longed for him to be in that field once more, and in her mind he was, picked out by a single beam of light from the night's moon, which now wept for him. The image was a joyous intrusion into her profound sorrow.

Isabel entered the walls of Teruel and made her way to the graveyard. A blanket of red shrouded the distant Muela as the first light prepared itself for the day's performance. She called insistently for attention from those who lived in the diggers' camp and her call was answered quickly.

The dancing flames of that morbid place reflected back at her from the verdant irises of a girl whose face was veiled by dark-brown locks.

'Doña Isabel! Why, it is very early!'

'Oh Beatriz, it is you.' Isabel hugged her tight and unleashed the pent-up despair that had been welling inside her throughout the night. There was something special about their touch, a spark that seemed to flow between them, enough to make Beatriz flinch as their hands connected. It was a feeling that only one other person had ever given Isabel, and now he was dead. Beatriz had been a child last time Isabel had seen her, but now the girl was adolescent. She was stunned by how much they resembled each other.

'Beautiful young Beatriz. Every time I set eyes on you, I am more convinced than ever that you must be a long-lost sister!'

'Why thank you Isabel, I would be very proud if that

were the case!'

'Beatriz, in the dead of night, I believe that my wretched husband brought the body of Diego de Marcilla here? I need you to take me to him.'

'Are you sure you want to see him? His body is terribly disfigured, and night is not the time to visit the dead.'

'I know what his body is like!' Isabel snapped. 'I saw how that bastard mutilated him. I was there. He forced me to watch.'

Beatriz could see the sorrow oozing through Isabel's flash of anger. She reached out to take her hand, and once more the charge in their connection surprised them both. Beatriz led the way past lines of decaying corpses and on towards where Diego lay ready to be buried as soon as the sun provided enough light. She stepped back silently as Isabel knelt over him, not wanting to intrude in the lives of those of a higher status, and also a little disturbed by Diego's body, whose face still spoke of the anguish with which he had died.

When she saw him, Isabel's guilt fuelled a seismic outpouring of grief that seemed to shake the very soil on which she stood. She was truly distraught, and her grief so touched Beatriz that she forgot any sense of her place in the world and moved forward to comfort Isabel.

Though Diego's lips were grey and lifeless, Isabel leaned forward to kiss him. Her desperate tears fell on his ashen face and drew dusty patterns as they streamed over the contours that she knew so well. She kissed him for the last time and his icy lips gave nothing in return. At that moment, the finality of lost love hit her with its full force and she knew that she had lost Diego forever. Never again would she caress his face or gaze on those resolute eyes. She stared heavenward, incandescent with rage.

'Make no mistake, Don Pedro de Azagra, I am holding you responsible for this. You forced us apart with your presence, flirting your wealth in front of my poor father. You made me deny my one true love, to the point where I couldn't even give him the kiss that would at least have comforted his last moment. Then you disfigured his poor, helpless corpse in an act of vindictive depravity. All because of a missing day. Are you responsible for that too, you bastard? You have filled my soul with torment, and I will not live without my Diego. My grief is too raw, the chasm inside me too deep. I cannot go on, but I promise you that the love I share with Diego will never die. I curse you, Don Pedro de Azagra, curse you to be tormented by our love for ever. May it be a love that you will never know, yet one you and your family yearn for every day of your miserable lives.'

A darkness drew over Isabel as she knelt there clutching Diego's hand, a darkness that she knew would take away the sorrow. The knowledge that she had spurned Diego was too much for her to bear, and she had no desire to return to the ogre to whom she was married. She called for death to release her from the misery of life, and it answered. An instant pain burned through her chest as she felt her heart tear from end to end. She flailed a hand at Beatriz who quickly established a fizzing, smouldering connection. Isabel gripped tighter and tighter as the pain from her chest consumed her, to the point where her desperate nails brought tears to Beatriz' eyes.

With her other hand, Isabel reached for Diego's lifeless fingers but with one last, cruel twist she was destined to never quite reach them. In her final moments, her life surged through that smouldering connection with Beatriz, and when the last of her force left her body, she fell dead at Diego's side.

Lauren was crying uncontrollably now and James held her tight. He had felt Isabel's death and he knew that Lauren had too. For a while, she was too distraught to trust her voice and James held her patiently and silently. He knew that she would speak when she was ready.

'Are you okay?' James asked, after a time, when he could bear the silence no longer.

'Yes. I'm okay,' she said, her voice cracking with emotion. 'It's just so tragic that they couldn't be together.'

'I didn't believe that a love that powerful could exist!' said James.

'No, neither did I.' Lauren was regaining her composure. 'That's what so intrigued me about their story. It made me want to know more. It had me hooked. I needed to make sense of it, so I summoned the memories of Beatriz …'

'We've got hers too?' James interrupted.

'Yes, and everyone since.'

'This is just too …'

'I summoned the memories of Beatriz,' Lauren continued, determined to finish her story. 'I skipped through her entire life in search of a mere morsel to satisfy my hunger. I was conscious of the disrespect I was showing her by doing so, and I promised myself I would revisit her story at another time, when I was ready to open my heart again. Right now, everything was about Diego and Isabel.'

'Did you find anything? I'm desperate to know what happened next!'

'Well, I learned through Beatriz that Don Pedro de Azagra was furious when he heard the news of Isabel's death. He accused her of being an adulterer and ordered both their bodies to be buried separately, in unmarked graves.'

'What a vindictive bastard.'

'Yes, but get this. Rafael de Segura was inconsolable when he heard the tragic news. He knew he had sequestered Isabel and that, ultimately, he was responsible for her demise. Five years earlier he'd had the power to make her happy but had chosen wealth over her welfare. He bribed the gravediggers to bury them side by side so at least they could be together in death.'

'So he came through in the end. Such a sad story.'

'It got worse for him, I'm afraid. Don Pedro's fury knew no bounds. He slaughtered Rafael for allowing them to be buried together and took Isabel's sister, Maria, as his wife.'

'The poor girl. I can't imagine how awful her life with him would have been.'

'But the story doesn't end there. I couldn't find anything else in Beatriz's memory about Diego and Isabel, but I felt there had to be more than that. On the off-chance, I went to the library. I wasn't sure what I was looking for, or how I might find it, but I thought I'd give it a go.'

'What did you find?'

'Well it seemed that their story became something of a legend across Spain. None of the books told the story in the kind of detail that we witnessed, though, and over time the events and the endings had changed. I decided to turn my attention to the town of Teruel. I wondered what it was like today.'

'And you found it?' asked James.

'I leafed through the pages of a guide to Spain and was surprised at the town's prominence. I discovered that, as well as being renowned for its Moorish architecture, Teruel is known as the City of Love.'

'How appropriate!'

'It's no coincidence, James. It's known as the city of love precisely because of the legend of Isabel and Diego!'

'You're kidding me!'

'No. They are *Los amantes de Teruel*—The Lovers of Teruel,' said Lauren.

'That's incredible!'

'And there's more! In the mid-sixteenth century, a grave in the beautiful Moorish church of San Pedro was uncovered, which appeared to contain the bodies of a man and a woman who had been buried together in the thirteenth century.'

'Isabel and Diego.'

'It's claimed that it's them, but nobody really knows.'

'I reckon it's pretty likely, considering what we know, don't you?' offered James.

'Yes. For centuries, people have visited their final resting place, and they've now built a separate mausoleum within the church to hold their bodies. They were reburied in two new tombs that were sculpted to include the shields of the Segura and Marcilla families.'

'Wow!'

'But you need to see the tombs.'

'Why?'

'They're side by side.'

'Well I'd assumed as much.'

'They are a work of art—they lie, reaching out to hold each other, but destined never to actually touch!'

'That's so poignant! I guess that maybe somewhere in this tragic story there's some crumb of comfort,' said

James. He certainly hoped so.

'Yes, they are together in death at least. What's special is that their memory lives on after all this time. Every year Teruel celebrates the wedding of Isabel and the whole town re-enacts the scenes from the thirteenth century.'

'We have to go there. You and me. It'll be like a sort of homecoming.'

'Yes, one day, James. We must.' It sounded so beautiful when Lauren talked about them as a couple. James knew that he already loved her. How could he not? As well as this historical connection, these incredible abilities, she was the most amazing girl he had ever met. He had no doubts that Lauren felt the same way too. It wasn't something she needed to express, it was there in her every touch, every thought, every glance.

'So why do we feel connected to them?'

'Look, I can't answer that fully. From what I can tell, there's a direct connection through every generation since.'

'So we're descended from them?'

'No. We're not related. But we are physically identical in every way. No matter which lifetime I've explored it's always you and I,' said Lauren.

'And are they all tragic?'

'I'm afraid so. It's the same story every time. We are desperately in love but something tragic always keeps us apart. I haven't come across a lifetime in which we found a way to be together.' As she heard her own words, Lauren turned her attention to the swelling grey mass of the sea, where the waves continued to smash onto the beach. That was it! 'The Ancient Tide!' she exclaimed.

'What?'

'The sea.'

'What about it?' quizzed James, wondering what other mind-blowing information he was about to find out.

'For millions of years it has sent its foot soldiers to the shore. Each wave sacrifices itself on the shore, and for what purpose?' She paused for effect, suddenly aware of the profound nature of the realisation. 'The pursuit of a greater good.'

'What are you saying?'

'Well it's only a theory but maybe nature is determined for us to be together. Maybe it keeps sending its own foot soldiers, knowing that one day we will make it.'

'You think?'

'Don't you see? It makes such sense!'

'I suppose it does, kind of,' James agreed, 'but do you know what? I reckon this is our time. All those who have gone before us have eroded the barriers to us being together. I mean, it's nearly the twenty-first century. If we can't choose to be together now, then there's no hope, is there? Unlike Diego and Isabel, we are able to make the choice to be together. The choice that all the others have been denied through history. We have the world at our feet. There are no obstacles for us to rally against. It's just you and me, Lauren. After nearly eight hundred years of trying we'll finally be able to share the love we have and live out our lives together. Fulfilling our destiny. I can't wait to be with you Lauren, I want to wake up to you every morning and celebrate our togetherness. I'm so glad you found me.'

'Oh James, I wish it was that simple!'

'What do you mean? I don't see how anything about the desire that we have for each other can be complicated. You feel it, don't you?'

'Of course I do! But that doesn't mean we can be together!'

'Why not?'

Lauren paused for what seemed like forever, while James' heart thumped vigorously in the back of his throat. Then she spoke three dreaded words.

'James, I'm married!'

*

A little further along the sea defence, hidden from view, stood a raging eavesdropper. Fury bubbled from his lips and spittle dribbled across the whitening whiskers on his chin.

She was damned right about that, he spat. She *was* married. She'd been stringing the Jordan boy along all this time, made him think they could be together. Everything she had done to date had been a barefaced lie. It was about time she told him the truth. There was no way those two sickening lovebirds would be together; he would see to that. She wasn't free to love who she wished. She had a husband. Him. And he wasn't going to let her go.

He'd heard enough, and slipped silently away. Unseen. Unheard. Over the years, he'd learned to do that well. It was what people like him did. He headed along the curving concrete wall and towards the harbour. He needed a drink. Any bar would do, and when he found one, he would drink to the two of them being together one day. But not in this world. Death had a wonderful way of bringing people together. In the meantime, they could enjoy their fiction for all the good it would do them. He knew the real story and that gave him the advantage.

7

JAMES' SLEEPING BODY provided the perfect base from which his mind launched its nightly missions. Closing his eyes triggered the release of a perpetual worm, which wriggled through the vast mass of content that was now inside his head. It was indexing. Exploring. It was like being locked in a library overnight, and just picking random books off the shelves. The truth was that these were a far cry from any trawl through literature. They weren't the hefty autobiographies that frequently aided sleep; neither were they tales that one read or heard. They were real lives to experience, personal stories relayed in multiple dimensions, in which each protagonist called James' name from their cranial archive and begged him to unlock their memoirs.

Considering the enormity of the day's events, it was no surprise that James' dreams had been plentiful that night. Each was an emotional rollercoaster that always ended in tragedy, and he woke regularly to find himself sobbing uncontrollably into a sodden pillow. Such was the burden of the gift he had received.

He was snatched from one such episode by a purposeful

rapping on the front door, which ripped through his rest, like rapid gunfire. It wasn't the timid, 'Sorry to interrupt you' version that belonged to a concerned neighbour, questioning their authority to interrupt the peace; neither was it the zealous rapping of a Jehovah's Witness, keen to share the joy that the impending end of the world would surely bring. This was a demanding and assertive banging that insisted on a response. It dared him to ignore it at his own peril.

He peered reluctantly across at the clock, through dry and painful eyes that confessed immediately to their tortured night. It was 10:15. He had slept through the alarm and most of the morning, though he was stunned that he had slept at all. His mind had been racing when he climbed into bed and it was still lapping endlessly now he was awake.

The pounding on the door continued, each time with greater fervour, rattling the door in its setting and questioning the strength of the lock. James staggered fuzzily across the room and did his best to avoid the still-damp clothes that had been discarded the night before. He found himself stepping through the house in time to the door's unrelenting beat, like rowing slaves tied to the oars of a trireme. His pace picked up with every stride, until he found himself leaping down the stairs two at a time to silence the infernal racket.

The door shuddered from further impact as he

fumbled with the lock. James was wondering who, or what, could be so important as to need entry so urgently. He found out soon enough, when the door flew open with the clicking lock. He retreated instinctively, and narrowly avoided the painful blow that its swing aimed at his temple. What was left of the sleepy fog inside him cleared instantly, vaporised by the piercing stare that confronted him.

James had been so focused on his destiny, so lost in trying to understand the newfound purpose he had discovered, that he had forgotten all about work. It had crossed his mind occasionally, but at the time it had been like worrying about the bite of a mosquito while standing in front of a salivating tiger. Suddenly, in the cold light of day, all his attention was forced back to the thirsty mosquito.

'James! Thank God!' Nick's anxiety was clear.

'Nick!'

'Where the hell have you been?'

'I …'

'Why haven't you called me? Did you not get my messages?' James hadn't even thought to check his answering machine when he had returned home the night before. That had been a mundane reality he just hadn't been ready for.

'I didn't know you'd called, Nick, sorry!'

'What's going on JJ? You didn't show up for work. You

didn't call. You didn't respond to my messages. I was worried about you, man. I thought something had happened to you!'

'I'm okay.' said James, though he wasn't entirely sure that was true.

'Well I'm glad. But where the fuck were you yesterday?' That was a question James didn't know how to answer. He found himself trying to summarise the events of the day before in his mind, and almost laughed at how ridiculous it sounded. He had been on his way to work but a strange calling had forced him to the beach. There, he had met the girl of his dreams and it turned out she had a telepathic connection with him. Then she had loaded up a thousand years of lifetimes inside him stretching all the way back to Diego and Isabel, and he had collapsed on the beach. No, he wouldn't be going with that version.

'Honestly? It was just all too much for me yesterday,' James said, convincing himself there was a slight grain of truth in his words. It made the necessary lie that was coming next a little more palatable.

'What do you mean?'

'I had every intention of going to work, Nick, I nearly made it to the front of the building. I just couldn't go in. For some reason, I felt an overwhelming sense of panic. The closer I got to work the worse it became. In the end, I just had to get out of there. I knew I needed to speak to you, but I really couldn't face you or anyone. I just wanted to be alone.' The emotions of the day before were still raw and James felt his eyes fill with tears as he spoke.

'It's okay mate, I understand.' Nick reached for James and brought him into a hug. 'I've been there too. More often than you'd think and more often than I'd like. At times like these you need your friends, JJ. You need company. You need to talk. Being alone just isn't healthy. It makes you think too much, and thinking's dangerous. Come on, let's try again, get yourself dressed and come to work with me now. We'll go together.'

He hated lying to Nick, the man was such a good friend, but what choice did he have?

'James! Get a move on!' James had been daydreaming a little there and Nick jolted him to attention with his words, and an assertive hand to the back that guided him towards the bathroom. 'Now get in the shower and get dressed. I'll be downstairs having a cup of tea.'

As James entered the bathroom, he saw Nick enter his bedroom and open the CD tray. He picked up the incumbent disc, full of songs that had resonated with the frustration James had felt over the last few months, and threw it across the room.

'And stop listening to this maudlin crap. You need real music.' Moments later the house filled with the smashing cymbals and ripping chords of The Jam's 'Modern World'.

James rested the back of his head against the closed bathroom door, and exhaled deeply in relief. He ran the hot shower, and the bathroom quickly filled with a cleansing steam that immediately invigorated his pores. Before stepping into the shower, he went to assess the extent of the effects of his restless night in the misting mirror, but what he saw was so disconcerting that he knew he would never look in a mirror again. What had once been a single reflection was now a kaleidoscope of faces from many eras, each bursting with an inner sorrow, demanding to tell its own tragic story. Staring at his reflection like that brought home a stark realisation. He just didn't know who he was any more, and he recoiled at the thought, before stepping under the steaming shower in search of refuge. Its ferocious heat reassured him and forced him back to reality.

He finished the shower and dried himself off, noticing that even his body was the same as that of Diego de Marcilla. He dressed to the tuneful and inspirational 'Life From a Window' from the same album, and headed down the stairs to the kitchen, where Nick was sitting with his feet on the table, hands behind his head, looking like he owned the place. He smiled supportively, drained his tea and stood, thrusting a ramshackle sandwich in James' direction.

'Made you some breakfast.'

'I guess it's the thought that counts,' said James, eyeing the sandwich with disdain.

'Eat it at work. We're late.'

'Since when did you start caring about time?'

'Since one of my employees failed to show up for

work!' With that he was out the front door and into his Daimler so quickly that James barely had time to lock up on the way out. He sidled into the leather seat next to Nick, and it struck him that the car and its owner were the perfect match, both around the same age, grand and immensely powerful, with a dash of panache.

It was a little surreal that they were heading to work like this, the day after what had been a life-changing revelation, the details of which James couldn't share. Instead, in the relatively short journey, Nick found a way to fill the silence, something he was highly adept at, with stories of his antics of the last few weeks.

The call centre was abuzz when James arrived. This was the peak time for callers, and he took his seat sheepishly, doing his best to ignore the scowls of his two hundred colleagues. Most were in their late teens and early twenties, bar a few long-suffering stalwarts in late middle age who clung to their roles with gollumesque fervour. They feared the empty lake that lay ahead when eventually the precious that was their employment would be stolen from them.

Everyone else was convinced that their tenure was temporary, such was the exuberance of youth. They had latched onto the labour market in their late teens, but the excitement of a regular wage meant that many would never leave.

James threw himself into his daily dose of discourse. It

wasn't long before the events of the previous day began to make their way to the surface like a breathing whale, though he suspected a whale could stay underwater for longer than he could suppress thoughts about Lauren. It was all so fresh, so vivid. He could still hear the sound of the sea as it broke on yesterday's sodden sand, could still hear the gulls calling yesterday's chorus, and above all he could still hear those three words that Lauren had suckered him with.

'James, I'm married.'

After her revelation, they had sat silently, still holding each other but not talking. The silence was more noticeable because they had so many more ways to communicate. It wasn't that either of them was holding back. Instead they were quiet because James was charged with breaking the ice, and felt helpless to do so because he was devoid of the tools and technique required. He had no idea what to say. He had spent the day growing to love her in a way that he had thought was impossible, had shared the un-shareable, yet in one sentence she had ripped down all that they had built, and was asking James to pick up the pieces. He lost himself in her expectant eyes, wanting to overlook her monumental words. So deep were his feelings for Lauren that he felt just maybe he might be able to. All he needed was the slightest sign of encouragement, some bait that he could take. None was forthcoming.

Eventually the pregnant pause between them ran its

full term and an image began to incubate inside James'
head, demanding nurture. Lauren had lost patience
waiting for him to respond and was now answering the
questions that she knew James was unable to articulate, by
showing him her memory. He found himself once more
viewing the world through her captivating viridian gaze as
she stared, half at a dull pistachio basin beneath her head
and half at stark cream hexagons of an outdated linoleum
floor beneath her.

She was crying, though not tears of misery. These
were the tears of fear, fuelled by a frantic heart that
strained beneath her trembling body. Piercing pain
stabbed into the nerves of her face and James felt it as
clearly as if it were his own. Crimson dripped steadily into
the dull green bowl and thinned into paler hues as it sank
down the gentle slope and gathered once more on the
steely lip that dammed its progress. She raised her eyes and
stared into the stark, dry mirror. This was no preening,
post-shower gaze into a warming, vapoured mirror, it was
a cold inspection in a bathroom that had become a place
of refuge. Her left eye reflected the wildness of that fear,
but her right was concealed by the hand she had pressed
across her face. It was clamped against a weeping wound
whose red tears trickled across the valleys of her knuckles
and streamed to her elbow, where gravity grasped them
and pulled them to the basin. James could feel Lauren
hesitate before inching her hand away gently, mindful of

the gushing source beneath. The ensanguined fissure across the bridge of her familiar nose gaped, though a congealing clot was already forming at its surface. Its gore detracted from the rubric swelling that added new and unwanted contours to her perfect face.

Boom!

Any sense that Lauren's fear was subsiding vanished as the flimsy, yellowed door buckled under attack from the other side. The tiny bolt made half an effort of protest, before fleeing to the floor and taking its socket companion with it. Lauren cowered, covering her wound in a mixture of fear and shame, seeking out what little protection the corner of the room was prepared to offer. Seconds ticked by in a psychological torture that prolonged the dread that was now consuming her. Her attacker knew. He could smell the fear that filled the bathroom and he inhaled its narcotic like a weekend partygoer, waiting for the fix to take effect. Finally, as the odious opiate kicked in, he swung the door open.

The sight of his uniform surprised James, and he relaxed momentarily in the surety that the arrival of the police meant that whatever had happened to Lauren was now over. But something was wrong. Lauren's panic was increasing, not reducing, and the beat of her heart was exploding in James' eardrums. He felt her instinct processing its options. Fight or flight. To stay would be accepting whatever came at her, like a victim. Running at least meant she had some control. Within moments she was breaking for the door. It was no more than six paces. Lauren covered them in half that number as she picked up speed from the adrenalin of survival. James took each with her, willing her to break out.

Despite Lauren's speed, it still took vital seconds to cross the bathroom. She reached the door, desperate for escape. But not before the element of surprise had disappeared. By the time she reached her assailant, he had already processed his response. He threw her back into the bathroom and against the heartless tiles. They offered no mercy as Lauren's back crashed against their fierce resistance. James could feel their chilling kiss as she lay there, stunned. Through her panicked eyes, he watched as her attacker strode towards her. The patent Doc Martens sole on his black boots squeaked their impending aggression as they strode through the drops of blood that covered the floor like flicked fountain-pen ink on a teenager's school shirt. James winced as the steel toe cap crushed against Lauren's ribs and unleashed a ferocious pain that screamed through her body. A second followed, and then a third. The first had been agonising and, mercifully, familiarity and expectation dulled the pain of those that followed.

As Lauren winced on the floor she looked up at the aggressor who was leaning over her, dominating her. He drove a fierce hand through his thick black hair and

restored order to his disobedient parting, then scratched
his whitening goatee, while his hateful black eyes burned
with fury across the chiselled, mature face that Lauren had
once felt safe with. Now she looked at it with nothing but
fear and hatred.

'If you ever leave me, I'll kill you. Do you understand?'
he spat. His face was so close to Lauren's ear that despite
the overload of pain James could feel the hateful droplets
land on her skin. Then he turned and crossed the gaudy
bathroom, half-closing the now redundant door behind
him. It was an act that symbolised his disdain for her at
that moment and also hid his transgression from sight, as
if shutting out his grizzly violence would delay the
unstoppable arrival of a profound remorse.

Lauren lay wincing and bloodied on the hateful
hexagons, watching through the partial opening as her
husband began to change out of his uniform with
nonchalant cool, fumbling through a myriad of clinking
wire coat hangers for clothes that would cleanse him of his
wrongdoing. Once he had dressed, it was as if he had
replaced the evil genie in the bottle. His socked feet
padded across the carpeted bedroom, and triggered the
tell-tale hiss of a starting record as the third side of Pink
Floyd's *The Wall* kicked in with 'Hey You'. As it morphed
into 'Is there anybody out there?' the unmistakeable and
sickly waft of marijuana crept through the useless door
behind which Lauren lay, conscious yet unmoving. She

was a hidden shame that he cared not to revisit.

Lauren was crying, yet dry of tears, thankful merely for the solitude in which she could hide away her excruciating pain. Her eyes gazed across the bloodied floor that had born witness to the assault. Behind them was a deep ache, worsened by the flood of fluorescence overhead that convinced her they were better closed, though doing so intensified the ubiquitous, unbearable pain that was ready to burst out of her. As strains of 'Comfortably Numb' floated through the air at her, unconsciousness took away any pain.

Her broadcast ended there and James found himself back on the beach. He was seething. Fury was rolling and boiling inside him, like a core of fiery magma, seeking a weak spot in his outer crust through which to erupt with volcanic vengeance. Right at that moment, he knew that he was capable of murder. He wanted nothing more than to seek out that snake and stand on his throat, to control him just like he was controlling Lauren. James imagined himself slowly increasing the pressure on that pulsing and submissive windpipe, revelling in the gasps as his captive flailed for undeserved air. He would point at the fear in his eyes and make reference to Lauren's, then crash one of the man's own hateful Doc Martens down on his face. Again, and again. That was what they were for, wasn't it? James wanted to see the pattern of that legendary tread tattooed on the bastard's choking face.

Not for the first time in his life, James was seeing red, this time the colour of his eternal lover's blood. It was not in his nature to sit idly by and watch someone be so helplessly dominated. He was a catalyst, a stretcher of boundaries, an agent of change. He wanted to make it right, to free Lauren from the nightmare of her existence. A fierce searing need to avenge her coursed through his body, kept at bay only by his need to keep her safe.

James looked across at Lauren and saw the deep misery in her eyes, sadness she had shielded from him until now. He reached over to her and held her. He had seen her trauma and relived her suffering, felt her pain and her shame. With every protective bone in his body, he supported her, his arms taut with the fury of vengeance as they smothered her with the kindness and love that she deserved. He didn't ever want to let her go. It was as though, by embracing her, he could rid her of the callous cruelty she faced at home. Each tearful tremble fuelled his anger, and the images of retribution were played over and over in his head.

'No! That's not …' There was no hiding his potent surge of revenge from the intuitive Lauren.

'Yes, it is! He deserves everything he has coming to him. I am going to make him suffer!'

'Yes, he does deserve everything he has coming to him,' she said calmly, 'but you deserve what the future has in store for you too!'

'What do you mean?' James was puzzled.

'Well your, I mean our, future is whatever we want it to be. We need to find a way to be together, forever.'

'We will find one. And watching his pain will make it all the sweeter.'

'That's not the way!' Lauren insisted.

'It is!' James' inner fury sneaked from his lips before he could stop it. 'And we're going to go and sort him out right now.'

'No, we are not!'

'What do you mean, we are not? Don't you want to be free?'

'Of course I do. I want to be with you. But you're not going to do anything to him.'

'Why not?'

'Think about it. Let's say you get lucky and get the better of him.'

'Well thank you for the vote of confidence!'

'James, he's a policeman. He knows how to handle himself.'

'And I don't?' said James indignantly.

'Maybe you do. But, like I was saying, if you get lucky and you get away with killing him, you'll have the whole police force tracking us down.'

'And if I don't get lucky?'

'If you don't get lucky then either you or I, or both of us, could end up dead.' As annoying as it sounded, and as much as he didn't want to listen, James knew Lauren was beginning to make sense. 'Considering that we have just discovered we have a history of missing out on our destiny, I'd say that confronting him was a pretty high-risk strategy for us to take! Wouldn't you?'

'Okay. Okay. You've got a point,' James conceded eventually. The red mist had begun to subside and some of his self-protective questions and fears were now beginning to find their way to where they were needed. 'I agree that we need to think about it more, but the fact is that he's not going to stop. If he can do it once he can do it again.'

James noticed Lauren sheepishly avoid his piercing stare. At that point it was clear that this wasn't the first time.

'How many times Lauren?'

There was no answer. She said nothing.

'How many times?' James pushed harder. He needed to know.

'Four? No, Five.'

'What! That's it, we're going to sort it out right now! I'm not going to run the risk of it happening again.' The crimson haze was well and truly back. He stood to leave and held a taught, quivering hand for Lauren to grasp and follow. 'I'm taking you home to pack your bags, and then you're coming to live with me until we figure out what to do.'

'Stop! James! If I thought that would work, I'd be with

you in a heartbeat. Don't you get it? Even if he wasn't there when we packed up, he'd find us. He's a policeman, remember? He knows how to find people and, whether he does it himself or not, he knows how to hurt us too.'

'But you're not going back!' James reaffirmed. He was scared witless at the thought of confronting a raging bull, but protecting Lauren was paramount, far more important than his own safety. When the moment came, James knew he would stand ahead of Lauren and fight for her, though he was beginning to question whether this was that moment. What she had said undeniably made sense. It would be easy for a policeman to find them at James' house, and then what would they do?

'What's the alternative?' said Lauren. She was a voice of reason, calming the storm. She'd had far more time than James to process the violence.

'Let's run away,' James replied. 'We can figure out where to after we make the break.' It sounded impulsive and ill thought out, even as it passed his lips, but at least it was action. That was the way he hustled and made things happen. It had worked well for him so far in his life.

'But we don't have anything! We've no money, we've no plan, we've nowhere to go. And we need to get it right, because he'll find us, and then he'll kill us.' Once again James knew she was right. They had nowhere to go and he certainly had no money, the monthly cycle of earn and spend was one that he enjoyed, but it didn't mark him as one of the bank's more solvent customers.

'Why can't we report him to the police then? There's a law against what he did. It's called assault. Grievous Bodily Harm.' It all seemed clear to James.

'You don't know the police very well, do you?'

'No, I …'

'Well I do. I'm married to one of them and I can tell you that they close ranks and protect their own. You'd have to have overwhelming evidence, and even then they'd probably find a way for it to go missing. Even if you did actually make the charge stick, he'd still have time to come home and dish out his own justice.'

'Alright. Alright. I get it.' James was resigned. This was a battle he was not going to win. 'You've held on to this for a while Lauren. This is the first I've heard of it, and I can't stand the thought of anything happening to you. I want you to be safe. I want you to be with me.'

'I'm safer than you think. He doesn't do it all the time. He's possessive and doesn't want to lose me. If he thinks everything's normal, then I'll be safe.'

'So what happened last time?'

'That was the night that we met in the cl …'

'What?'

'Yes, I was late home and he got himself worked up. I stayed longer than I should have. When I wasn't home at the end of his shift, he convinced himself that I'd been with another man. Let's be honest, he was right.'

'Oh Lauren, how the hell did you end up with this arsehole?' Guilt began to poke him with an accusing finger. He had been the one who kept Lauren at the club far longer than she had wanted to stay.

'It's a long story. The short version is that I felt safe with him.'

'Well that's ironic. What did your parents think of him?'

'My mum didn't want me to marry him.'

'And your dad?'

'He died a long time ago.' James sensed the sadness in Lauren at the mention of her father. He wanted to share her pain, but now wasn't the time. Instead he held her tighter, wanting her to know that he wasn't probing further because it wasn't the right time, rather than because he wasn't interested.

'Did your mum come around in the end?'

'Yes, but one time when he was being really nasty, Sean told me the only reason she accepted it was because he threatened to pass her name and address to some pretty nasty people.'

'Sean. That's the first time you've mentioned his name. I'm not sure he deserves one. It humanises him.'

'James! Honestly! You need to forget about him. He's just an obstacle standing in the way of us being together.'

'Pretty big obstacle if you ask me. Have you told your mum what he does to you?'

'No. He won't let me see her. I haven't seen or spoken to her since the wedding.'

'Jeez. The guy is a prick.' James broke off their embrace in a frustrated protest and stared out towards the endless tide that fascinated him so. Not one of those waves ever won. They self-sacrificed for a greater good, one whose motives they didn't even share. That would not be him; his life would mean something. He wouldn't fall into the traps that pride, anger and revenge would set for him. He would keep his eyes on the ultimate prize. Lauren. Everything else was merely a distraction. Nothing was more important to him than being with her.

'You know you're the one I want to be with, right?' said Lauren. James thought it was incredible to hear those words. It was astonishing to think that they shared centuries together, yet they had known each other for mere moments. He turned to her.

'So do you have any kind of plan? I'm struggling to be anything other than angry!'

'Well our only choice is to run off together, but we need to plan it properly. We'll need enough money, know exactly where we're going, and work out how to minimise the chances of him finding us.'

'Sounds a lot easier than it is! How do we do that?'

'We start by being patient. We'll have a lifetime to spend together, so we need to do it properly.'

'You mean lifetimes, don't you?' Lauren smiled at his

flippancy. 'How long exactly, Lauren?'

'If we're to give ourselves the best possible chance, we probably need to use the rest of the year to save and plan.'

'The rest of this year! That's eight months! I was thinking you were going to say one, tops! Eight months is too long!'

'Is it? I'd take being together in eight months over not being together at all, possibly even being dead. Wouldn't you?' Lauren's pragmatism was irrefutable.

'I suppose one day I'll be thankful that at least one of us has some patience, but I can't say I'm feeling it right now!'

'And I think in eight months' time you'll be thankful for a whole lot more!' Lauren was beaming. If James had any doubts at all about her love for him, that one smile would have conquered them. The fact was, he had none. The two of them shared such a phenomenal bond. Their destiny was to be together. A fool could have seen that.

'Let's set a date then,' said James. 'New Year, new start?'

'New Year's Day?'

'Yes! The first day of 1992. I have a sneaky feeling that'll be the best year ever.'

'And every year after will be just as good!' added Lauren. They kissed, this time with greater freedom, as though they had guessed the first digit of destiny's combination. James' body was on fire. The warmth convected through his every nerve ending and radiated through his soul. It was liberating. Inspiring. Empowering. At that moment, he felt he could move mountains.

As with all good things, the embrace came to an end and James and Lauren resumed their planning, but the intensity of their togetherness was never far away.

'And I know just where we should go!' James was so excited when the thought popped into his head.

'Where?'

'Well, we're the two latest lovers in a long line that connects us all the way back to …'

'Teruel! I love it! James you're a genius!'

'There's something just right about it isn't there? It'd be so fitting that we're finally together in a place that means so much! Imagine it. You, me, underneath that Portuguese oak where it all began.'

'I can see it now. It's beautiful.'

'We just need to work out how to get there. How about we meet once a week and put some details around the plan?'

'You don't get it, do you?' Lauren's frustration crept to the surface, and her words were like a sharp slap to the face.

'Get what?'

'He watches me, James. Like a hawk. There's no way that I can meet up with you now. It's too risky. We had to meet today, we had no choice, but we can't risk it again. We mustn't leave any kind of trail. We can't call each other, we can't meet up, nothing. That way he won't know we're together.'

'That way I won't know we're together either!'

'Yes, you will. You're forgetting. We don't need to meet up!' Lauren whispered, leaning forward to kiss James. As she did so she threw open her mind to reveal the most sensuous and erotic thoughts. 'And there's no trace.'

8

THE REMAINING DAYS of the year passed in slow motion, flowing like honey from an upturned container. In September, the Bank of England declared the recession over. Not that it made any difference to the real people, who struggled in the following months just as they had in those that preceded them. All the while, the upper echelons of society with their ancestral wealth sailed through the financial crisis in luxurious cruisers, and threw unwanted strawberries from their fizzing cocktails over the side at the floundering masses.

James withdrew from his former life as much as he could, and with each passing day his savings grew. He knew that his friends, Nick in particular, were worried about him, but he didn't care. The fact was that he was happier than he had been in a long time. He counted each day, each hour with the same precision as Diego, eight hundred years earlier. Destiny awaited him, and it felt good.

When it came to the day-to-day drudgery, James was all over the place. All too frequently his body would present itself at events and conversations without coordinating the arrival of his mind. It was as if one had grown sick of waiting for the other and had decided to hurl itself into the abyss of action, determined to prove a point. His mind was constantly preoccupied. There were just too many distractions. If he wasn't obsessing over those precious moments that he had shared with Lauren, counting the compounding returns on his emotional investment, he was exploring countless memories. All his mind needed were seconds of inactivity. Then it would be smashing through a jungle of experience, trying to make sense of a millennium of lifetimes whose neglected branches so intertwined that they were near impossible to pass. He sometimes wondered whether he would wake up one day, and find that he'd been placed in some kind of asylum, though rested, safe in the knowledge that in her ransacking of the country, Thatcher had all but closed the last of them too.

At the start of the year, James had been a naive and self-absorbed youth, burdened by the choices of the generation that came before him. Now he felt he had perspective. It would have been impossible not to. The gravity of the situations that his predecessors had faced seemed almost planetary in their scale as his mind spun through the galaxy of memories, through times where human life counted for little. In particular, he found the aggressive thuggery of the medieval world confronting. It was an age that had fascinated him at school, yet the reality was so deeply terrifying at every level. He wondered how anyone had survived in those times. Even those born into privilege frequently had it stolen by stronger or richer foes in an almost evolutionary development of power. Lives were trivial in that dog-eat-dog world, and survival was an art that few were able to master.

In each lifetime, the lovers were invariably kept apart by societal norms that showed no mercy to poor luck. Of course, there was always that unyielding yearning, satisfied by a series of fleeting moments together, yet frustrated by what seemed like an eternity of absence. Whatever the era and regardless of location, circumstance conspired to constantly keep them apart until an inevitable and desperate event brought their lifetimes to a miserable and unfulfilled end.

*

Fate, it seemed, was a thief. It had mercilessly stolen Sabine Dreschler's life from her since the day she had been born. It had brought her nothing but misery. For as long as she could remember, she had been a prisoner. Even now, so many miles from her beloved Schwerin on the northern coast of Germany, she wasn't free. It didn't seem fair that fate had asked so much of her, and yet given her nothing in return. What right did it have to expect her to continue to do its bidding?

She was on her way to England. She wished she was
heading somewhere else, but she had no choice. It was her
destiny to meet someone there and she was already ten
years late. For every second of that decade, she had felt the
strain of delay, and that was just another cruel offering
from fate. At least she was now reaching the end of her
journey, the white cliffs ahead reflected the morning sun
like a mirror of fire. She hoped it wasn't an omen of what
was to come.

Sabine wondered what England had in store for her.
She hoped it would be kinder than her twenty-eight years
in East Germany had been. For the last ten she had been
locked and tortured in the bowels of the
Hohenschönhausen in Berlin. The high, beautiful house.
That was what those words meant, it was what those
bastards had called their prison. It had most definitely been
neither. Its name was just a cruel joke that diverted
attention from the misery they inflicted on those poor
souls who they held deep underneath the ground. What
they had done to her in that hell-hole was appalling. With
their pliers, shocks and drugs, they had stolen the very joy,
the spark, the joie de vivre from her soul. She was now just
a shell of the girl she had once been. They had even robbed
her of the sun, a miracle she had always taken for granted.
It was so long since she'd seen it that even now, almost
two weeks since her release, Sabine still feared its daily rise
and fall.

The collapse of the East German regime on 3 October 1990 might have opened the door to her cell, but no-one had the key to unlock the poor helpless girl inside her that she had hidden away from the merciless Stasi. She had concealed it so well that even she couldn't find herself any more. To all intents and purposes, that girl was now gone.

Her childhood in Schwerin had been little short of idyllic, she remembered. Life had been frugal but comfortable. Like others, her family had plenty of food, and everyday necessities were cheap and abundant, but any luxuries were priced outrageously. Sabine had never seen a television, yet she never felt deprived. It was just the way life was. Simple. It was a standing joke that the Minister for Television was the only person in East Germany who could afford to own one.

Manfred Dreschler, her father, was a veteran of the German Army, the Wermacht. He had fought, and nearly died, for his country during the Second World War. Like so many, he had been swept on by rhetoric and false promises. He had believed in the Reich, felt that they were changing the world, until the reality of what was happening became apparent. At that point, fear had motivated him to fight, fear of the enemy and fear of his own side. Rumours of the death camps circulated surreptitiously through the ranks and sickened the fighters at the front line. The stories were so atrocious that many refused to believe them. Those like Manfred, who did, would have surrendered had it not been for fear of the dreaded SS.

Near the end of the war, he was captured and mistreated by the Russians, punished as an individual for the actions of an entire nation. At the end of the war he returned, a broken man, to a broken Germany. One in which the dream that had been promised to millions of Germans had turned out to be a nightmare.

Manfred was a hero to Sabine, though she knew little of his time in the army. He refused to talk about it. Whenever the subject was raised, she saw his eyes glisten with tears. He had seen horrors, she knew, but they were filed away in a closed book that he refused to open, memories that were just too painful for him to revisit.

He was more forthcoming to her about his disdain for the communist oppression in East Germany. He regaled her with tales of life before the war, told her how the country had been on its knees in 1932, just waiting to be put out of its misery by a vindictive and unforgiving continent. His were stories of freedom and prosperity, of the pride of a recovering nation. Like everyone else, he had been swept up in a tide of optimism, had believed that they were reaching out to achieve greatness. But it had all been a lie. When the true horrors were revealed, shock reverberated through the nation and it brought a shame that he knew he would carry to the grave.

From the day he returned, Manfred had been careful

to be seen to support the communists publicly. It was safer that way. He knew that the government watched all the returning heroes like hawks. They had seen too much, achieved so much, that they represented a high risk of subversion. Privately, however, he shared his real thoughts with Sabine. He wanted her to know that the whole way of life they led was a lie. He warned her about the network of informants who fed a stream of information to the Stasi. He wanted his daughter to yearn for the truth, in the hope that one day she and others would break free. But above all he wanted her to be safe. The secrets that father and daughter shared brought them together. Their bond was unshakeable.

The Stasi's reach was truly sinister. It was an organisation to be feared. Anyone, anywhere could be an informant. Information was power, and the Stasi thrived on it. Its officers forced people to do their bidding, or face jail. As a result, wives informed on husbands, sisters on sisters, brothers on brothers. Unfortunately, during the summer of 1979, most of which Sabine spent with her cousin Heike, she discovered the true extent of the nation's treachery. They were both seventeen, and it was an age of discovery, the best time of their lives. The two of them felt free as they rambled through acre after acre of countryside and swam in the cool lap of the Schweriner See without a care in the world. Its pure waters lapped against their bare skin, and the beating sun warmed them as they dried off on the river bank.

The best part of that magical summer was their sexual awakening. Neither of them was short of suitors. Heike was a voluptuous German beauty, tall and blond, and Sabine saw many a man transfixed by her heaving chest. She played on it too, for free cigarettes or booze. It was incredible what a confident woman could make men do, Sabine thought. She herself was a short brunette with striking green eyes that reminded most men of the forests of Mecklenburg, a classic beauty with a face that screamed for attention from men of all ages.

The two girls talked for hours of their latest crushes and their desires, and they giggled at the way the most powerful men went weak at the knees in their presence, something they used to their advantage. They talked of their experiments with love. The time that Heike let a boy touch her breasts, the time Sabine allowed a married man to kiss her in exchange for a bottle of Schnapps that the two girls shared at the side of the lake. They traded all manner of secrets. Among them, Sabine let slip her father's true feelings about the regime. That information was all it took to destroy him.

Heike innocently shared what she had learned with her mother, and within hours it was passed to the Stasi. At midnight the following night, they came for Manfred Dreschler in a terrifying raid. He was dragged, protesting, from his bed. It was then that reality hit Sabine. There was nowhere for her to hide. She could blame the Stasi, her family or the regime as much as she liked, but deep down she knew it had been her who had betrayed her father. He had trusted her with his innermost thoughts and she had been unable to keep them to herself. As the Stasi took him away, Manfred gazed at her for what would be the final time. It was a heart-wrenching look of love and forgiveness, one that would haunt her for the rest of her life.

From that day onward, guilt imprisoned Sabine. She fell into a depression that was fanned by a fear that she might never be able to trust anyone again. She distanced herself from everyone, feeling worthless and undeserving, and lived in paranoia, second guessing the motives of all she had previously held dear. Overnight, every treasured childhood memory suddenly seemed inconsequential in the absence of her father, and revisiting them served only to reinforce the awful mistake she had made.

In the end, Sabine had little choice but to move away from her beloved Schwerin. There were just too many ghosts there for her. In early 1981 she made a new life for herself in Berlin, where, amid buildings still pock-marked by war, she was able to revel in the anonymity that the big city afforded her. Berlin was no match for Schwerin; it was all function and no form, drab and dreary in a way that complemented her inner mood. Her daily existence was banal, and she became a slave to routine, accepting each miserable moment as part of the punishment she deserved.

One morning in July, colour entered her monotonous world for the first time in years. On her daily trudge to the factory, she tripped in one of the many potholes that lined the streets, which sent her sprawling across the pavement, her fall broken by one of the hundreds of puddles that had accumulated in a society that didn't care. She lay there for a moment, sopping wet and trying to contain her embarrassment, feeling that the longer she stayed there, the less people would notice. When she sheepishly lifted her face for the first time, she saw a strong hand held out towards her and was surprised to see eyes trained on her, smiling in a way she hadn't seen for years, tempting her to take his hand. They were eyes that appreciated her, that knew nothing of her past; a piercing blue-green gaze that took her back for a moment to the beautiful Schweriner See. Sabine felt drawn to the owner of the eyes instantly and, when he wiggled his fingers in insistence, she reached to grasp his hand.

When their hands touched, a charge flew through her body. It was pulsating and electric, sizzling with a power so exciting that she let go instinctively. Realising the extent of her surprise, the stranger reached forward and touched her arm in gentle reassurance and, as he did so, his presence seemed to effervesce through his fingertips and sparkle on her skin. His touch was magnetic. Magical. She felt drawn to him, even though they had never met. His grip seemed to cut through the years of hurt and inadequacy that riddled her body. For the first time in years she felt light entering her darkened soul. The winter inside her began to thaw but, as it did so, he seemed to invade her, his words entering straight into her mind.

Sabine. Don't fear me. I am Karsten Maier. We are meant to be together.

Sabine was shocked at his intrusion. It was too much. Her body had been intrigued by his touch, but the words, more so the way he had communicated them, terrified her. A blitzkrieg of fear stormed through her body and her sense of self-preservation kicked in. Instinctively she ran.

As the days went past, she dwelt on the experience and relived the moment a hundred times and as she did so, familiarity numbed the fear. She became more and more intrigued by those words. On reflection, they were the most calming, beautiful words she had ever heard, though she wondered whether 'heard' was the right description. Sabine started to kick herself for having fled, and she cursed her instinct for having torn her away from what she felt was such a pivotal moment in her life. She began to long to hear those words once more, and lusted after that fizzing touch. She wanted to stare into those congenial eyes, and lose herself in them. In that single moment, she had felt free. Alive. And she wanted more.

Every day, she passed the spot where she had fallen, and found herself loitering there for a minute or so longer each time. At first it was a subconscious dithering, but soon it became a conscious five, and then ten-minute, stop. She was desperate for the mysterious Karsten Maier to show himself once more, and she promised herself that, the next time they met, she wouldn't let him go. Her wait became longer and longer each day. Whenever she left, she instantly wished she had given him another minute. The idea that she might not be there when he eventually turned up, was unbearable. Finally, she resolved to stay until she saw him again, no matter how long that took. The factory had already become used to her arriving late, and she no longer cared about the cold shoulder that would be orchestrated amongst the workers to communicate the collective disdain. All that mattered to her was Karsten. She had to find him. He had opened a window of excitement in her dark and claustrophobic life, and it was one she needed to crawl through. So she waited. Ten minutes became twenty, twenty became thirty. Sabine became riddled with self-doubt and even began to question her own recollection, wondering whether the magical Karsten might have just been a dream. But despite her inner turmoil, she remained there, rooted to the spot and determined not to leave. Not until she knew for sure. And her perseverance was rewarded, though not at all in the way she had expected.

I feel you waiting there Sabine. I cannot come, even though I want to with all my heart. I need you to meet me. Now. At the Fernsehturm. Come quickly.

Sabine was already committed. It was impossible for her to ignore his request. She was at the point where she would have broken out of East Germany if this enigmatic stranger had asked her. Nothing was more important to her than Karsten. There was little to lose except the darkness that still tormented her, and everything to gain. She pined for that touch, longed to look into those eyes once more, and needed to understand why he could talk to her that way. Without a moment's hesitation, she left.

Unfortunately, Sabine had been noticed. Berlin was a society that thrived on high routine and it was uncommon to be just waiting somewhere, ostensibly for nothing. There were queues of course, some of which lasted for hours and went on for several blocks. Nobody would have given her a second glance if she had been in one, but she wasn't. She appeared to be just waiting, and that was not something to be recommended in Berlin in 1981.

She headed across the city and down Karl-Liebknecht-Str. to the Fernsehturm in Alexanderplatz. It was East Germany's tallest building and the very antithesis of the nearby Marienkirche, Berlin's oldest church. The old and the new were together. Religion and the regime, almost side by side in a concrete desert.

Instinctively she knew where to find Karsten. She could feel him. It was as though he was a blinking beacon, guiding her towards the chevron steps that surrounded the stark and ominous tower from which the televised lies were broadcast to so few. There, at the entrance, he sat. Sabine was exhilarated to see him. Her heart leapt in excitement. She had none of the fear of their earlier, brief encounter, just a feeling of calm familiarity.

'You came, Sabine.'

'Of course! I had to!'

'Were you followed?'

'Why?'

'Were you followed, Sabine? I must know!' he demanded.

It hadn't occurred to Sabine to check. She wasn't a criminal. In her life, she had done nothing wrong, other than betray those closest to her. The idea that she would be constantly looking over her shoulder was ludicrous. She had seen enough of the Stasi in her life to date to fear them, but it was a fear that was always in the background, like a constant ache. She had no reason to be so immediately concerned about them.

'I, I don't know, Karsten.'

He scanned the vicinity with those vivid blue-green eyes, before focusing back on Sabine. The way that stare made her melt was uncanny.

'It looks like we're safe.'

'What have you done Karsten? I don't want to be involved. I can't. The Stasi. They terrify me.'

'I've done nothing Sabine. Nothing at all.'

'Then why would they be after you?'

'They've been watching me since I was eight. It was the day the wall went up and the authorities blocked us from leaving the city. I ran to help a dying girl who had been shot trying to cross the barbed wire they had erected the night before. Everyone else just stood there staring at her, but I felt compelled to go to her. I reached down to touch her and from then on my life has never been the same again.'

'Why?'

'I need to show …'

He was interrupted by the sound of heavily booted footsteps thudding towards them, accompanied by the unmistakeable rattle of weapons. It was a sound that Sabine had heard once before in her life, and one she had hoped never to hear again.

'Police! Stay right where you are! Both of you! Maier, your time is up! You are coming with us! There's no escape for you this time, no-one to hide you. It is time for us to find out the truth about what happened that day twenty years ago!' The officer in charge spat the words with a contempt that was clearly born of long-term frustration, as though he personally had been seeking Karsten for all that time. Sabine froze. She looked to Karsten but his eyes were wild. Thoughts of her father flew through her head. It was happening once more. She had betrayed someone to the Stasi again. How would she ever live with herself?

'Sabine, I …'

'Silence!' snapped the Officer.

Instantly, Karsten's words filled Sabine's head.

I can't let them take me.

And with that he made a break for freedom. Almost instantly the crack of gunfire filled the Alexanderplatz. He fell to the floor with a sickening clump and his blood began to trickle along the cement grooves, tracing around the pavers like a gruesome grout.

Sabine. Come. To. Me.

Without hesitation, Sabine rushed towards him, expecting the weapons to target her as well. But at that point the police weren't interested in her. They had their man and were approaching him to check he was dead. Sabine reached him first. He was still breathing.

Take my hand Sabine.

Karsten's life was draining away. Sabine could see it. There was no way he could be saved. All she could do was to comfort him in death, and she reached for his hand. Immediately their fingers touched, a tidal wave of power swept through her body. In seconds, she absorbed Karsten's memories, his thoughts. It was as though his entire life had transferred through her fingers. But it was more than that. There were other lives, other names. Ilse. Joachim. Molly. Edward. Diego. Isabel. Then the names became a blur as the tide engulfed her completely and she felt the onset of blackness.

When Sabine awoke, she was in a cell. It was little more than the size of a grave and even less homely, the only furniture a wooden bed and a toilet seat that covered a metal bucket. The walls were a damp and mildewed yellow and there was no window. She was cold and alone, frightened and confused. She had no idea what she had done, where she was or how long she had been there. So many questions circled her mind, but no answers were to be found. All she knew was that she had not just witnessed Karsten's death, she had felt it. In that one miserable moment, he had passed something to her. Something she didn't understand.

From then on, every day was the same. She sat silently in the early hours of each morning, listening for sounds. Something, anything to indicate where she was. The call of a bird. The rumble of a train. But there was nothing other than the screams of distant torture, which echoed through the unforgiving walls, haunting her consciousness, just as whatever had been passed to her besieged her dreams. Occasionally, she wondered whether the screams might belong to her father, but the guilt that came with those thoughts was too painful for her to contemplate.

Time was meaningless in the near-constant darkness. The lack of sustenance meant she was always hungry and, as a result, she could never be sure whether the opening door would bring the latest helping of rotting meat and moulding bread, or whether it would signal the next bout of torture. As a result, she quickly learned to cower at the unlocking of the door. Within days of her arrival they had removed all her toe nails, exposing the sensitive underbellies. Then they had kept her awake for days on end, forcing her to confess to made-up allegations, which she did, despite the knowledge that her admission would commit her to a long prison sentence. Anything was preferable to the pain she was made to endure. What they were doing to her was creative sadism.

After her confession, occasionally they came back for her, trying to extract more and more falsehoods to incriminate others she had never met. Once, they even injected her with drugs and placed her in a rubber cell. She remembered nothing of that experience at all, other than that in her first few lucid moments, she felt heat. The heat of a summer sun. It was the only time she would feel it for the next decade.

At night, when she was allowed to sleep, Sabine was restless. Her mind trawled through the lifetimes that had been passed to her. Whenever she closed her eyes she found herself there, in someone else's life. She saw what they saw, felt what they felt and cried when they cried, though each time the tears were too much for her. There had been so much sadness in her life so far that she had no room, or desire, for any more. Whenever she came across misery she withdrew. It was too painful.

She was able to glean just one thing. She had been

entrusted with a legacy, an ancient responsibility. It was one that needed to be passed down to someone else. It wasn't a welcome realisation, considering her situation, and merely added pressure inside her. She knew she had no control over her release and no means of escape. Even if she had been free, she had nowhere to go and no funds. She could only hope that one day she would be free, and that, if and when it happened, she wasn't too late. In her waking hours, she began to plan what she needed to do when she was eventually freed. She had to believe that one day the door would open for good, and when that happened she would need to take action. At least she had plenty of time to prepare for it.

Finally, on that milestone day in 1990, East Germany ceased to exist. The country was absorbed once again into Germany and, in a flurry of shredding, the Stasi disbanded. Sabine's cell opened for the last time, and she left behind the tomb in which she had been imprisoned for so long. But she wasn't free. She learned quickly that the concept of liberty was just an impossible dream for her. She knew she could never escape from the torment of the abuse she had suffered, and it dragged behind her like a ball and chain.

She stepped gingerly into a world in which little had changed. The only difference was that the hundreds of administrative buildings looked even shabbier. She began to smell the fresh air and she shrank from the sun's glare. For the first time, Sabine traded knowing glances with the other inmates, as they all left the Hohenschönhausen Prison, hundreds of them, kindred spirits. They each knew what the other had been through, even though they had never met and would never speak of it. Each of them knew the violence and torture to which they had been subjected would never leave them.

Like Sabine, they too tried to come to grips with the end of their ordeal, struggling with the uncertainty of the day, a feeling so opposite to the certainty of the gruesome routine inside. None of them knew where to go or what to do, and so they secretly hankered for the security of their cell. They were lost.

Sabine, at least, had purpose. This was the day she had hoped for, and she knew what she had to do. For ten years, she had protected an ancient secret that had been passed to her, and now her job was to ensure it survived. At first when she had developed her plan, she didn't know where she needed to go but, as she became more familiar with the lives of those who had come before her, she began to learn answers. By the time of her release, she still didn't know exactly where she needed to go, but inside she felt an overwhelming calling to England, where she knew a girl would be waiting for her.

The trouble was that Sabine had nothing. No possessions and no money. Without the latter, she would be unable to make the journey and she had no choice but to beg. Society was so appalled by the treatment of prisoners in East Germany that those with money took pity on her and her fellow inmates. It turned out that even the East Germans had not known about Hohenschönhausen Prison. It had been kept so secret that it didn't even show up on maps. It was no wonder those who worked there had been so vile and depraved, Sabine thought. It was because they worked with total impunity.

Most of the citizens spared what they could. It was as if they each carried a small amount of guilt, even though it was far from their fault. Those who could give nothing donated clothes. Some, of course, refused her begging, and occasionally she would recognise one of her former torturers. She was astonished that they felt so little shame they could still live in the same area. She wondered what inner turmoil they suffered and how they were able to live with themselves. None of them gave her money, and neither did she ask. Whenever they came past, she blocked their way and stared accusingly into their eyes. Without exception, they failed to returned her gaze. In those moments, their shame betrayed them, and Sabine knew it was as close to an admission of guilt as she would ever receive.

For the best part of a week, she skimped and scraped together the fare for a train journey. There was no need to pay for shelter, sleeping under the stars was such an advance on where she had spent the last ten years, it was like all the world's luxury hotels rolled into one. And it was free. She lived off scraps that she found, or had been donated. Even some of the foulest morsels were more appetising than what had been served to her in the prison.

Calais would be her destination, she had long since decided. It was a port, though much smaller than her home port of Rostock, which she knew so well. In some ways, it would indeed have been ideal if she had been able to travel to England from Rostock, she felt pulled to the marshes, the forests, the lakes, craving a return to the beautiful region of Mecklenburg where she had grown up. After such a long time away, Sabine dreamed that a visit would feel like a homecoming, a return to normality, an opportunity to wipe clean the filthy and miserable slate that had been her recent life. But she also knew that terror had amplified her longing for Schwerin, that she had held on so tightly to her childhood memories, preserved them as so precious, that reality could never match her expectations.

She suspected that her family would be long gone, and no-one would recognise the homecoming queen. The reality was that there had been a point in her life when she had been so miserable in Schwerin, so alone and paranoid, that she had moved to Berlin.

There were other reasons not to head to Rostock too. True, it was a huge port, but it opened to the Baltic. Any crossing from there to England would have to take her around Denmark, and considering her lack of any identification it would be a journey that she would have to make by trawler. Desperate as she was to make it to England, the idea of a week on a trawler in swelling seas, seemed almost on par with her time at Hohenschönhausen.

Heading to Calais would mean that Sabine had to evade whatever border controls there might be between Germany, Belgium and France, but she felt sure that borders of that size were impossible to seal, and that one way or another she would be able to sneak from one country to the next. She bought her train ticket for just under three hundred marks. It was a sign of the guilt that the Berliners felt at the sight of her desperate, tortured soul that she still had a hundred or so marks left, money she would use to pay a fisherman to take her to England.

Sabine boarded the train and snuggled into the firm seat that she would occupy for the five and a half hours to Düsseldorf. It amused her to hear those around her cursing about their discomfort. To her it was the most comfortable place she had rested for as long as she could remember. Within minutes she was asleep and reliving the memories of those who had come before her as she always did in her dreams. A smile flickered across her dozing body as once more she saw a vision of Karsten Maier. Tears lubricated her tired eyes as her dreams momentarily turned to how life might have been under different circumstances.

She woke to the perpetual clack of the train traversing

a number of points, which meant they were entering
Düsseldorf. Out of the window, for the first time Sabine
caught a glimpse of Western society. What struck her was
the care and deliberation with which they had constructed
the buildings. Sabine had heard stories of how the city had
been ravaged by Allied bombing during the war and yet,
unlike Berlin, what had replaced those damaged buildings
was beautiful. It was a vision of a thriving community. Her
eyes absorbed every tower, every park and every bridge.
She felt envious, jealous of the life others had been allowed
to lead by fate.

From Düsseldorf, she boarded a train to Aachen, her
nominated crossing point. From her geography lessons at
school she knew it was the place where three nations met,
Germany, Holland, and Belgium. Her plan was to sneak
across the border into either of the other two and continue
her journey. Her previous experiences of border crossings
were frightening. She'd had no reason to pass through any,
but had seen first hand how those entering the west were
interrogated by border police in Berlin, so her assumption
had been that all crossings in the world were the same, and
she was astonished to find the border to three countries
was completely unmanned. Those were in the process of
adopting the Schengen Agreement, and had long since
abandoned any desire to patrol their borders. As a result,
Sabine walked straight into Belgium unchallenged.

She skipped easily through the light forest, and onto

the Route des Trois Bournes, which took her into Gemmenich. From there she caught a bus the thirty minutes or so to Liege, where she boarded another train to Brussels and on to Mouscron. There, once again, she strolled across into France without so much as a sniff of border security. Never in her wildest dreams could Sabine have imagined that travel between countries could be so easy and, when she boarded the train again at Lille, she began to suspect that crossing the channel might be the hardest part of her journey.

She was right. The French fishermen refused to take her across the channel. Only a Spaniard, Carlos Alvarado, relented. He was the captain of the *Belouga*, a small fishing seiner no more than thirty feet in length. Compared with some of the vessels, it seemed ancient and the deck stank of putrid fish. She found it odd that a Spaniard was operating a French fishing vessel, but her need to cross the channel was urgent. Oddly, she wasn't the only one needing transport. Already aboard was another passenger, huddled on the deck in a long sou'wester, clearly on the run from something and not wanting to be seen or recognised. More worryingly, there was something about him that triggered a primeval warning inside her. She had flinched when their hands touched during Alvarado's introduction. It was as though his very presence was an offence to her sense of touch. That kind of power was something she had encountered only once before in her life, but back then it had been so special. It had been a touch that she longed for, one that filled her with hope and excitement, whereas this was one that brought nothing but sorrow and fear. She was torn. Every instinct told her to leave the ship, but she had no other options. Her imprisonment meant it had taken her far too long to make it to England already, and she was acutely aware of the mounting urgency with which she needed to be there. She knew she couldn't afford to delay any longer. Besides, her certainty that her fate was somehow linked to a girl in England made her feel a little invincible, so she decided she needed to trust destiny to look after her, even though everything about the journey felt wrong. With a heavy heart, she surrendered herself to fate. All the while she remained on her guard, never trusting Alvarado or her creepy companion, determined to maintain as much distance from them as she could find on such a small vessel.

It was a tactic that worked for the first few hours of the crossing, and she began to relax a little, allowing herself to picture what might happen in England. She dreamed of finding freedom there, of somehow unlocking the fun that was buried so deeply inside her soul. A part of her wondered whether she would even recognise freedom when she felt it; it was a concept that had so far meant so little to her.

Sabine was jerked out of her daydream by the sound

of footsteps. They were close enough to hear above the constant whispering of the sea. She wheeled around to see the fugitive lurching across the rolling deck. He was closing in on her and she cursed herself for having dropped her guard momentarily. For the journey so far, she had kept him at a distance but now, in the middle of the channel, he was close, too close. His eyes were fixed on her, like a cat tracking its prey. She felt trapped, cornered at the prow, as he advanced. With every step, she felt more threatened. His every movement was menacing. Her heart was racing. Her head scrambled for options where there were none. She clenched her fists instinctively, knowing she had not come this far, not suffered this much, to fall at the final hurdle. Her life had been miserable but she lived for the hope of what was to come. It was something she was prepared to fight for.

In moments, he was on her. She felt his stifling malevolence, could smell his festering breath. He kept coming towards her. Looming over her. Intimidating her, just like her torturers had done. At the critical moment she cowered, hands across her face. Just as she had when they had shone those bright lights at her. Over the years, it had become a conditioned response to attack. The natural instinct to fight or flight had been nullified by years of torture and, although her mind wanted to fight, her body wanted to surrender. It needed mercy.

His assault was brief and violent. He swung a rusty

wrench, and it gave a sickly crunch as it connected with Sabine's head. Instantly her world went black and she slumped to the coarse painted floor of the deck. He went to work straightaway, undressing her with cold but efficient hands. One by one he removed her ill-fitting clothes, wondering what possessed such an attractive girl to wear such tat. In no time, she was naked and unconscious in front of him. She was a beauty alright and he thought briefly about forcing himself on her, giving himself a taste of what might have been, but her body was ruined by scars, the like of which he had never seen before. Only her face had been unmarked, until his attack. He fingered the scars briefly, wondering about the trauma she had endured. She was lucky he was putting her out of her misery, he thought. He hoisted her limp body towards the edge of the boat, surprised at its lightness. He rested her gently on his knee as he reset his grip, and then tipped her unconscious body into the sea, watching as she slipped into the distance, her pale and scarred skin glowing in the moonlight.

The icy entry into the sea jerked Sabine into consciousness. It took several seconds for her to understand where she was, seconds she didn't have. Water plunged into her lungs as she took her first, knowing breath. With all her energy, she spluttered to the surface and gasped for air, spewing the water from her lungs with every cough. She knew that within seconds she would be under again, and forced as much air in as she could. At least the water boarding in prison had given her experience of drowning. She wasn't going to panic.

But the water around her was scarlet with blood and her head screamed from the blow. Weakness began to take over her body and the cold seeped into her every bone. The effort to stay afloat began to take its toll and Sabine knew that she couldn't keep it up. Though she had survived much in her lifetime, she suspected this was the end. She had ignored her instinct and blindly followed what she had thought was destiny. It seemed that fate had deceived her.

*

The icy water snatched James back into the present. The shower had run cold and for a moment he was disoriented and began gasping for breath, fearing he was drowning, just like Sabine, who he now knew was the girl Lauren had found on the beach. He was filled with profound sadness at the misery she had endured, and now understood why her body had been so scarred. Fate had indeed been cruel to her, crueller than to most.

Sabine was yet another who had failed to drink from the elusory chalice that promised so much. James began to wonder why it should be any different for he and Lauren this time around. The more lifetimes his distracted mind relived, the more tragedy drew his tears. Foreboding trembled its way through his nerves and he found himself questioning whether he had chosen the right path. The trouble was that, now he had tasted the elixir that lay at the end of it, there was no turning back. He knew that his life was taking him down a track that had led to certain doom for everyone who had taken it before him. He found himself hoping for a miracle.

9

W HAT POOR SABINE had endured put Lauren's own experience into perspective. Whatever happened in the future, she vowed to relish every moment of her time with James. At least she had been given some. Poor Sabine had been denied even that.

It was hard for Lauren, living on the edge of safety with a possessive and violent man. She inched through the ashes of a relationship that her husband poked at in vain to rekindle. In the distance, the planned escape shone brightly, guiding her through a confused and frightened existence and towards a blessed release. She reached out to James when she could, and that tended to coincide with her husband working emergency extra shifts or, better still, nights. One of the beauties of police work was that there was always plenty of overtime on offer and, although Sean fell woefully short as a partner, he couldn't be faulted as a worker. If they had ever had a family, he would have made sure they wanted for nothing, but there was no circumstance under which Lauren would ever have brought a child into such an atmosphere of fear. That was a source of constant frustration for Sean, and he had tried to bully Lauren into motherhood on more than one occasion.

Another tangible benefit of the extra money was that she was able to siphon away some savings into an escape fund. Sean never kept up to date with their finances. All he wanted was to be able to go to the cash-point and withdraw money whenever he needed it, not sit for hours reconciling bank statements. It was Lauren's job to run the house and control the expenses, a role that suited the planner in her. He trusted her housekeeping implicitly, feeling that the control he exerted over her meant she wouldn't dare hide anything from him. He was wrong of course, and with each week the pile of ten-pound notes that she kept rolled up inside one of his old jackets, grew fatter. It had been difficult for Lauren to decide where to keep the money. She knew that Sean regularly went through her drawers, and if he found anything there would be hell to pay. His mistake was that he underestimated her intelligence. She knew better than to hide anything in any of her possessions, and so she hid money in his. He had plenty of clothes, but they quickly fell out of favour, and as a result his wardrobe was full of trousers, shirts and jackets archived in apathy. Not only did he never wear them, he rarely noticed them. But Lauren did, and she knew it was the last place he would ever look. Despite that, she still lived in fear that maybe by some random misfortune he would, and so whenever he lost something Lauren jumped in very quickly to help.

The other great thing about his work patterns was that it gave her more time alone. Time to think, to dream, to plan. Time to make contact with James. When Sean's work kept him away from home at night, Lauren could connect with James, and they would lie there with their minds in glorious harmony for the whole night, despite their distance. At those times the exhaustion of the following day was a mere triviality compared with the exhilaration of the night before. She always felt a renewed hope after those nights with James. They topped up her resilience to the point where she knew she could cope with anything. For once she had an outlet, a release valve through which her fears could escape.

She found herself yearning for her stolen moments with James. Even five minutes of exclusive togetherness brought reality to what sometimes felt like a fictional affection. In the agonising periods between them it was easy to feel as though it was all a dream, that somehow the escape was never going to happen. On those days, she headed to the beach, and just the feel of her toes on the sand made her feel closer to James. The memory of that special day together was so vivid she could almost relive it at will.

★

Lauren's haphazard contact played havoc with James' punctuality. He had always hated to be late and yet now was frequently left with no choice. Under normal circumstances, the mere thought of being late filled him with a panicked dread that upset his day, even if he actually arrived on time. The closer it was to the designated time, the more stressed he became. He had his suspicions about where this had come from. His dad's incredible propensity for tardiness had somehow pushed him the other way and made him over compensate to ensure he didn't end up the same. His father just seemed not to care about time at all. It wasn't that he lost track of it and found himself rushing at the last minute, there was *never* any rush on his part. Growing up, James had lost count of the hours that his mum and he had waited in the hall for the man at the agreed departure time, poised at the front door with coats and hats on ready to brave the cold, only for him to come out of the lounge and tell them he just needed a shave. James soon realised that was a euphemism for his entire bathroom and dressing cycle and he, unlike anyone James had known since, could and would sit on the toilet for thirty minutes, regardless of any impending deadline.

James found that he just had to start learning to accept being late. Nothing was more important than seizing that time, any time, with Lauren. Whenever he felt her reaching out to him, everything was placed on hold. Start times at work became a moveable feast and it stretched the friendship with Nick considerably. James was really torn about that. Nick had given him so much, but the fact was that Lauren had shown James a whole new level of relationship and it was one that nobody else could live up to. As a consequence, everyone else became less and less important. Fortunately, he knew that it would be hypocritical for Nick to pull him up on his timekeeping, considering his own tardiness. It would never cost him his job, though it might cost him a friend.

In the end, the New Year arrived like a tardy train, held up somewhere further up the track, and gathering lateness as it closed in on its destination. In the dying weeks of the year, James felt himself pacing the platform like an expectant passenger. It seemed that the passing of time was inversely proportional to the level of excitement about an event. Dreaded ones, like exam week at school, arrived in a flash, he recalled, but the thought of exciting ones possessed an innate ability to slow the passing of time to a crawl. James wondered if that was something to do with the amount of attention that he paid to them. He had spent as much time as possible avoiding thoughts of the former but had been so fixated on the latter that maybe it invoked the watched-kettle principle, and never boiled.

It was a strange experience for James to put himself to bed early on New Year's Eve. Since he had been an adult, every previous one had been an inebriated fuzz. His friends and colleagues gathered across Folkestone's many bars to rid themselves of the indomitable 1991, that had so compounded the misery of its recent forbears. They drank through its dying hours and held its abominable hand as it gasped its last breath, before turning their backs at the moment of its demise. For them, 1992 arrived in a vodka veil that lifted temporarily at midnight. They embraced it like a new wife, with whom they callously flaunted their hopes and desires in the lifeless face of the old one.

Instead of sharing the shenanigans, James spent a restless evening pondering the future. While 1991 had been a gruelling year for the entire country, it had bought passion and purpose for him. It had been a year that others would have preferred to see buried deep, like spent nuclear fuel, yet James felt he was on the verge of riding surging waters as they smashed through an enduring dam and engulfed all before them. He knew that he would begin a great adventure the following morning and his body tingled with excitement. It was so close. He could feel it. The next day he would be with Lauren. Forever.

At the same time, he felt he was laying his friendships on the altar, and perhaps sacrificing them forever in pursuit of a higher purpose. It wasn't that he felt the bonds would fail to survive distance and time. The roots that he had established, with Nick and Adam especially, were so deep that he knew he would be able to return periodically and gorge on future fruits. What he didn't know was whether it would ever be safe enough to return for the harvest.

The plan for the following day churned over and over in his mind as he wrestled with sleep. It had been the source of much disagreement between Lauren and he, as they planned their escape. Some things had been simple to agree, like using the ferry and trains rather than taking a flight. Other aspects were more controversial. Lauren had insisted they should make their way separately to Paris, to avoid any hint they might be together. James, on the other hand, didn't want to waste another moment of his life without Lauren. He had also been concerned about the prospect of Lauren's husband returning home while she was in the process of leaving.

They were such a great team, however. They had so many channels through which they could communicate. They understood each other. They could hide nothing. In the end, they had been able to reach a compromise that met both of their base needs. James would watch Lauren's exit from the pub opposite, and had promised not to show his face at all, unless the worst happened. He had no real desire to remain apart from Lauren any longer than necessary, but he accepted the logic of them travelling to Paris separately, even though they shared the same itinerary. At least this way, James felt he could be certain that Lauren had made the break. And if anything happened, well, at least he would be there to protect her.

After the usual restless night, James was up and at it early on New Year's Day. So early in fact, that he spotted the odd reveller staggering home from the night before. He had been too excited to sleep in any longer, yet there was nothing for him to do now he was awake, other than wait. His bag had been packed for more than a week and the house was clean and ready for the incoming tenant. Truly these were the longest hours of his life. He set himself meaningless tasks. A walk to the shops to buy a newspaper. Making a cup of coffee, but none of them performed the job of passing time to any satisfactory level.

As the time to leave approached, James found himself having to physically hold himself back. He knew almost exactly how long it would take to reach Lauren's street, even though he had never timed the walk. That would have been something we would have done too, multiple times, if he had been able to. But, once again, his thoughts had betrayed him. Lauren knew that if she gave James her address, he wouldn't be able to resist passing by on the off-chance of running into her. So, she had withheld it until that morning, and it turned out that she lived closer than James had thought.

Finally, the clock struck eleven and that signalled the time for his departure. As he left the house, it was with a sense of finality that surprised him. Closing the door turned out to be not just a physical act, but a symbolic one too. Not only was he sealing the house, he was letting his mum go, accepting, drawing the curtain on his former life, moving on. He paused for a moment's reflection and wondered what his mum would have thought of his plan. To some it might seem like a flight of fancy, a risk, but James suspected that she would have viewed it differently. All she had ever wanted was for him to be happy and she would have seen the way that his eyes sparkled whenever he mentioned Lauren. He whispered a silent farewell to his mother and closed the door to their family home for the last time.

It was no more than a ten-minute walk to the Richmond Tavern, one of Folkestone's many forgotten pubs. It was off the beaten track, on the corner of Margaret and Harvey Streets. James had been there once or twice before, though he couldn't think why. Its location was such that he could only ever have been passing through on his way into or home from, town. Inside it was compact and old fashioned. The central bar took up nearly all of the space with padded stools around it.

He bought himself a pint and sat down. There were just two window tables. One was occupied even at this early hour, by a hooded regular who was hunched over his ale and scratching the white hairs of his goatee pensively. James felt sorry for him; drinking alone at such an early hour could never be a good thing. At least he had a reason for being there. He took a seat at the window, overlooking Harvey Street. The view could not have been better. Across the street was number thirty-three. It was distinctive, the only house on the street that sat back from the path. In its style, it and its right-hand neighbour, seemed like an afterthought. The rest of the houses in the street were typical Victorian terraces, but it was almost as if the planners had miscalculated the number to be built. Numbers thirty-one and thirty-three were wedged in the middle. They had none of the bay windows and their roofs were significantly lower, so different they couldn't possibly have been part of the original plan. He wondered whether perhaps a bomb had landed there during the war.

James had bought a newspaper and was pretending to leaf through it, though his eyes really were fixated on the cream rendered building opposite. The windows were heavily netted and he could see nothing inside. Assuming the plan was in motion, Lauren would be frantically packing the belongings she had earmarked to take. From the outside, everything seemed perfectly normal. It was only because James could feel Lauren's presence that he even knew he had come to the right street. Through their connected minds, they were each able to discreetly register that the other was in position, so there was no need for her to pull back the net and wave to him. He could sense the anxiety that riddled Lauren's mind. At one point the feeling of her pounding heart reverberated so strongly through him, he had to check that the table he was leaning on wasn't vibrating. Despite her obvious fear, the plan seemed to be going well so far. Her husband had clearly left the house as planned, and that had triggered her activity. In less than ten minutes, James expected to see a taxi draw up and Lauren emerge with a mid-size backpack.

Something was niggling at James though. On the one hand, he was on edge and willing the plan to work. They were within touching distance of a life together, and he was praying that nothing would stand in their way. On the other hand, a growing dread seemed to have taken root inside him. It was a feeling he had experienced fleetingly before, one that seemed to accompany each of his meetings with Lauren like a minor chord tempering their harmonious liaison. He didn't think it was emanating from Lauren as such; it just seemed to be around her, as if it was following her. This time, the dread was anything but brief and imperceptible; it was ever present, and with each minute it was increasing, to the point where it was beginning to suffocate him. He wanted nothing more than to leave the tavern. It felt unsafe.

A metallic amber Mitsubishi Galant pulled up outside number thirty-three. The only feature that distinguished it as a taxi was the white roof sign that bore the word. The driver beeped his horn to announce his arrival to Lauren, though to James it felt like it was an alert to the world. His heart raced as the engine idled. This was the moment of truth. If all was well then Lauren would emerge, climb into the taxi and set off for the port of Dover. If it wasn't, well, James didn't really want to consider that scenario.

To be fair to Lauren, her timing was impeccable. It might have felt to James as though the taxi was waiting for the best part of a year outside the house, but in fact Lauren appeared almost immediately after it arrived. Relief flooded across James and Lauren's mental connection as, without so much as a look towards the tavern, she climbed into the taxi and was off. The journey had begun.

James swallowed the remainder of his beer. He needed it after the stress of the last fifteen minutes and briefly considered ordering a second. It was an automatic reaction, one that he was beginning to learn to tame. This wasn't the time or the place for a second beer. He needed to make his own way to Dover and that meant a walk to the train station. Besides, he needed to leave the bar. Even though Lauren had left, it still felt oppressive and James couldn't understand why. There was no reason for him to stay here now and he needed no excuse to leave. He stepped through the door and out into the street, taking the opportunity for a last glance at Lauren's former home. She wouldn't be needing it any more. Good riddance to her former life. He had no sympathy for her husband.

Behind him, the pub door flew open with enormous force. Before he could complete his turn, James was knocked to the floor by someone barging past him and he hit the pavement with an almighty thud. It was no accident. He knew he'd been pushed. His heart pounded as he waited for the follow-up assault. But it never came.

His nerves had been on edge anyway, but now they teetered over and were plummeting fast towards the ground. It wasn't so much that he was sprawled across the path, or that he was attracting attention at a time when he wanted to maintain a low profile. It was the push itself. He had felt a charged hand connect with his back in the moment before his fall. That touch had set off fireworks of dread inside him. It was almost the opposite of the electricity, the gravity, with which he had always felt drawn to Lauren. This was hateful. Spiteful. Vengeful. Its ferocity made James freeze on the spot. There was something otherworldly about the sensation and James didn't like it one bit.

The assailant was nowhere to be seen as James picked himself up. He had mixed feelings. Part of him wanted to know who, or what, had shoved him. The other part was grateful that he didn't know. The one clear thing was that he didn't want to feel that particular touch again. Ever.

He gathered his thoughts and set off for the train station. It was no more than fifteen minutes away and he was still on schedule. At Dover, he knew he would feel Lauren's presence once more, and he surrendered to his longing as he walked. It was far more preferable than dwelling on what had happened outside the Richmond Tavern.

★

As usual he had been watching her from the comfort of what had become his favourite bar. It couldn't have been better placed, almost built to be able to watch the house. It was a very civilised way of stalking his wife.

The usual tranquillity of his surveillance had been spoiled by the arrival of the boy. So, it had begun, had it? The game was afoot. Pretending to read the newspaper? What a farce. Anyone could see that he was watching the house.

Fury welled inside him as the taxi pulled up. Moments later, he watched as she left with her belongings. He couldn't intervene. It was too public. This wasn't the time or place to act with impunity. Street confrontations were for amateurs. Professionals like him were able to keep a lid on their emotions and kill in cold blood. He knew where she was going, he had already done the research. He also had the taxi registration and, if all else failed, the driver would tell him where she had gone. He had ways of ensuring that.

He watched the boy leave and stand gawping at the house over the road. He had sensed an opportunity and followed him out of the pub. The boy needed to understand what he was dealing with. With the element of surprise behind him, he had pushed the boy to the ground with a trained arm. He considered a follow-up, but it was unnecessary. The boy would go where his wife went, she was what he wanted. He would deal with them together.

He slipped around the corner and watched as the boy picked himself up. He could feel the fear coursing through the boy's body and he liked it. There would be plenty more of that coming, he would make sure of it. Once the boy had disappeared, he doubled back to Harvey Street. He had business to take care of before he could follow.

He slipped a well-worn key into the lock of number thirty-three and let himself in. The house still smelt of his wife, an aroma that had changed much over the years but was still uniquely hers. It was a pity that he would have to kill her.

10

THE TRAIN FROM Folkestone Central was on time, and James made his connection. In less than half an hour, he arrived at the port and immediately sensed that Lauren was there. Trying to stay away from her was tearing him apart, but he knew she was right. What was another few hours apart compared with the security of their life together? At least the compromise he had forced meant he knew she was safe. He could relax, though he wasn't sure that was the right word. He felt more like an antelope on the savannah, jittery and watchful. It was only a matter of time before the lion came after them.

Despite being on edge, he still felt relief and excitement and he could feel it in Lauren too. He knew that the greater the distance they could put between them and Folkestone, the more their chances increased. This was their moment to share in the rewards that at least a hundred predecessors had chased and failed to reap. Destiny was at their fingertips and James felt exhilarated. Together they had the power to make a loser of legacy.

As usual, there was a delay in the ferry's departure and that led to an uncomfortable extra hour or so at Dover.

Not only was there nothing to do in the crowded ticket hall, but James jumped every time the automatic doors slid open. It was nerve-wracking in the extreme, and he was grateful when he received instructions to board the bus that would take him to the ship. Danger was behind them, not ahead, and he made sure that Lauren left on an earlier bus before he boarded one himself.

Aboard the ship, they worked hard to avoid seeing each other, knowing that locking eyes would make keeping their distance nearly impossible, so intense was their desire. There were several hundred witnesses on board and each had the potential to betray them under questioning. It was a risk they couldn't afford to take. The fact was that tracking two people was easier than one.

The vast diesel engines droned incessantly as the ship began to sail, and their vibrations throbbed through the green painted floors as the vessel wobbled its way out of the harbour. The toothy smile of the white cliffs began to shrink in the background and James felt a sense of loss as he left them behind. England was his home, his birthplace, and he felt as though he would never return. He locked his eyes on the fading coastline, staring at the growing distance for as long as possible. It was like waving goodbye to a favourite cousin as they left after a glorious weekend.

The prevailing south-westerly wind that rampaged along the English Channel, caught occasional spray and flicked it onto James' ruddy cheeks. It was icy, and the wind infused every drop with its unrelenting bitterness as each pricked at his skin like a shard of the sea. All around were seagulls, nature's airforce repelling a vanquished foe.

Finally, James turned his back on the beautiful British backdrop and zig-zagged his way to the bow. From the distant fog, Cap Gris-Nez began to appear. It was France's perennial sentinel. For millennia it had stood, staring forever in stalemate at its English counterpart across the sea. Those two wily campaigners had seen some action over the centuries, he thought. The sentinels of two opposing cultures that sought periodically to rule the other. Those great headlands had watched a million hopeful invaders depart with bellicose intent, and many of them now lay at the bottom of the sea. Romans. Normans. Plantagenets. Tudors. Napoleon. Nelson. Throughout history, the nations had quarrelled like brothers sparring for control. It was ironic that the two countries had now almost completed a tunnel under the sea that would connect them forever.

In spite of their proximity, and the similarity of their coasts, the two countries could not have been more different. In recent times, Thatcher had decided Britain wasn't going to make things any more, it was going to provide services instead. Such a thing could never happen in France, James thought. There was too much collective pride in everything French. 'Made in France' meant flair and innovation, if not always quality. Only France could have produced and sold in millions a van that looked, and most likely drove, like a mobile Anderson shelter. Only the French could have made an icon of the underpowered and unsightly 2CV that had fended off its successors for forty years because they just didn't have that *je ne sais quoi*, that quintessentially French factor that drove the population to purchase those Citroëns in droves.

The chill of the channel wind was becoming unbearable, and James stepped over the raised lip of a portside door. He was greeted immediately by the warmth that insulated the passengers from the bitterness outside. He craved a coffee to replenish some of the heat he had lost while saying goodbye to the land he loved, so he made his way to the restaurant and took his place in the kind of orderly queue that no self-respecting Frenchman would ever have joined.

Standing there in the queue, James could feel Lauren's presence. He knew she was there, in that room. Closer to him than she had been for far too long. His eyes longed to glance across the crowded self-service restaurant and feast once more on what they had been starved of for months. He wanted her. Needed her. He could sense her resolve wilting with his presence too. She wanted nothing more than to throw her arms around him in an incendiary cocktail of joy and relief. She was tantalisingly close. It wouldn't be long now until they could be together.

Knowing that if he set eyes on Lauren there was a chance the dam would breach and nothing would be able to stem the flow of the tide of togetherness, James lowered his head, determined to maintain the distance they had agreed to. He poured his coffee and teetered across the room. With each lurch, scalding liquid slopped into the saucer. He rebuked himself for his blistering choice, as the growing brown pond sizzled against the captive tips of his fingers. He slammed what had begun to resemble a boiling lake onto a nearby table and cursed his screaming hands. This was all part of the English disease, he grumbled to himself. Why did they have to serve hot drinks like this? On the one hand, it was lucky that the saucer was there. If it hadn't been, then at least half his coffee would be trailed across the floor by now. On the other hand, he had spilled half his coffee precisely because it was balanced on an ill-fitting saucer that effectively acted as a slippery tray. He was sure that a hundred years ago it was extremely quaint to be served hot drinks like this in one's drawing room, the saucers no doubt perfect to balance a tasty biscuit, or rest a finely crafted silver spoon. That was what cups and saucers were designed for. In this rolling setting, they were outdated, impractical and downright dangerous.

Through the window, James could see the Cap as the ship entered its welcoming arms. The weak winter sun flooded through the windows, making the artificial light inside seem woefully inadequate as it placed all those out of its direct reach into shadowy obscurity. The land moved across the many windows like a nature movie, as the vessel turned to reverse into the expectant harbour. As it did so, the sunlight passed across the passengers closest to the window and picked out their features for the darkened crowd to inspect. For one beautiful moment, its glorious spotlight shone on Lauren as it had the day James first saw her. Her hair gleamed like freshly polished ebony and her skin glowed like a soft and soothing night-light. She was even more beautiful than James remembered. Blinded to the inside of the ship, Lauren shielded those glorious eyes from the sun with her hand and turned towards James. Briefly their eyes locked, and they both felt the dam begin to crack.

She smiled, just as she had that cold day in February, almost twelve months earlier. It was a smile of release, a smile of joy and passion, a smile of fulfilment, one riddled with history. Then, as the ship continued its turn, the sunlight moved and plunged Lauren back into shadow, though their minds remained locked together in a loving embrace.

*

'Lauren, I'm home!' Sean Kennedy shouted his customary greeting as he walked through the door of number thirty-three. He wasn't a big fan of the early shift. Being at work

for a six o'clock start meant staggering out of bed before
five. On the plus side, it meant that he returned home at
2.30, and the whole afternoon lay ahead of him. It would
be a chance to talk to Lauren. She had been acting pretty
strangely on New Year's Eve, and he wanted to know
why.

'Hello?' He was surprised when there was no
response. Usually Lauren was so scared of him that she
made sure she acknowledged him. That wasn't something
he was particularly proud of so he did his best to bury
those beatings deep in his memory. He was always full of
remorse the morning after and he couldn't bear looking at
the damage he had done to that sculpted face. It didn't help
that she flinched whenever he moved. All he had to do was
reach for a piece of toast and she would visibly cower.
He'd turned her into a gibbering wreck, but at least she
was his.

Of course, it was always her fault that it happened. She
knew him well enough by now to know what set him off
and, if she pressed his buttons, well then she shouldn't be
surprised by the result. It wasn't as if he could control it.
Once the rage set in there was only one outcome.

'Lauren?' he shouted this time. 'Where are you?'
Nothing. That was annoying. Confronting her had been
playing on his mind all day. He wasn't going to get angry.
He was just going to talk to her and find out what was
going on. She was up to something, he could tell. Always

standing at the door, waving him goodbye, as if she was waiting for him to leave. She had better not be thinking of leaving him. If she was, well she wouldn't make it out of the house alive. After all he had done for her. Bitch. He rammed his fist into the wall, and the instant pain of the impact snapped him out of the simmering fury that was coming to the boil.

Usually, by now, Lauren was cleaning the house or doing the washing. She rarely went out. She knew that he didn't like that. So, where was she? Come to think of it, the house looked a little different. He wasn't able to put his finger on what it was, but his instinct rarely let him down. Police work honed the skills of observation and, if he felt that something was out of place, he was usually right. It was … it was messy. Yes, messy. That wasn't like Lauren, she never left the place like that. She learned a long time ago that he liked it tidy. Something was definitely wrong.

He climbed the steep and narrow stairs, all the while calling to her. There was no response. She had to be out but, if that was the case, then why had she left the door to the wardrobe open? That was sloppy. He walked across to close it and stopped dead in his tracks. Her clothes were gone. Not all of them, but enough for him to notice their absence. The hackles on the back of his neck began to stand. He could feel his anger rising once more. He darted to the bathroom. Her toiletries were gone. She couldn't have left him, could she? After all, she hadn't taken all of her things. Maybe she had gone away on some holiday. If she had, boy would she be in for it when she returned. But, deep down, he knew she wouldn't have done that. It wasn't worth the repercussions.

A thought struck him. Her jewellery. Had she taken it? He went over to the box he had given her for Christmas, and emptied its contents onto the bed. A lot of it had gone, but she certainly hadn't taken all of it. In fact, everything he had ever bought her was still there. Everything. Including her wedding and engagement rings. With a yell of exasperated fury, Sean picked up the box and hurled it at the wall. It smashed into tiny pieces. She'd left him. Stupid bitch. Didn't she know he would find her? What did she think he did for a living? He knew people. And, when he found out where she was, he would kill her. Nobody left Sean Kennedy. His rage teetered out of control. In a frenzied assault, he tore every remaining item of her clothes and threw them across the room. Picture frames with images of the two of them together shattered as they ricocheted off the wall. Then he took the photos and ripped them to shreds. There was no stopping him. He didn't care any more.

He bounded down the stairs, intent on wreaking havoc in the front room. But he never made it. As he stormed through the doorway, someone was waiting for him. He didn't see the baseball bat primed and ready for him. All he felt was the force of its impact across his face. Immediately, he slumped to the floor.

When he regained consciousness, his head seared with pain. He wanted to raise a hand to the throbbing source but he couldn't. His wrists were bound together. So were his feet. What the fuck was going on? Was this some revenge that Lauren had cooked up for him?

'Welcome back, my friend.' Whoever this was, they spat the words with a Spanish lilt and an air of supreme confidence.

'Who the fuck are you? Get out of my house?'

'Make me! Oh sorry. You don't seem to be able to.' His subsequent laugh infuriated Sean.

'Untie me, you fuck! Then we'll see who is able.'

'And why would I do that?' said his captor.

'To prove you're a man? Make it a fair fight?'

'I have no interest in making this a fair fight!'

'Then you need to know I'm a copper. The entire force will be after you. Let me go now, and you'll live.' Sean was becoming desperate, but his words were met with a howl of derision.

'I know exactly who you are my friend.' With that he flipped Sean onto his back and showed his face for the first time. Sean had been right. There was no doubt he was Spanish. Not the suave, loafered kind that strutted around the streets of Madrid. No, this man was swarthy, wild and gypsy-like. His thick black hair was slick and unkempt. His shadowy eyes were hidden even further by weighty eyebrows. It was difficult to put an age on him. He could have been late thirties, but the white hair that had taken over his beard, aged him. Only his moustache remained black. If it hadn't been for the diamond earring in his right ear, Sean would have assumed he was just some burglar, but it, and the unnerving air of assurance that surrounded him, suggested he was someone used to being in charge.

'Yes, but who the fuck are you?' Despite his training, Sean wasn't going to give him any respect. This was his home, an invasion of his personal space. He was surveying the room, considering his options. Training had taught him to remain calm, to make decisions with a clear head, but it had also taught him to resist the initial onslaught. It was too late for that.

'I am the last face you will see on this earth!' With that, he withdrew a jewelled, silver dagger and rammed it between Sean's ribs. He let out a scream of pain.

'You Spanish fuck. You'll pay for this,' he wheezed through grimacing lips.

'No. You are the one who is paying my friend. You are the one who dared to marry my wife. You are the one who beat her. Do you not understand that is my job?'

'What the fuck are you talking about? I get it now, you're some kind of fruit loop!' he choked with intense agony.

'But she doesn't look at you the way she looks at the

others,' the Spaniard continued.

'What others? What are you going on about?' The pain was making it difficult for Sean to concentrate on the conversation.

'Oh, I see. You don't know about the others? Well I'm not going to tell you. All you need to know is that she's an adulterer. And she will pay for it.' He readied the knife for another strike.

'Hold on! Don't you see? That's what we both want. She's left me. I want her dead too. Let me go, and I'll help you.'

'I don't need your help! Who do you think I am? Some amateur? Besides, she's not the only one I want dead. I have killed all those she has cheated on me with. That, my friend, includes you.' With that he sliced the stiletto across Sean's throat in a mortal blow, and watched his face contort in pain and shock, then blanche as the blood left his body.

The Spaniard wiped the dagger clean across his victim's chest. It was his signature. A final act of disrespect. Something that allowed him to savour his work a little. He had developed a passion for dismembering his victims. He didn't always have that opportunity, but when he did it was something he indulged in. There wasn't a lot of time, as he needed to keep on the trail of his quarry, but he felt a little bit of chopping wouldn't hurt. Five minutes. That was all he would allow himself. It wouldn't be enough but at least he could practise for when the real work was done later. He set about his business with vigour.

When the time was up, he wiped his hands clean on one of the many strands of his wife's clothes strewn across the house. She smelled different to how he remembered. Sweeter. It was such a shame he would never lie next to her. He shook the thought out of his head. He wanted nothing from her. Nothing at all. Nothing, except revenge.

Just as he had slipped silently into the house, so he left. He wasn't worried about the body. Sooner or later they would find it, and then what? They would never find him. What was more important was staying close enough to the two lovebirds as they made their way to Spain.

11

THE FRENCH COUNTRYSIDE passed in a blur as the train made its way to Paris. Lauren had maintained her distance from James so far, and it wouldn't be long now until they could be together. They had chosen different carriages, but were comforted by each other's presence aboard. She knew James could feel her fear; she couldn't hide it. She was on a knife-edge, startling at every opening door, and nervy at every stop. By now, Sean would have discovered she had left, and the hunt would be on. At first, she had been scared in case he came home early; now there was no question that he would know. It felt real.

Lauren had no plans to return to that place, but even still there could be no going back, now she had laid down her cards and shown her hand. She imagined his rage at finding her rings, that last vengeful slap in the face that told him their marriage was over, confirmation that she cared so little for his affection that she didn't even want his diamond. He would be furious. He would destroy everything. But nothing she had left behind was important to her. Anything of significance had made its way into her bag, jewellery, trinkets and photographs, memories of happier times. Pictures of her beloved father.

Lauren cast her mind back to those torturous moments after Sean left for the day. She had wanted to leap into action the moment the door signalled his departure. Instead she had waited, watching the clock and counting down the nervy hours until eleven. She had chosen that time specifically. Towards the end of the shift was safer than the beginning. In the past, if Sean had forgotten anything, he had made a point of returning. Sometimes he had even swung past in the squad car if it was important enough. Lauren wasn't prepared to take that risk. Eleven had been the right time. By then he would have been more than halfway through his day and it wouldn't make sense to come home for something he had forgotten. That didn't make the waiting any easier though. They were truly the longest few hours of her life. The pressure inside her was enormous and it had taken every ounce of her self-control just to wait. As those last seconds elapsed, Lauren leapt into action.

For the previous eight months, she had meticulously planned what to take, had known exactly what was coming with her and was at peace with all the belongings that were not. Leaving them behind was a price she was happy to pay for her freedom. Everything she was taking had been strategically placed, and it was just a matter of systematically working her way through it all. The idea of a full, dry run had crossed her mind on more than one occasion, but that was risky. All she could do was go from room to room, pretending to pack.

The worst thing about it all had been the wait for the taxi. She had called it at eleven-fifteen, knowing it would take somewhere between five and ten minutes to arrive. She only needed five to pack her belongings, and the few moments she waited by the door for it to arrive, were among the most terrifying of her life. The relief that she felt when it pulled up outside had been enormous.

The train pulled into the stunning Gare du Nord, and Lauren made her way across the concourse to the entrance. The station was glorious from the front, a work of art in itself. Sculptures lined the building, each representing cities in France and Europe. If there was any doubt she was in Paris it was now erased. Only the French could design a station like this. It was incredible. The plan from here was to cross Paris in separate taxis and meet at Gare d'Austerlitz.

Lauren smiled at James longingly as the taxi drove off, and then pondered the beauty of the city briefly as it whisked her away to her destination. She marvelled at the spectacular Notre-Dame from the Pont d'Austerlitz, beautiful, even at a distance. When the taxi arrived moments later at the station, she was so excited that she almost forgot to pay the driver and her error was pointed out to her in no uncertain terms. After apologising profusely, she made her way to the agreed meeting point, under the white sign for platform eighteen, and waited.

It wasn't long before she saw James sprinting across the concourse towards her, and she was torn between annoyance at the attention his impetuousness would surely bring, and the joy she felt at his arrival. As he approached, she gave in to the latter and threw her arms around him triumphantly. From now on she knew they would be together forever. Nothing would separate them. It felt incredible.

The station was noisy. A diesel choir monopolised the airwaves as the expectant engines idled noisily under the intricate iron of the roof's triangular pitch. It somehow exaggerated the number of trains at Austerlitz at that time. It felt busier than it actually was. There were no more than four trains in sight, and yet they roared like forty. It was late afternoon and the shadows from a thousand roof-lights contorted by the second as the sun began to withdraw. Even in France the winter days were short, though the time difference made it feel as if the sun stayed later than its English counterpart. Everything on the continent seemed to start later and finish later, so it was no surprise that they had found a way to make the sun do the same. At that point, time seemed irrelevant to Lauren anyway. She didn't care about the seconds slipping away, or the minutes passing, all she cared about was the oneness she felt with James. She felt his hands pull her slight frame towards him as she kissed him more and more deeply, and felt his eyes imprison her in dreamy blue-green as she gazed upon them properly for the first time in months. Her senses exploded as their bodies and minds connected. It was total immersion. An invasion, yet one she submitted to readily. It was what Lauren wanted. Everything she had dreamed of and much, much more.

She tempered what was fast becoming a frenzied clinch, as they had to deal with the practicalities of the onward journey. The plan was to take the night train to the end of the French line, in the Catalonian town of Portbou. It was the gateway to the rest of Spain. There were, of course, slower and more devious routes they could have taken that might better disguise their path, but they felt putting a whole country between them and Lauren's raging husband would make them safer. Besides, having crossed Paris, they knew the trail would be difficult to follow. Even if he managed to trace them to Paris, there were an infinite number of onward destinations. Why would he think they were heading to Teruel, of all places? Until relatively recently, neither of them had even heard of it!

The last counter measure they employed was for James to buy all the onward tickets. To date they had been careful to travel alone. Even though they were now together, they were convinced that anyone trying to follow Lauren would assume she would be buying her own tickets.

Thankfully France had yet to trial any of the CCTV crop that Thatcher had planted in England and was now being carefully cultivated by Major. That meant even that scorching embrace on the platform wouldn't give them away. There would be no video evidence of them together and it wasn't as though what they were doing would make them stand out from the crowd—public displays of passion were common place in France. The French had none of the self-conscious prudery that riddled English culture.

James' rudimentary grasp of the French language also made him the best candidate to procure the tickets, even though every Englishman knew that the French way was to let you stutter bravely through a sentence and then respond to you disdainfully in English. It was cultural. A collective rebellion against the slaughter of a beautiful language by the barbaric Brit. The ultimate insult to the pretenders who felt years of study of the language somehow made them understand what it was to be French.

He looked at the lengthy queue in front of the solitary ticket booth, and chose to buy a coffee to enjoy during the wait. James and Lauren walked over to the café together, lost in each other's company. It felt good to just enjoy being together, even though their every touch echoed the eons of embraces that had been shared by all those who had come and loved before them. James felt that celestial cogs were beginning to turn now he and Lauren had finally broken clear of the obstacle that had kept them apart. It was as if a vault was opening and, as each lock turned, so he was beginning to glimpse more and more of what was inside. There was no turning back for the two of them now. They were about to reap a harvest that had been sown eight hundred years earlier. Through their locked hands, they felt what Diego and Isabel had felt as they had lain, exalted in each other's company, by the side of the surging Guadalaviar river. Between them, they could feel the ancient joy of that skip through the streets of Teruel that Diego and Isabel had shared, on their way to ask permission to be married. Any thoughts of how tragically things had turned out for them were nowhere to be seen.

Lauren was James' illicit drug. He couldn't get enough of her. In those early days, seeing her had launched him euphorically skywards and then cast him ferociously into the depths of despair when they were apart. Now he surrendered himself to a total addiction, a life in which the two of them would soar together in an unrivalled high. From now on James knew that even the most mundane of activities would light up his senses. The short trudge to the terminus coffee shop was like an amble through a technicoloured field of tulips, and their vivid and perennial blooms tickled the tips of his fingers as he made his way from one side to the other. Yet this was just day-to-day drudgery. These were just perfunctory duties that needed to be accomplished in order to continue their journey. If such basic togetherness thrilled to this extent, James could only dream of the rapture that awaited when he made love to Lauren for the first time.

'I think you should hold that thought, don't you?' Lauren smiled as she said it, then touched his lips tantalisingly with hers.

'And that's supposed to help, is it?'

They ordered their drinks and sneaked a further embrace, in which they stoked the passionate fires inside each other. Before they reached a point of no return, they parted company. Lauren's role was to purchase food for the journey ahead, and James made his way to the end of the ticket line, which had barely moved forward in his absence.

He juggled the searing coffee between his hands as he walked. That was one of the drawbacks of liking it hot and black, the cup gave no protection at all from the steaming liquid inside, and typically it had the capacity to melt skin. He was well practised at passing the cup from one hand to another, just before the heat became unbearable, but it was a little trickier with a suitcase and Lauren's backpack. Every ten paces or so he followed the routine of stopping, placing his suitcase on the floor and swapping the hot coffee into his other hand. As he crossed the station, the stops became more and more frequent, as both left and right received less time to cool between juggles. At that rate, he knew it wouldn't be long before the cup felt like molten lava in either hand and needed to be dropped. Fortunately, before the eruption he reached the queue and was able to rest the cup on the floor.

James could see this was going to be a lengthy exercise and was grateful for his blistering cup, as the south-easterly breeze whipped in through the station approach and imparted its chilling cordiality. The coffee at least made the wait more bearable as he stood there. There were clearly many non-French speakers in the queue, and the booth was manned by a moustachioed jobs-worth who had perfected the art of communicating solely by shrug. It was a peculiarly French gesture that everyone in the nation seemed to have perfected. So widespread was it that James wondered whether it was taught at school. He laughed to himself that perhaps while he had yawned through 'double maths', or scribbled through 'double art', the French had gesticulated through 'double shrug'. However they came to learn it, it was the standard response to befuddled foreigners and was hardly an endearing quality.

At least James had studied French. He suspected that a number of the travellers who hadn't would fail to articulate their destination or preference correctly and might end up on a mystery tour. He was determined he would not be among that number and practised hard in the minutes leading up to his moment of truth, whenever it eventually arrived.

'*Deux billets sur le Wagon-lit à Portbou. Nous voulons un espace privatif de couchette s'il vous plait.*' James impressed himself with his request. Somehow, he had dredged the ability to ask for a private sleeper from the silt of his psyche.

'It is entire,' replied the ticket seller, in a form of English that was barely recognisable to James.

'*Qu'entendez-vous* "entire"?' James was indignantly reinforcing that the ticket seller could speak to him in French. His version, while not perfect by any means, was at least understandable.

'There is none berth.' The ticket seller continued to speak to him in basic English, even though it was clear that James' French was good. James found it incredibly frustrating and uncannily like so many other conversations he'd had in France over the years. In Spain, they congratulated tourists on attempting Spanish. In Germany, they worked with them, pleased that anyone would try to communicate in their language, even though most of the population spoke English to perfection. In France, they treated foreigners who attempted their language with disdain.

'So, there is no couchette?' James gave up talking in French and decided to just speak to the ticket seller in English. It was clearly what he wanted.

'Non.' James' heart sank a little. He had hoped that the private compartment would mean that Lauren and he could add their own rocking motion in time to the swaying carriages as they made love throughout the lengthy journey. Now there was a chance they would either be confined to a restless night in narrow and uncomfortable seats, or worse still would have to revert to a Plan B. He hoped a new plan wouldn't be necessary because they didn't currently have one.

'Can I book seats then?'

'*Quoi?*' this was ridiculous. James had given up speaking to the ticketseller in French because he had insisted on responding in English. Now when James spoke to him in English, he didn't understand.

'*Vous avez deux places ensemble?*' James was becoming irritable now and his tone did little to hide it.

'Yes.' The man proceeded to print the tickets as James handed over the best part of two thousand French francs. He then mumbled his way through some very specific information that James doubted even a French person would understand. This public face of the French railway had insisted on speaking to James in English throughout their conversation, and James had received the message loud and clear that he was not worthy to converse in the man's native tongue. Now, when it came to important information—maybe relating to safety or boarding instructions—the ticket officer rattled off words that James had no hope of understanding, at a speed so fast that they sounded like just one continuous word! For all he knew this could have been a typical send-off for every foreigner, one that sent them into a tailspin with concern over what critical information they had missed, when actually the message was, 'Now fuck off back to your own country!'

James grabbed his still-hot coffee from its temporary residence on the counter, and stepped to the side of the ticket booth. He was holding those liberating tickets in his left hand while he inspected them. It wasn't clear what they said but they did appear to meet the minimum criteria of being for travel, that night, to Portbou, and with two seats next to each other. He began to relax. He knew that, at the very least, he and Lauren would be able to continue their journey. Come morning they would be approaching Spain, with almost a thousand miles under their belt. That was a decent head-start in anyone's book. Even though he was disappointed they weren't travelling in style, James allowed himself a smile as he stowed the tickets away in his wallet.

It was at that precise moment, as he juggled the coffee, tickets and wallet rather precariously, that someone chose to barge past him. His coffee flew out of his hand and the hot liquid spilled down the front of his jeans.

'Fuck!' James yelled instinctively, both in annoyance at the loss of his coffee and in anticipation of the scalding pain that he expected would sting the skin of his left thigh at any moment. Sure enough, in mere seconds the tingling on his nerve endings became unbearable. He patted at the spillage intuitively as he turned to curse further at the culprit.

He or she was nowhere to be seen. Though the concourse could have been busier, there were enough people to prevent James from pinpointing who had just knocked into him. There was certainly no-one walking away guiltily. He cursed aloud, attracting much unwanted attention from across the concourse. His only consolation was that the fierce heat that had been searing his leg had subsided to just an uncomfortably moist warmth.

Something else began to bother him though. It was a feeling. One that nagged at him like a demanding toddler. It poked him. Prodded him. It grew and grew until James began to recognise it for what it was. Dread. That same overwhelming sense of dread he had felt before, at the Richmond Tavern. He felt the screams from future disasters ringing in his ears.

He didn't know where it had come from. Only a matter of moments before, he had been relaxed. Now he was tense and uneasy. His mind searched frantically for the source. It wasn't the ticket seller. He might have been infuriating but eventually he had done what was needed. He couldn't possibly have triggered such a primal warning. James knew it wasn't the coffee stain either; that was an annoyance, but it was hardly life threatening. No. Something about the scene itself was troubling him but he couldn't quite put his finger on it. His brain played the moment again and again like a commentary team debating a contentious decision. With each review, he gathered more insight. It was the jolt. The accidental knock that had sent the coffee over him. Something was wrong with it. What was it? It didn't seem right. It was on the tip of his tongue.

An icy fear streaked down James' spine. On its malevolent meander, it woke every sleeping hair on his nape. They responded to the alarm like slumbering soldiers and screamed warnings of danger to their comrades. Something had indeed been wrong with that bump. James recalled it clearly now. It had been no accident. It had been a deliberate and lingering touch. His skin tightened at the memory of the fingers clasping around his forearm. He felt the weight of the grip and the jerk of the deflection. And through the touch he felt rage. Fury. Festering resentment. A need for revenge. One that he had felt before.

Panic began to flow through his body, from that very spot where those dire digits had left their indelible mark of dread. It was an unspeakable fear. Ancient. Inherited. One that had lain in wait to pounce at this very moment. It brought with it a total desolation.

His instinct was to flee. Every muscle in his body wanted out of the station, but his fear had somehow magnified gravity and rooted him to the spot. At that moment, he understood how onrushing headlights enslaved a deer whose instinct had been to flee.

Then he remembered Lauren. Convinced that

something must have happened to her, he abandoned his luggage and sprinted towards the entrance to the platform. His heart was racing as fear turbocharged its four cylinders. He felt the bewildered stares of returning commuters as he charged across the concourse. But he didn't care. He knew if anything had happened to Lauren life would be unliveable. He would never forgive himself. His panicked eyes searched with all the thoroughness of a four-year-old as they darted at random. He was desperate to catch sight of her. To know she was okay. As seconds ticked away, the anguish heightened. It was inflating like a balloon inside him. Then relief burst it as his eyes finally locked onto Lauren.

She was waiting exactly where they had agreed and, in that instant, he felt silly, as if his emotions had swept him off his feet and convinced him to elope. Despite his best efforts, there was no disguising his distress from her.

'James! Are you okay?' she placed her hand supportively on his chest, and James could see it moving as his pounding heart strained to catch up with itself.

'Yes,' he lied. 'Just got a bit spooked. That's all.'

'What on earth happened? And where are the bags?'

'Shit!' He felt even more foolish and avoided her gaze. He had left the bags at the ticket office. He could only hope they would still be there when he went back for them.

'And this is normal behaviour, is it?'

'What?' James was surprised by Lauren's lack of

empathy.

'Abandoning our bags and sprinting across the station.'

'No. I, er,' James was forced onto the defensive. 'Look, I, er, don't know. My mind just ran away with me. I was convinced something terrible was happening. I needed to find you. I just bolted.'

'For God's sake James. You think I'm not jittery? Everywhere I look I see Sean. I'm terrified. But I'm not running around in panic.'

'Okay, I'm sorry.' She had not spoken to him like this before. It troubled James. It wasn't the reaction he'd expected. It wasn't normal. He sensed something was wrong. 'Is everything alright? I sense …'

'I'm fine!' Lauren interrupted. 'I'd be even better if I had my things.' Despite her irritation, she drew James close. He felt almost all the remnants of despair dissipate immediately, replaced once more by that heady excitement that came with their togetherness. He was conscious that a small part of the foreboding remained, cocooned for protection against a predatory joy that threatened to devour it.

James left Lauren once more and returned to the ticket office. He couldn't help noticing the ticket-seller shrugging Gallically at his latest victim. He really had perfected it. James found himself involuntarily trying to copy the perfect frown, but he couldn't force the corners of his mouth down far enough.

The abandoned bags were starting to attract attention. Just like England, France had learned to be suspicious of unattended luggage. The country's recent history was littered with bomb attacks and assassinations by Hezbollah and Action Directe, and, despite the arrest of most of the latter's leaders four years earlier, the French remained on alert.

Sheepishly, James stepped into the growing throng that was beginning to surround the bags, and reclaimed them to a volley of derision.

'Espèce d'idiote!'

'Vous-voulez vos sacs a explosé?'

Those were just the few words he understood. They were right. He *was* an idiot, and the bags *could* have been taken away and exploded. Still, his fear had been very real. He recalled it vividly. And he wondered what was wrong with Lauren. She had been angrier than he had expected, on the attack, as if she was hiding something. James was sure there was something she wasn't telling him. It began to play on his mind.

12

T HE BLUE ANACONDA snaked beguilingly into the platform. It was longer than any train Lauren had seen in her life. Cleaners appeared from a multitude of points along the platform and began readying the train for departure. It was a while before they could board as the couchettes needed to be prepared for those who had been lucky enough to secure a berth. She had been disappointed they weren't able to share a private cabin that night, as she had shared similar lusty thoughts to James about how they would pass the journey. For so long she had wanted to feel him against her naked body and yet again she found she was having to suppress her desire. It didn't seem fair. They had waited so long already. In some ways, this was harder than being apart from him, she thought. James' presence this close to her pressed every one of her buttons. Unfortunately, their passion would just have to wait, putting distance and time behind them was far more important.

She knew she would be in Spain within twelve hours, having left behind relatively little trace, and she took so much comfort from that distance. Sean couldn't touch her this far away, at least not until he found her. In the meantime, she knew she was free. She thought about him briefly, and deep down a part of her felt sorry for him, though she dismissed it quickly. Even though she had thought she loved him once, she had lost that feeling a long time ago, and now she knew a love that was in another universe in comparison. She had discovered that love was tender and reciprocal, love was something to share, love was total trust and security, it was breath-taking and exhilarating. It wasn't danger, and it certainly wasn't fear and domination. It had been a long time since she had felt as safe as she did now, though she was conscious that the hunt would be on. He might even have found she had headed to Dover, but from Calais the trail would begin cooling and Lauren was convinced that it would be stone cold at Paris. James' little scene with the bags hadn't helped though. The last thing they needed was unnecessary attention, and people remembered things like that. She was still furious, though it was hard to stay mad at him; she loved him too much.

There was nothing to do now other than wait to board the train. Under normal circumstances it would be an agonising hour or so, one that had travellers cursing. It was different for Lauren. She had been apart from James for so long that every hour with him was one to celebrate. At last they had each other. They needed no-one else. They had all the time in the world and plenty to talk about.

She knew so little about him and wanted to know more. She asked about his mum, Katharine. It was clear how much grief he still carried with him and Lauren wished she could have met her and been there for him when she passed away. It was so hard to lose a parent. From now on life would always feel a little empty for him, something she knew all too well after the death of her father. From experience, she knew it was easier to cope with grief when it was shared.

James was happy to talk about his mother, though his sadness was clearly still raw. He had been close to her, at least, as close as she would allow anyone to get to the emotions she had kept locked inside her. It turned out that things had never been easy for Katharine Jordan. Her Protestant parents had named her after Katharine Hepburn, who had won an Oscar the previous year for her role in *Morning Glory*. They admired Hepburn's free spirit and independence and had hoped their daughter would develop similar traits. Unfortunately, the Anglicised name they gave her singled Katharine out as a Protestant in the Catholic world of 1930's Dublin. Every day she walked the gauntlet to school, flinching from the stinging stones that were hurled at her heretic body. Even when she arrived, school offered no respite. The Sisters of Mercy saw to that. Lessons were a cycle of censure from the harsh and austere nuns, who were at least indiscriminate in their near daily beatings. Katharine always felt a sense of justice when her bullies were on the receiving end, though she knew those tormentors would take it out on her later on. Each day was harsh and confronting. As a result, she learned to bury her emotions deep beneath the surface. That was how she kept her soul safe in the face of such abuse. Her feelings rarely saw the light of day, and any outings were fleeting, even to James.

Listening to the story, Lauren began to understand why James struggled to talk about his grief. He just hadn't learned to do it. She was so glad they were able to share each other's minds. It didn't matter that he couldn't express how he felt; she already knew.

Katharine had left for England as soon as she was able, spurred on by a need to feel like she belonged somewhere. It being a Protestant country meant she was no longer ostracised by the hatred that had so deeply indoctrinated the suburbs of Dublin. Despite her belief in God, Katharine felt that religion had a lot to answer for. On the one hand, it brought people together and preached peace, but on the other it made people intolerant of others. Zealots developed sinister motives and repeatedly warped interpretations of ancient words into convenient excuses for ungodly acts. Worst of all, faith made the believers blind to manipulation.

James was more scathing when talking about his father. In the early 1960s Katharine had had the misfortune to marry Henry Jordan. From James' account, Lauren learned that Henry was an extraordinary man. He was gifted musically, but was either too lazy to nurture his talents or lacked the determination to follow through. Either way, it seemed that he ambled idly through life with no grand plan other than to spend as much money as he could on a lavish lifestyle for himself. His was a world of privileges where he was the only recipient and everyone else was there to ensure he received them. His relationship with Katharine was one where she gave and he took, remorselessly. Most of the fight had been smashed from her back in Ireland, and all she wanted was someone to be good to her. If she'd had that, she could have coped with anything. Sadly, Henry was unable to deliver. As the years passed, the irony that 1960s society was relaxing its social taboos while he had signed up to a supposed life of monogamy, was not lost on him. He spent more and more time away from home, pursuing the high life with whatever willing women he could find. At weekends he would return, ostensibly to see his family but really to recover from the week's exertion and revel in the pampering of a wife and child. Eventually he traded Katharine for another model after numerous test drives. Even then, she had wanted to forgive him. Deep down she had known about his philandering all along but had chosen to ignore it. The security of a husband, a father for her son, had been more important than faithfulness. When he chose to leave, her world began to collapse, and it was the blow that finally broke her. She kept her emotions bottled and firmly corked as always but her misery ate away at her from the inside. Six months later she was gone. James hadn't spoken to his father since. He held him personally responsible. Henry had put himself before his family and that was something James could never forgive. His face visibly angered at the mention of his father's name.

By now the train had departed. There was something soothing about the gentle rocking of the carriages as they swayed at speed. It was comforting for both James and Lauren as they shared each other's sadness. The carriage was only partly full, giving a little more room than their two narrow seats would have offered otherwise. There was enough space for each of them to occupy a double seat if they wanted, but they were unanimous in sitting together. After all the time apart, Lauren couldn't bear even the distance of the aisle to be between them. She did feel a little sorry for James though. The seats were plenty big enough for her small frame but woefully inadequate for him. At least it was clean, but she doubted that the oxymoronic cocktail of dread and exhilaration she was feeling would be sleep-inducing anyway. She snuggled up to James, relishing the reassuring contact.

James was struggling to sleep too. The size of the seat didn't help, and neither did Lauren's constant fidgeting. As annoying as it could have been, he found it endearing, though it wasn't conducive to sleep. The other problem was that a sense of dread was also growing inside him. He wanted to tell Lauren about his experience at Austerlitz and the encounter outside the Richmond Tavern, but he also wanted to protect her from it, whatever *it* was. He did his best to bury his fear, trying to ignore it for a while, but it had taken a cancerous root inside him and was growing malevolently. The less he focused on it, the stronger it was when he returned. He tried to distract himself with the speeding views and thoughts of what would be their new life together, but all the time he found himself drawn back to the events at the station, shivering at the memory of that unwelcome hand. Worryingly, he had begun to believe there were distinct similarities between the feeling of the fingers at the station and the push at the pub. There was a similar blackness about them, a disconcerting rage. It made him even more uncomfortable to think there might be a link between the two.

In the same way that Lauren's first touch had exploded inside him, so this one had detonated. The difference was that the emotions that touch had triggered were the very antithesis of what he felt from Lauren. He knew he needed to disclose it to her. He chose to share the memory, rather than tell, and reached out to Lauren's mind. As he did so, he was stunned to find she was blocking him out. It was now beyond question that something had happened earlier. He sat bolt upright and his movement roused her from her half-sleep.

'What is it you're not telling me, Lauren?' he demanded.

'Nothing. Why?' she said sleepily.

'You're blocking me out. It's as if you don't want me to see something.'

'And you're not hiding your thoughts from me?' He couldn't help noticing that she was attacking again. It was proof that she was holding something back.

'Well. I …'

'Exactly! So don't be such a hypocrite. Tell me whatever it is you're keeping to yourself!'

'I honestly don't think I can explain.'

'Then don't. Let me see.'

Lauren entered James' thoughts easily as soon as she was invited. He tried to take the opportunity to explore her thoughts too but she was having none of it. Her mood darkened as she felt the malice of the mysterious touch James had witnessed.

'No wonder you were spooked! I feel as though someone just walked across my grave!'

'Yes. And it's really worrying me. Until then I felt like we'd won, we were free. Now I feel like maybe the odds are stacking against us. I'm just not sure I understand the game any more.' Lauren didn't respond. After her experience in Paris, she knew more than she wanted to and she wasn't ready to share it with James just yet, if ever.

'And there's more,' James continued. He shared the memory of the push outside the pub, just after Lauren's escape. There was no question that the senses were identical. The direct link between the two meant someone, somewhere, knew who they were and where they had fled to.

Lauren gripped his hand tighter. James had expected her to be more perturbed than she actually was. Instead her response was matter of fact.

'That's why you've been so damned quiet!'

'Yes! I can't make head or tail of it.'

'So let's not try!'

'What do you mean?'

'That no matter who it was, or what they wanted, we're never going to be able to work it out,' Lauren said calmly. James was surprised at how readily she was trying to rationalise the situation. She should have been petrified by his two hateful experiences but instead she was playing it down. There was definitely something she wasn't telling him. He was convinced. But he had no idea how to push her to share. He hoped that somehow she would fill him in before it was too late.

The conversation fell away quickly and both Lauren and James returned to the preoccupation of their own thoughts. It had been a long day and it wasn't too long before they fell asleep together, locked in an awkward embrace that could only be the product of a plane or train seat. Outside, James could see Paris dispersing. The suburbs were becoming less and less dense, though the train line was still cordoned off by endless spirals of barbed wire. There was something vaguely familiar about the way the steel thorns glinted in the moonlight.

*

It was 13 August, 1961, Ilse Schaeffer's eighteenth birthday. She had set an early alarm, eager to start what she knew would be a special day, yet she needn't have. Her sleep was far from sound and she spent much of the night mulling over the events that were now more than half a year ago, and playing down the excitement that was brewing inside her.

Seven months earlier, her beloved Joachim Kemmer had left for West Berlin with his parents, and since that day she had vigilantly ticked off the days on the calendar. The passing of each one brought her closer to the return of her soul mate. Snow had surrounded them the day he left, as they shared a farewell kiss under the feeble winter sun. Their steaming breaths clouded around them like a shroud of secrecy. Ilse knew he didn't want to leave her, but he had no choice. For a while now the two of them had known that the love they shared was way beyond what normal people felt for each other. It was a love they felt privileged to share. An incredible love that had been around long before them. They were like indulgent tenants who occupied an ancient and joyous property. Ilse and Joachim knew their love would outlast them. It made them all the more determined to enjoy their time together.

They adored each other's company. They walked to and from school together. They shared every waking hour. When they were unable to be side by side, they could feel each other's presence, to connect their minds at a distance. That made it so much easier for them to avoid the disapproving eyes of their parents.

Joachim's family had been desperate to return to the West for a while. At that point up to a thousand East Germans were crossing over to West Berlin each day. It was clear that Western life was casting a giant shadow over the East. The perennial brain drain had left an intellectual void in East Berlin and, by the time 1961 arrived, the two societies were poles apart. The Kemmers were weary of the repressed way of life in which those who fought for freedom struggled to make ends meet, while those who restricted it lived lavishly. The government handed down arbitrary punishment and reward. Control was total and the Kemmers found the duplicity unbearable.

Ilse's father, Johann Schaeffer, was a bigwig in Ulbricht's inner circle. The family wanted for nothing. Johann could hobnob with the best of them, although even he was mindful to tread carefully, such was the paranoia that pervaded the state. Before every social function—and there were many—he would brief Ilse and her older sister Gisele on what they could and couldn't say. Specifically, he would make sure they knew who to be careful of. The retribution for a wrong sentiment was formidable, and both he and his colleagues were just one accusation away from a fall from grace or something worse. That was not a fate that Johann wanted for himself or his family.

On that freezing day in January, Joachim and his family had crossed into West Berlin to make a new life. Like most East Germans, they still had a network of family in the West. The break-up of Germany after the Second World War had split families apart like that. It was just one of the many prices that all Germans had paid for the aberrations of the generation before. The Kemmers knew they would have to work hard to adjust and establish themselves to a life in the West but, even so, anything was preferable to the iron fist under which they lived in the East.

After their illicit embrace, Ilse had hidden in the shadows, peeking through vivid, yet teary, green eyes as the Kemmer family slipped out of their home, carrying as many of their possessions as they could safely conceal. It was heart-breaking to see her Joachim leave like that. As their embrace ended, she had gazed at him for a while without speaking, storing that handsome face in her mind. Whenever she wanted, Ilse was able to recall his image, the vivid blue-green eyes that absorbed her love and returned it with interest. His short and swarthy chestnut hair, which spiked slightly in defiance of gravity, and those tickling whiskers that teased her pale cheeks whenever the two of them embraced.

As he walked away, Ilse knew he couldn't turn and look towards her for one last time. She wasn't supposed to know he was leaving. The family needed to keep their departure a secret and they wouldn't thank him for confiding in anyone, especially not the daughter of a key member of the Politburo. Everyone knew the government was becoming more and more concerned about the number of people crossing the border, and they were beginning to prevent migration with increasing vigour. The Kemmers would have to avoid the major crossings and sneak over the border as it was, so the last thing they wanted was for anyone to know of their plan.

Instead of looking longingly over his shoulder to the waiting Ilse, Joachim reached out and spoke straight into her mind.

Ilse. I love you. I will return for you on your eighteenth birthday and I will take you back with me.

Thrilled as always by the special bond they shared, Ilse responded in similar fashion.

Joachim. I love you too. I will count the days while you are away and I will be here waiting for you.

From that day on, Ilse struck through every day of the next seven months on the standard-issue calendar on her cracked bedroom wall, counting down to the day they would be reunited. The seasons progressed. Spring arrived with a flurry of yellow *Osterglöckchen* and their trumpets dripped with the rain as their stalks swayed in occasional winds. In May, the temperature began to lift and sunshine cast its happiness across the East's grey existence. Much of the damage from the war had been removed but, where once there had been rubble, there were now just empty blocks. No grandiose plans existed to reconstruct the city like its Western twin. East Berlin was hauntingly stark, and vast government buildings had been constructed at the expense of recreational amenities. It was so bleak that even the joyous sun seemed to lose its radiance and give up hope by the end of each day.

All the time, Ilse's mind was absent. Her school grades deteriorated and she became forgetful. She just couldn't concentrate on anything. In the middle of class, she found her mind wandering, dreaming of her life across the border with Joachim. Whenever she closed her eyes she saw his boyish face smiling at her, telling her that it wouldn't be long until they were together again.

Eventually her birthday arrived. She leapt out of bed and embraced the day, as she made that final mark in her calendar with frenzied precision. From now on she would make her own choices, even though she knew her father would disapprove. Now that she was at the age of consent it just didn't matter, nothing would keep her apart from Joachim. She headed downstairs, knowing she would have to suppress her feelings for just a little longer while she shared breakfast with her family.

'*Zum Geburtstag viel Glück! Zum Geburtstag viel Glück,*' the familiar birthday song rang out as Ilse came down to a special breakfast that morning. Gisele and their mother Magda beamed as they sang, while Johann watched stoically on. Any sense of frivolity was a sign of political weakness and he had long since trained himself to abstain. Instead he spoke to his youngest daughter.

'Happy Birthday my dear Ilse. Eighteen already eh? I can't believe it!' He parted her long dark locks and kissed her pale forehead.

'Thank you, Papa.'

'And look at you. So beautiful!' added Magda, as she threw her arms around Ilse's slight frame.

'Thanks Mama.'

It was a special day for them too, Ilse knew how much they loved her. It would be painful for the whole family when she left with Joachim, but there was no alternative. She had made up her mind to go immediately the words had passed his lips, and had not had any second thoughts since. It was a choice she had reinforced every morning for seven months exactly and, when the time came, she would leave without hesitation.

Ilse had been miserable without him and today her mood was greatly improved. Already she could feel that he was on his way. He was like a flare in the distance, lighting the way. The butterflies that had been loosed inside her stomach made breakfast more of a task than a joy, and her father was disappointed when she didn't touch the bratwurst he had procured for her, through some favour or other. Instead, she picked at them absently, her mind a million miles from the family that surrounded her.

After breakfast, she rushed up the stairs and threw her belongings into a small bag, already clear on what she was taking with her. There were plenty of things she would have to leave behind, including trinkets she had cherished through the years. Each held treasured memories of friends and family but they had to stay, and she left them behind with a ruthless disdain that reinforced their lack of importance compared to the love of her life.

When her bag was packed, she slipped out of the side door of the house and walked to the corner of Wöhlertstraße and Chausseestraße. There were no farewells to her family, for they would have asked where she was going, and might even have followed her. It was awful to sneak away like that on such a special day, but there was no alternative. She walked to the spot where Joachim had left her back in January. His presence there was strong, and with each passing second, she could feel him getting closer. Soon they would be together.

As she reached the corner, she was confronted by pandemonium. The scene was one of complete chaos. It wasn't clear what was happening, but hundreds, if not thousands, of East Germans lined the streets, looking towards the West. Ilse could see nothing but the backs of heads. At her height, she was useless in crowds and usually avoided them at all costs. All she knew was that something was clearly wrong. Many of the crowd were weeping and there was an air of enraged defiance, coupled with a sense of fearful submission. Ilse was alarmed. From such a low vantage point, there was little hope of establishing the cause, so she barged through the armpits of those in front of her until she could see for herself what was happening. When she reached the front, she wished she hadn't. What she saw tore her dreams away from her in an instant. She stared incredulously at what lay before her, desperate to rewind the clock and return to the blissful ignorance she had enjoyed moments earlier. Ahead of her there should have been wasteland, the deserted buffer zone that separated the enclave from the East. It was ground that thousands had carefully sneaked across, including the Kemmers. But it was no longer barren. Overnight it had changed. Now it was a sea of razor wire.

Ilse knew from her father that the Politburo had been threatening to do something about the brain drain for a while. The action they had chosen, however, dismayed her. They could have found ways to entice people to stay. Perhaps a better standard of living, better housing, more equal distribution of wealth, or greater freedom. Instead they had responded by building an impassable barrier to prevent people from leaving, one that would slice anyone who tried to cross. What did that say about their attitude to life and humanity?

There was no break in the wire as far as the eye could see, and Ilse was filled with total and utter sadness. The whole of West Berlin had been sealed off. It was surrounded and inaccessible. Nobody was coming in or out, without a damn good reason, and Ilse knew that love was not one of them, no matter how intense or ancient it might be. She stared forlornly across the arid void as the morning summer sun picked out each individual barb and made the wire twinkle like the very antithesis of a Christmas tree. Across in the distant West, Ilse could see Joachim. He too was distraught, incredulous. She could sense his mind churning, clutching at straws. He was desperate, as was she. Today was the day they were supposed to be together, forever.

Their eyes remained locked on each other until their gaze outlasted the day. The sun cast longer and longer shadows, and eventually the darkness hid him from view. Still he remained there though. Ilse could feel him. Their minds were locked together across the impassable barrier and stayed that way throughout the night and into the next morning, until Ilse was interrupted by Gisele.

'Ilse! There you are! We've been looking for you everywhere!'

'Oh Gisele. Look what they've done.' Ilse was sobbing inconsolably. Gisele took her in her arms, putting aside her own astonishment at what confronted her in order to console her younger sister.

'Ilse. Don't fret. We were prisoners here anyway. You know that. Papa would never have let us go over to the West. What does it matter that there is now a barrier to stop us?'

'I don't care what Papa wants. I'm eighteen now. I can do what I like. At least I could if the state hadn't just made all of us prisoners overnight!'

'Oh, come on! Nothing has changed! For our family things are just as they were yesterday,' said Gisele. 'Come home with me. You must be hungry—you missed your birthday dinner!'

'No. I will not leave.' Ilse was defiant. Gisele followed her gaze across the blockade towards Joachim.

'Who is that, Ilse?'

'It's Joachim. Joachim Kemmer. Yesterday was the day that our love was going to be complete. Then someone built this damn blockade overnight and stopped us. This is as close as I can get to him and I'm not going to move from here until I …'

'Ilse!' Gisele interrupted. 'You can't be serious! You can't go over to the West.'

'Yes, I can, and I will. I will find a way. The only thing I want in life is to be with Joachim. Nothing else matters to me. Not you, not Mama and not Papa.' With that, Ilse resumed her listless gaze across the killer wire as she dismissed her fussing sister. She felt awful for what she had said to Gisele, but she was distraught. She would make it up to her one day.

Her remorse was short-lived. Almost immediately it was pushed to the back of her mind. In those moments she had spent remonstrating with Gisele, Joachim seemed to have disappeared. Ilse was heartbroken. Tears streamed down her cheeks as she cursed his lack of determination and wondered how his love could be so shallow that he could let her go after just twenty-four hours. She started to question whether their love was actually so special after all. There was no doubt about her love for him. She had been prepared to wait here until they found a way to be together and couldn't understand why it would be so hard for him to do the same.

Ilse's wailing caused Gisele to return. She comforted her once more with a sisterly hug, unaffected by her earlier harsh dismissal. With an arm around her sister's shoulder, she began to usher her homeward down the Wöhlertstraße. As Ilse took those first few grudging steps home, she felt resigned and defeated. And then she stopped. At first, she wasn't sure why, but then her senses told her that she had been wrong to dismiss Joachim so easily. She turned her head and looked towards the other side of the wire. Joachim was there. He was walking forward, holding something. What was it. She couldn't quite … wire cutters. He had wire cutters!

'No!' Ilse screamed at the top of her lungs, pushing Gisele to the floor as she ran towards the wire. 'No Joachim! That's not the way!'

He was striding towards the barrier, one hand on each handle of the wire cutters and he was close enough now that Ilse could see the steely determination etched across his face.

I love you Ilse. I will not be without you.

Don't do it Joachim! No!

With that, he cut into the first wire and a collective gasp murmured through the gathering crowd as they began to grasp what was happening. Then silence. So silent was it that Ilse could hear the snip as he broke the second wire. He never made it to the third. Within moments the innocence of the entire East German nation was lost. The night before, a barrier had been erected to keep citizens in. They were about to find out the lengths to which their captivity would be enforced.

Crack! Crack!

Two very clear and chilling shots rang out. The crowd flinched in shock at the noise, before the true realisation of what had happened settled in. It wasn't lost on Ilse though. She sensed the bullets penetrate Joachim's heart and began to feel the life force drain from him immediately. She was overcome by a need to be at his side and hurtled towards where he lay, fighting off the despairing grabs of concerned onlookers. She tore through the barbed wire on the Eastern side and it lacerated her skin as it clung to her and dragged behind her like a bridal train. Ilse threw herself at Joachim's body as it lay motionless in a growing scarlet pool. Around her was just emptiness and wire. Even Joachim was empty.

Crack. Crack.

This time Ilse's own pain seared through her chest as first one and then another bullet smashed into her body. But still she clung to Joachim's lifeless hand. The pain was overwhelming though not as complete as her grief. She knew it would be only moments until she joined him in whatever afterlife there was. She could hear the onrushing crowd in the distance. They were all thudding feet and gasping shock. They wouldn't be able to save her, Ilse knew. Then she heard footsteps, closer, lighter ones. She felt a touch on her hand, and with the last of her energy she turned to see a boy, no more than eight. There was something about his blue-green eyes and the quirky shape of his chestnut hair. It felt right that he should be holding her hand. Instantly, among her misery and pain, she felt a slight comfort. With her last breath, Ilse whispered.

'Karsten ...,' and everything she had ever known, passed through her body and into the boy.

13

JAMES WOKE EARLY the following morning as the sun streamed through the carriage window and illuminated the town of Argelès-sur-Mer and the rugged green foothills of the great Albera Massif beyond. The Pyrenees seemed more like large, undulating hills here on the eastern coast, unlike the sheer peaks of the central district. What they had lost in scale, however, they retained in their beauty. On the western horizon, James could see the outline of the higher mountains in the distance. He remembered that those were the same ridges Diego de Marcilla would have crossed almost eight hundred years earlier. Even in 1992 they were intimidating, and he bristled with pride in the knowledge that an ancestor-of-sorts had made such an epic journey, at a time when all the advancements we now took for granted in the twentieth century were not available. James was in awe of the determination that had driven Diego across them, but he knew where it came from—it was the love he felt for Isabel, a fierce love that James knew well. He felt the same about Lauren. He would do anything for her, anything to be with her.

He wondered what kind of relation Diego actually was. There was no traditional family link between them, just as there was none between Lauren and Isabel. Yet they had to be descendants. There didn't seem to be an adequate term. James felt that perhaps he was an heir. Maybe Ilse had described them best as tenants. The only problem with that word was that it didn't imply permanence. James didn't want to ride on the coat-tails of an ancient love, he wanted to own it, to live it, to reap the reward. Though he was beginning to realise that perhaps sharing eternity with Lauren wasn't going to be as simple as he had thought.

Fear and uncertainty were still breeding inside him and the same horizon he had been admiring was starting to shroud in an inescapable doom. He had done his best to control his growing anguish, but he knew he wouldn't be able to hold it back forever. Whatever it was that Lauren was refusing to reveal wasn't helping. It disturbed him. He had given her several opportunities to share whatever it was, but she hadn't taken them. Instead she had gone on the attack, put the focus on him. She seemed to be doing everything she could to avoid disclosure.

James wondered what on earth it could be. He knew it wasn't any kind of deceit or wavering commitment, their love was no flash in the pan. It was genuine, complete, glorious, ancient. Lauren's feelings for him were beyond question, as were her motives. He knew that meant there was only one reason for her to conceal information from him—she was trying to protect him. The fact was that she hadn't been the same since the incident at the station, and he was in no doubt his histrionics had probably unsettled her, but he knew there was more to it. Even now, as she slept beautifully on his shoulder, he could feel the turmoil and terror inside her. It was eating away at her.

It gave James an idea. He wondered if perhaps, while Lauren was sleeping, her guard might be down. Enough to let him sneak through her defences and see if he could find out what had spooked her so badly. It was one of those things he knew he shouldn't do. He didn't suppose there was an established etiquette for entering someone's mind but, whatever the ground rules were, he was sure it was something that wasn't done without invitation. Having said that, Lauren had very clearly invaded his mind when she had forced him to the beach that day. It wasn't the same thing, but James clung to it as a justification for what he otherwise might have feared was a betrayal. So, he began to explore Lauren's dreaming mind as she dozed on his shoulder. There was an art to probing another's mind and it was one he was still learning. He clumsily turned over piles of irrelevance. It really was like looking for a needle in a haystack. Whether it was by fortune or skill he wasn't sure, but eventually he found the thoughts he was looking for. He unlocked the moments when

Lauren saw him running, panicked, towards her and he felt the pounding of her startled heart as his freaking form flew into view. With sheepish hindsight, he blushed slightly at the sight of his own distress. It was the second time he had seen himself through Lauren's eyes and it was no more pleasant than the previous, puckering glimpse. James knew there was something he was missing in the scene and he replayed it, over and over again. He was nudging the images back and forth, like a DJ scratching a living from their artful swipes. He knew what he was looking for was there, waiting to be discovered, but it remained elusive. The more he concentrated, the further away from the answer he seemed to be.

In the end, he pulled away and distanced himself guiltily from Lauren's inner thoughts. He felt terrible. When he had entered her mind, he had felt justified. Now that he had finished, he felt as though he'd abused her. It was an awful feeling. He had tried to take something that she hadn't wanted to give him. It was sneaky and dishonest. It wasn't him. In that instant, he hated himself for doing it. He had risked everything he loved. And for what? He'd found nothing. There was no turning the clock back of course; the deed was done.

He tried to focus on the film reel of scenery that flickered across the carriage window. He cursed himself for being unable to pinpoint what he knew had been right at the tips of his fingers. If he had at least managed to find something, his intrusion would have been vindicated. Whatever it was that was concerning Lauren enough to withhold from him was tantalisingly out of reach. That, and the way he had tried to locate it, tortured James.

WHACK!

The door at the far end of the carriage flew open and James' insides made a dash for the outside as the noise startled him from his torment. His dragster heart roared to full throttle from an idling start, fuelled by the high octane dread he had been consuming since Paris.

'Montrez-moi vos billets.' James had never been so glad to see a ticket inspector in his entire life. He sucked in a gasping mix of air and relief, and his inner revs began to fall. He hadn't realised quite how on edge he had been, and laughed at his silly reaction, though there was no humour in his mood. He had thought that the fear inside him was well contained, that it was safely tucked away under lock and key, only to be allowed to surface under strict conditions. Instead, it had been plotting its escape, waiting for the right distraction in order to make an all-out play for freedom.

James knew he would have to learn to control this kind of panic. It was something he was beginning to feel more and more frequently. He felt out of control and he didn't like it. It was something he needed to tame, for fear that it might rob him of any ability to take action. If a time came where he had to stand and fight, he wanted to be ready, present and capable, not a quivering jelly that was simple to overpower. The last thing he wanted was to be rooted to the spot if whatever event he so dreaded ever materialised. The speed with which the fear had just exploded out of its vault astonished him. He had never experienced quite such a rushing terror before, even at the ticket office back in Paris.

But Lauren had. Now he thought about it, the closest feeling to this that James had felt had belonged to Lauren. In those memories that he had so surreptitiously raided, he had sensed the same intensity inside her as she had watched his anxious approach. Her fear had been ripping her heart from its very moorings, such was its ferocity. The odd thing was that he hadn't felt the same explosive rush. He ought to have done. Lauren should have been relatively calm while she was waiting for him, but she hadn't been. He had felt her terror. He had heard her muscles screaming for oxygen.

In that moment, James understood. There had indeed been something wrong with that scene. Until now he hadn't grasped it, but it was crystal clear. Lauren had certainly been scared witless by his frantic appearance earlier that day but, considering the scale of her fear, he should have felt the explosion inside her. He hadn't. All he had felt was her fear at full speed. Her senses were already on fire with adrenalin at the moment she had caught sight of him. There could be only one reason. Something else, something completely separate from what had happened to him, had terrified her.

Lauren began to stir from her oblivious slumber and immediately the guilt James had felt at prying into her inner thoughts returned. It was something he knew he would have to confess to if he wanted to challenge her about what had really happened. He watched the delicious drowsiness that fogged her waking and held Lauren close as her thoughts cleared. For a while, he paddled around what he knew would be troubled waters. He tested the temperature with his toes as he engaged her with pleasantries about how well she'd slept and how she felt, then he threw himself headlong into the subject like a bather entering the icy English Channel at the first glimpse of sun.

'Lauren, you need to tell me what happened.'

'When? I've been sleeping!'

'Back at the station. What was it that terrified you?'

'I told you. You freaked me out. I'm not having this conversation again.' it was what James expected. She was straight on the attack, holding back. He knew that he had no choice but to confess his trespass.

'Lauren. I know.'

'You know what? Stop talking in riddles!'

'Back on the platform when you were waiting for me.'

'Oh not again, James. I …'

'No Lauren, this time we're going to talk about it.' James asserted. 'While you were sleeping, I entered your mind …'

'You did what! How dare you!' Lauren exclaimed as she slapped his cheek instinctively. Though he felt chastised, James admired her fight.

'Who's the hypocrite now Lauren?' countered James.

'What do you mean?'

'Well, I accept that entering someone's mind without invitation is poor form—'

'Damn right it is James!'

'But it's not as though you haven't done it.'

'When have I done it?'

'When you forced me to the beach!'

'That was different.' Now Lauren was backpedalling.

'How was it different?'

'You had to come; otherwise we wouldn't be here.'

'And you have to share what you witnessed in Paris. You can't keep it from me. I need to know what is happening,' James said, with an air of finality. He told Lauren what he had seen and felt. He left her no room to manoeuvre and she knew her thoughts had betrayed her to James, as his had so often to her. She was furious at his intrusion but knew she had no choice other than to share what had happened.

'Okay. Look I'm still not happy with what you did, but I'll tell you. Promise me you'll never do that again though.'

'Deal. You too.'

James sensed the wall she had built to protect herself

begin to crumble, revealing a mind that was tortured by terror.

Once more, he found himself looking through her eyes. The minimarket at the station had been crowded. It was an overpriced oasis in which the proprietor milked unprepared travellers for every centime they had. Lauren had been shopping for food for the overnight journey, most of which they had now consumed. There was nothing unusual in her recollection at this point. She paid the shopkeeper, and James empathised with her irritation at his insistence in conversing with her in pigeon English, despite her reasonable attempts to use his language. James chuckled as she too was a recipient of the legendary Gallic shrug.

She packed two plastic bags, one in each hand, and a lengthy baguette poked from the top of each in a kind of doughy symmetry. She clinked towards the door as the solitary bottle of red wine she had purchased to share with James jostled for space in a battle with the two mugs that it would be consumed with. As she approached the exit, one of the bags snagged on a sharp corner of the food shelves and teetering tins threatened to topple before her supporting hand reassured them. A single, suicidal jar took the plunge though and smashed to the floor. The shopkeeper waived his arms and cursed in his native tongue. He chastised Lauren's clumsiness and strode towards the sloppy mess that lay on the floor, kicking away the larger pieces of glass with angry feet. Lauren made motions to help in the clean-up but was quickly waved away by the agitated man. He was so rude that she felt no need to insist on helping him. She turned to leave the store and, though she carefully watched where she placed her feet, her shoes crunched on rogue glass shards that stuck to her soles and scratched the floor with each stride. She departed to a chorus of French curses and responded with her own Gallic shrug. It wasn't as though there was any more she could do. She had said sorry. She had offered to help. The gesticulating shopkeeper had refused any assistance, so Lauren was at peace despite his agitation. Instead, she continued towards the place she where had agreed to meet James. Behind her, the commotion continued. She was surprised the man couldn't let it go. It was just a jar, for God's sake. What was wrong with him? She decided to turn to see what was happening, why he was still so angry. Immediately she wished she hadn't. As her eyes locked on the entrance, a pistol shot of fear gunned through her body. There in the doorway stood a familiar figure. He was half-hidden in the shadow of the awning but his features were unmistakeable. She flinched. Her bags clattered to the floor and commanded unwanted attention at the very moment she needed invisibility. Lauren scrabbled to pick up the contents. Her hands shook as she fumbled on the floor. Surely it couldn't be him, she thought. It wasn't possible. She hoped desperately that her eyes were deceiving her. She knew she needed a second look, though it was the last thing she wanted to do. She had to know. With all her courage, she raised her eyes once more, forcing them in a direction that they resisted vehemently. What they saw left her aghast. Slick, thick and unruly locks with dark tendrils that curled rampantly between his ears and shoulders. The badgered mottle of his goatee. Black, deep-set eyes that bored into her as she stared incredulously. There was no question. It was him. If she'd had any doubts, they were erased by the sly sneer with which he acknowledged her. It sent shivers down her spine that she knew would never leave. It was an ancient and knowing smirk. One that she had seen at least once before. It had flashed across those same lips just seconds before that cold and violent hand had smashed Isabel across the room. Eight hundred years earlier. She had no idea how, or why, but there was no mistaking Don Pedro de Azagra, the dreaded Lord of Albarracín. The man who had butchered poor Diego's lifeless corpse.

*

It brought joy to Don Pedro's blackened heart when he had made them aware of his presence. He feasted on James' fear, he tasted Lauren's terror. He was out in the open now. For so long he had lurked in the shadows, waiting for history to repeat itself again. He had waited, bided his time. He had been patient for long enough; now he was closing in on the time for revenge.

He loathed seeing them together. It was a reminder of his wretched fate. He could smell their love; the air was foul with it and its stench was overbearing. The rotten fumes from the noisy iron monstrosities had been nauseating enough, but it was better than the aroma of these two. To his finely tuned instinct, they were positively rancid.

Just like all the others, they were rubbing his nose into the sham that had been his marriage to Isabel. They'd made him feel impotent and emasculated again, just as their kind always did, century after century. He asked himself when this infernal coupling was going to end. He was sick of it. Did they think he wanted to stalk them across the earth for eternity? If they did, they were wrong. All he wanted was for all this to stop. To be able to die like everyone else. But he couldn't. And he knew who was to blame. All this was her doing. Isabel. Even when he spoke the words in his head, he spat them. She had never loved him; she hated him. And the bitch had gained her revenge anyway. Eight hundred years of misery.

Don Pedro had allowed himself one little reward this time. There had been no reason to alert them to his presence; in fact, it would have made the end game far simpler had he not. But he couldn't resist it. He wanted to watch the fear flow through their eyes. They had been fleeing a false enemy after all. One that would not be coming after them. They could be certain of that. The bigamist had died a painful death as his throat was sliced. Unlike many of Don Pedro's victims, his body was still recognisable. There hadn't been enough time to indulge in his hobby, but what he had left was certainly a work of art. Perhaps more Picasso than his usual da Vinci, but beautiful work nonetheless.

He had laughed and laughed as he watched the boy sprint across the concourse in search of the cheating whore. He hoped the coffee still scalded, that it scarred the boy's skin for what remained of his brief life. He would be like a trembling lamb to the slaughter. The whore had been the best, of course. This latest slut in a long line of harlots, a line that had somehow been ignited by the woman who had paid lip service to her short-lived duty as his wife. Like all the others, this one's resemblance to Isabel was incredible. A little part of Don Pedro lusted after her just as he had each and every one of them before her. As far as he was concerned, she was still his wife, yet he had never fucked her. He wondered what it would be like. It wasn't too late.

The fact that after all this time he still thought about her that way, made him want to hurt her even more. No. He didn't want her. He wanted vengeance and release. The terror that had spread across her face as she recognised him was priceless, perfect. It spread satisfaction across his ancient countenance. He saw her pale skin turn whiter still and watched the blood drain from those fulsome lips. For once, he felt those glorious emeralds trained on him. It made him feel alive. He didn't care that it was the look of a startled rabbit. He'd long since accepted that it would never be more than that. He had sworn to rid the earth of the love these two had for each other. And he could feel the end closing in.

14

T HE TRAIN SCREECHED to a halt as it entered the tunnelled glass of Portbou station. James and Lauren exited the train, like cattle, to bilingual prods that they assumed were advising them to prepare their passports. It was a token gesture. The Spanish customs officers didn't seem to care less who was entering the country. The lovers now had the entire landmass of France between them and Lauren's husband. They should have felt relief, but they found none. Neither of them was sure who they were running from any more. They had carefully planned their escape and mitigated the risk, because the fear of Lauren's retaliatory husband was real and tangible and, even though they had such a distance under their belt, they still expected to be looking over their shoulders. The trouble was that everything they had previously considered and planned for, seemed insignificant in the face of the events in Paris. They were on a knife edge, gripped by a fear they didn't understand.

James scanned the jostling passengers with a wary eye as they filtered through an eternal customs check. Lauren smiled sweetly at the swarthy Spaniard who welcomed them to his country in perfect English. It was eight in the morning and the sun glistened across the mighty Mediterranean, which lapped its way into the welcoming arms of Portbou's tiny bay. In fact, the town below looked so delightful they chose to delay their onward journey to Barcelona by a couple of hours. It was an opportunity to shake off their recent confinement and take in the first air of their new Spanish life. They stowed their belongings in two of the plentiful lockers, and exited the station.

Being a frontier town, Portbou existed only for its station, and yet it had that peculiar Spanish seaside beauty that made it a tourist destination in its own right. It was uncanny, James thought. He had visited most of Britain's seaside towns and each had a cheap and cheerful charm that heralded from Victorian innocence, and was unfortunately accompanied by facilities that had not been updated since. Yet here, in a town that just happened to be by the sea and made no attempt to be anything other than a by-product of the changing gauge of the rail line between France and Spain, was everything that the British aspired to in a holiday destination.

They strolled silently down the slight incline to the beach, through what James assumed was an occasionally bustling and vibrant village. That morning it was deserted. The shuttered doors magnified its emptiness with their cold and unwelcoming greeting and the concrete reinforced the silence between the two lovers. In the hour or so since Lauren's revelation, they had exchanged few words as they wrestled with the enormity of it all, drawing what comfort they needed from each other's mere presence.

Throughout the walk down to the sea, their hands remained locked together. Lauren gripped James so tight that any blood had long since left her fingers. It was a clasp of determined confusion, one that celebrated their togetherness, but at the same time betrayed their fear. When they reached the promenade, even the soothing familiarity of the rolling waves couldn't distract either from the foreboding they felt. They perched on the protractor shaped wall at the end of the Carrer de Cerbère and looked across the curious grey sand into the azure beyond. Out to the dark, lizard rocks of Cap de Portbou that basked in the unbroken sunshine. It truly was glorious, and in different circumstances they would have rejoiced, but today their focus was elsewhere. Eventually, James broke the silence.

'I don't understand any of this, Lauren.'

'Neither do I. We've been focused on getting as far away from Sean as possible only ...'

'... to find there's something far greater for us to worry about?'

'Yes. Exactly. I just don't know what it is!'

'I can't make any sense of it at all,' said James.

'I'm really scared James. Every time I close my eyes I

see that menacing sneer. It was awful.' Lauren was once more on the verge of tears and James held her close to him in a reassuring promise that he wasn't convinced he could keep.

'Those times …' Her voice faltered and her tearing eyes glistened from her inner turmoil. '… when he hit me … I genuinely feared for my life. I thought that was real fear … and I'd lived through it. I felt strong for it. I knew I was a survivor.' James held her close as she shuddered at the recollection. 'But now, now I feel a different fear. There's something ancient and intended about this and …'

'Hey. It's okay,' James lied. 'We're strong together, much stronger than we ever were alone.' They were brave words and he hoped that was how they sounded. He knew that when the time came he would fight to protect Lauren. Life wouldn't be worth living if anything happened to her and he would die saving her if that was what was needed, of that he had no doubt. What worried him was whether he could do enough. Would he be able to protect her? How could he know? He didn't even want to think about what forces were at work.

They sat there, entwined like muses for Rodin. James felt somehow that their togetherness would be a saviour. When he held Lauren. When she held him. Whenever they kissed each other. There was nothing else. No pain. No fear. Nothing. Just pure togetherness. It screamed of their combined power.

After a time, James broke what was becoming a monastic silence.

'You don't think that was really Don Pedro de Azagra, do you? Under normal circumstances I'd say it was impossible, but I'm not sure I know what normal is any more. Whoever it was, there's no question he knew who you were.'

'All I can say is, if it wasn't him, it looked an awful lot like him!'

'But how could it be him?'

'I don't know. I've been wrestling with it since the moment I saw him.'

'Me too,' said James. 'The only conclusion I could come to was that I'd be wrong to dismiss it. Is it really so impossible? A year ago, I wouldn't have believed what *we* were capable of. I don't even understand that!'

'Considering the connection that we share with Isabel and Diego, it doesn't seem a huge leap to think that, somehow, whoever that was, shares a connection with Don Pedro,' Lauren agreed.

'No, it doesn't. But his face hasn't appeared in any of the lives I've explored so far, other than in Diego and Isabel's story. Have you seen him?' James asked.

'No. And I don't understand why. If we were somehow all bound in the same legacy, surely we would have seen him before?'

'Do you think it was him who grabbed my arm too?'

'I don't know. I can only hope it was.'

'Eh? I don't get it?' James was confused.

'Because, if it wasn't him, that means there are now two people out there who want us to know they're around! I can't tell you how frightened I am, James. I know with absolute certainty that we are meant to be together, but now I feel that's only part of the story. He's clearly a part too, but where the hell does he come into it?'

'I just don't know Lauren. I just don't know.'

'What do you think we should do?'

'What can we do? We can't go back, and I'm not going to give up the chance of a life with you now that we've come this far. There's nothing in England for us. If you ask me, we keep going. Stick to our plan. If there's something we're meant to find out, then I'm sure we will. I can't say I'm looking forward to that moment though!' With that Lauren drew James closer and as he finished his sentence she rewarded him with her prized lips.

After a time, they headed back towards the station through the grandly named, yet underwhelming Rambla de Catalunya and past the exquisite adoration that was the Church of Santa Maria. So strong was the faith in Spain, that even a town of no more than fifteen hundred, like Portbou, had a spectacular place of worship. This was no gothic intimidator like the English parish churches, but a warm and welcoming tribute to the love of God. It was decorated in lace-like carvings that drew the eye to its masterful point. Judging by the condition of the exterior and the tidy grounds that surrounded it, Catholicism was alive and well in Portbou, and the grounds were a stark contrast to the disdainfully littered graveyards of Folkestone's main church.

Before they boarded the train, James purchased what proved to be two delicious tortilla baguettes. He wouldn't have dreamt of ordering the English equivalent, an omelette sandwich. Not only did the Spanish have oily potato flans that tantalised the taste buds, they also had the linguistic pizzazz to pull it off. He was starting to realise that everything sounded better in Spanish. He looked forward to ordering *mantequilla* from now on, instead of butter. Already he loved Spain. How could anyone not be happy in a beautiful country with such a musical language?

The journey from Portbou to Barcelona was uneventful, and in no time at all, they arrived at Barcelona Sants. This was a city James had always wanted to visit and now he was here, although 'here' meant in the weaving subterranean passages between platforms. He knew he was in Barcelona, but the truth was he could have been anywhere. Above him was the city of Gaudi with its world-famous Ramblas, but all he could see were concrete walls and advertising boards. As they jostled along with their bags, hurrying for the train to Zaragoza, James glimpsed the exit. It was too much. He grabbed Lauren's arm.

'This way!'

'No. That's the exit. We need to go this way!' said Lauren, pointing to the platform.

'We've been travelling for more than 24 hours. We're tired. We haven't had a decent meal. As if that wasn't enough, we've just arrived at one of the most famous cities in the world.'

'James, we're not on a sightseeing tour, remember?'

'Believe me Lauren, I hadn't forgotten that for one second. I don't think I could. Right now, I need some normality. We both do. And where better? We're having lunch on the Ramblas.' Lauren was surprised at his spontaneity. It was something that she hadn't seen before and she liked it. She reasoned that he had not really had any opportunity to show it to date, such had been the extent of her control. Now she could feel the distance between her and Sean, she had begun to relinquish some of it and James was becoming more assertive. Every moment she spent with him she found out something new. She hoped this was the way their life would be from now on.

They searched for lockers at the station but none were big enough for their bags. It would be a hassle to lug a suitcase and backpack around such a throbbing city, but James was undeterred.

'But what if they're stolen?' asked Lauren.

'I know pickpockets are supposed to be rife on the

Ramblas, but I'd be surprised if they went off with a suitcase! Besides, who'd want my second-hand pants?'

'Thanks for that image James. I'm not worried about the clothes. It's the other stuff.'

'What other stuff?'

'I left my life behind yesterday. Everything I owned, bar a few things that were important to me. I've got photos, mementos. A set of earrings that my dad bought me. They were the last present he ever …'

'Sorry,' James jumped in, 'I didn't mean to be so insensitive. How about taking them out and putting them in a locker?' And so they did. They found a row of combination lockers and Lauren took a small shopping bag out of her back pack and placed it inside. Then she closed it and set the combination. A four-digit number was required. She chose one. 1603. The date they had first kissed.

*

'*Pa amb tomàquet,*' Don Pedro de Azagra grunted, '*y un poco de jamón de Teruel*'. He was hungry and the thought of that toasted bread rubbed in tomato and olive oil had him salivating. The traditional Catalan dish. Ha! He laughed to himself. It was no more traditional than smoking tobacco. If anyone had asked him, he could have told them there were no tomatoes in Spain until the sixteenth century. Even then, nobody had thought of putting it on toast like that until three hundred years later. Call that tradition? Teruel ham, now that was different. It had been around for centuries. He'd killed many a peasant for stealing the precious wheat, barley and corn that was meant for the pigs. How dare they? As if their hunger was more important than developing the sweet taste of a perfect ham.

He washed it down with a bottle of Ribera del Jiloca. As always, the waiter had raised an annoyingly inquisitive eyebrow when he ordered it. These days the Spanish thought it was a lower quality wine. It didn't have the reputation of Duero but that wasn't the point. It was Vino de la Tierra. Wine of the earth. His earth. Grown in the beautiful valleys of the Jiloca that, like everything else, had been spoiled over the last eight hundred years. Men had a lot to answer for with their bridges, their towns and their factories. They thought nothing of poisoning entire rivers with their indiscriminate dumping.

With every sip of that light, red nectar he remembered home. Albarracín. It was the source of the Jiloca river. As far as Don Pedro was concerned, that meant the wine from the Jiloca valley was his own flesh and blood, it always had been. Back in the day he had laughed as visiting noblemen spat out the Jiloca and demanded Rioja. Many had lost their tongues for doing so.

It was the wine that he had shared with the gorgeous Isabel on their wedding day. The day he had finally won her. The thought of her standing next to him at the altar in that stunning blue silk gown that he had paid so much for still made him hard. She was the most beautiful girl he had ever seen and those eyes sparkled like the sun on the meandering Jiloca river. Ever since he had first seen her, he'd wanted her. To caress those taut, tidy breasts. To nuzzle away those ebony locks as he kissed her fragrant throat. From that day on he had made it his mission to take her as a wife.

In the end, all the chasing, the threats and the bribes had been worthwhile, when that miserable merchant Rafael de Segura had finally caved. If he had been clever and accepted that Don Pedro was always going to get his way, Isabel would have commanded a pretty penny. But he'd taken so long that eventually Don Pedro had just held his sword to the quivering coward's throat and told him he was taking her. He had given nothing. Not one maravedi. Why should he have? The disrespectful bastard had made him wait for five long years. De Segura had been lucky he was still alive to see the wedding.

Isabel, of course, had been a shrew. She had taken a sip of that glorious Jiloca and spat it back into the golden wedding chalice, before passing it over to him.

'You may have taken me as a wife but you'll never have my love. That will always belong to Diego de Marcilla,' she had whispered venomously.

'I don't need your love,' Don Pedro had lied, although

her words hurt him more than any he had ever heard. He promised himself right then that he would never take her by force, that he would make her love him, make her want him. And then she'd spoiled it all. She had sneaked out in the middle of the night to kiss the dismembered body of that infuriating Marcilla. Even as a mutilated corpse he was more desirable to Isabel. Imagine that. Cuckolded by a festering monster. It was hardly good for one's ego. Even that Don Pedro could have forgiven, eventually, but not what she did next.

He hadn't heard the curse that she had screamed but he had felt the words cracking into his heart like a blistering arrow. And from that day he felt black and empty inside. He'd given himself over to a life of hate, hate for the way Isabel had refused to love him. Hate for the way she had preferred death over him. Hate for the special love he could still feel in the air, even though Isabel was dead.

He became more and more violent to those around him. His torture grew worse and worse. The punishment for stealing from him became instant dismemberment. And as for Isabel's sister, Maria, well, she had suffered. She wasn't Isabel and she never could be. He didn't need her to love him and he had taken her by force, every night, until he tired of her. And then he had let others take her by force. It was the least he could do to punish her for being related to the woman who had spurned him so.

Don Pedro flicked his arm across the table, exploding with the same rage and force with which he had struck Isabel when she interrupted his artwork. The Jiloca went flying and the red liquid seeped across the jamón de Teruel in a way that reminded him of the blood oozing from Marcilla's still-warm body. The fussing waiter was there immediately, dabbing at him with an infernal serviette. He deserved the slap that Don Pedro connected with.

'Bring me more wine, boy.'

'Y-yes sir, right away.' He cowered like so many before him.

This restaurant wasn't so bad, Don Pedro mused. The way dining had evolved over the centuries was one of the few things he felt were truly progress. This one, Cometacinc, was one of his favourites. It was nestled in the gothic quarter of Barcelona on the narrow Carrer del Cometa. The buildings weren't as old as him and many weren't authentic, but the closeness and darkness of the streets, the overhanging balconies and the stone façades made him nostalgic. This was a street where he didn't have to think about those iron machines that hared past in an infernal rush. The few that passed were like snails as they squeezed along the tight passages. It was a place where footfall on stone flags was the only noise. It was a place where the simple medieval times had stayed alive, at least in part. He always came here on his way back to Albarracín. Deep down, he felt as though this might be his last journey too. It would soon be over.

He tucked into the Jiloca-stained ham and tried to lose himself in exploring the countless memories he had built up over the years. Usually it suited him to reminisce. It relaxed him. But not this time. He felt on edge. Something wasn't right about the city of Barcelona today. There was a foul smell that he couldn't shake from his nostrils. It was one that he recognised and it was growing stronger. It was them. They were in Barcelona. But why? They weren't supposed to be here. They were heading to Teruel. He couldn't kill them here, that wouldn't be right. It needed to be at Teruel and it needed to be tonight. The anniversary of Isabel's death.

The chair scraped across the stone floor of Cometacinc as he stood. The timid waiter waved his hands to imply that there was nothing to pay. Fear. It always guaranteed a free ride, Don Pedro thought. He stepped into the chilly air and headed west. It was no more that quarter of a mile to the Ramblas as the crow flew but the weaving laneways almost trebled that. Occasionally a pickpocket would target him; the area was notorious. They learned very quickly to leave him alone, and he knew that one of them would never pick a pocket again. He wouldn't be able to without fingers.

At the Ramblas the air was thick with the stench of the lovers. Don Pedro hated that place. It was everything he despised about the modern world. Noisy and crowded. That was what happened when you didn't have wars any more. The population just grew and grew, and the world became like this. Didn't they realise there were now five times as many people in Spain as there had once been? And that was excluding the damnable tourists that swelled places like Barcelona to ridiculous proportions. He crossed to the central pedestrian zone, careful to avoid the cars that zipped past him. The world had come a long way, he thought. That didn't mean to say it was better.

The stink of love wafted along the wide thoroughfare that was flanked with restaurants where odd-looking tourists ordered food by pointing at photographs. The two of them were close, he could feel it. Out of the corner of his eye he saw them at a table, drinking Rioja and eating jamón. At least they had one thing right, he thought. It was a shame he wouldn't be able to introduce them to Jiloca. He bought a newspaper and sat in the café opposite.

'What would you like sir?'

'Bring me Jiloca!'

'But sir, we have no …'

'Bring. Me. Jiloca.' Don Pedro eyed the poor waiter with murderous intent as he spat the words with venom. Immediately the man scurried off on a mission to find some. He had seen the blackness in Don Pedro's eyes and knew immediately that his only option was to comply.

Don Pedro opened the newspaper and looked over the top of it at the two lovers. The way they gazed into each other's eyes brought back that familiar bile, which kept rising in his throat. It reminded him of Isabel's words.

'You may have taken me as a wife but you'll never have my love. That will always belong to Diego de Marcilla,' she had spat.

Once more he felt the rage boiling inside him. It was irrepressible, uncontainable. That day she had rejected him in a way that no-one had done before or since. If only he'd killed her then, he thought. That way he would have saved himself hundreds of years of torment. But he hadn't. And why not? Because he had wanted her to love him. She had been his one weakness. She was the only one to whom he had ever exposed his soft underbelly and she had plunged her words into it as if they were his own bejewelled stiletto. And it hurt. Cripplingly so. For a brief moment, he felt a tear preparing itself to break free. He was having none of it. Don Pedro didn't cry. He slapped it back into place with a hand that trembled with fury, giving over his mind completely to rage. It was the one thing he knew was more powerful than his sadness. For the second time in an hour, he smashed his arm across the table and sent the Jiloca, the poor waiter had finally found, crashing to the floor.

The rest of the customers looked over at him in shock but he didn't return their stares. He was fixated on the two lovers. They heard the crash and looked up. In that one second he saw their fear. They recognised him instantly. She, like a startled rabbit poised to flee. He, tortured but brave, almost insolent in the way he returned Don Pedro's melting hatred. He would have to die painfully.

*

The way those eyes stared at them was terrifying. James had seen them once through Lauren's eyes but it was different in the flesh. The horror of seeing him there, staring at them with such malevolence was unspeakable. Not for the first time, James' instinct was to run but he fought it bravely. He knew that sooner or later they would have to confront Don Pedro. The thought petrified him, but equally his desire to protect Lauren filled him with bravado. He was not going to let what they had go without a fight and, if that meant now, then so be it. He was determined yet intimidated. Bold yet shaken. Next to him he could feel the icy fear that weaved through Lauren.

'Run!' she shouted, ripping her back pack from the floor and sending several chairs around her flying. This wasn't the time for argument and James followed. They raced along the Ramblas towards Plaça de la Boqueria. Behind them, an agitated waiter waved a bill behind them.

'James! A taxi! Quick!' They threw themselves into the back of it and demanded to be taken to Barcelona Sants. As the taxi sped away, they stared desperately through the back window. With each yard, they felt the fire of adrenalin beginning to die, and an exhausting stress take its place. At each intersection, their hearts upped tempo again as they waited for an eternity at the lights. There was no sign of him behind them, but that did nothing to quell the urgency of their flight.

In ten interminable minutes, they were at the station. James thrust a handful of pesetas into the surprised taxi-driver's hand and they tore into the concourse. The next train to Zaragoza was in just two minutes. They needed to be on it, but that would leave no time to pick up Lauren's valuables.

'Lauren, your things!'

'They're safe. We're not!' she continued running towards the platform. 'We can always come back for them.'

The train was about to depart when they reached it. With a final sprint, they leapt through the closing doors and collapsed together in a heap on the floor. The train began to move. They looked around. All the passengers were staring at them. If only they knew, thought Lauren.

15

I N JUST OVER five hours, the train was close to Teruel. Along the way, the fleeting glimpses of Zaragoza from the scratched window had piqued their interest, but there was no way they were going to break their journey again. Nothing would have made them leave that train, so spooked had they been by the events in Barcelona.

'He's following us, isn't he James?' asked Lauren, already knowing the answer.

'Yes. It's almost as if he knows where we are going already.'

'So how about we change our plan? There are lots of other places we could go to. We don't even have to be in Spain!'

'We both know we need to be in Teruel,' said James.

'Yes, but it's not too late,' said Lauren hopefully.

'I don't think it matters to him where we go.'

'What do you mean?'

'I got a sense he knew where we were. It can't be a coincidence that we've run into him twice on our journey, can it?

'I guess not!'

'It's not like we've talked about where we're going. So how would he know we'd be at Austerlitz? In Barcelona? And we can feel his presence too. Now I think about it, I definitely sensed him in Barcelona, even if I didn't realise it. In which case, it seems logical that he can feel us too, don't you think?'

'What are you trying to say?' There was a hint of desperation in Lauren's question. She knew what James meant but didn't want to think about it.

'That, if I'm right, it makes no difference where we go. He will find us.'

'So what do we do?'

'We carry on with our plan. Sooner or later we'll have to face him and, considering that we're carrying a legacy that was born in Teruel, I reckon I'd rather face him there, wouldn't you?'

'You might just be right!' Lauren seemed to perk up.

'I know so. Come on, think about it Lauren, you said it yourself. There's a reason why these lives—this power— has been passed down. Despite all the tragedy, all the misery, it has remained unbroken. You called it an ancient tide that wears down its adversaries over hundreds of years. We're part of something much, much bigger than just the two of us. I feel as though in Teruel we will be stronger. Protected.'

'I hope you are right.'

'Me too!'

The last hour of the journey crept along like a weary tortoise. Despite his fear, James was full of hope. Full of expectancy. Excited about what lay ahead in Teruel. He felt as though perhaps he would be at peace when they arrived. Safe. In fact, it was like coming home.

The train weaved through familiar landscapes that hadn't changed in eight hundred years. The Universal mountains were spectacular, the mighty Muela de San Juan was like a beacon calling him home. Even though developments distorted the scenery, it was all still recognisable. Only the mighty Guadalaviar had changed. James' skin tingled at the memory of the cool embrace it had given Diego when he swam across it to Isabel. Back then, it had been raging, but now it was a mere trickle. It had been dammed to form the Arquillo de San Blas Reservoir.

In the distance were the familiar and foreboding ramparts of the tower of Andador, the walls of which were like the arches of a crown as they sat atop the head of over a mile of mountain. Those formidable walls were the gateway to Albarracín. It reminded James that, while the final leg of the journey to Teruel felt like a homecoming, it was by no means safe. He shuddered as the snarling image from Paris and the ruinous smile from the Ramblas sneaked into his mind. If it truly was him, then this was the land of Don Pedro de Azagra. They were going straight into the lion's den.

The day was rife with déjà vu. James spied the same gnarly Portuguese oak that Diego had proposed to Isabel under. Eight hundred years later it was even more beautiful, it's myriad of wandering tendrils etching patterns across the clear blue sky. James wallowed in the memories of that one delicious moment when Diego and Isabel had been happy. He had a strong sense that this was where it had all begun. That moment under the tree had made Isabel and Diego the founders of this long and uninterrupted line. Their love had been so strong that it had refused to die. James felt so privileged, proud of what had come before him.

The town of Teruel itself was unrecognisable on the approach. As the provincial capital, it had grown significantly over the centuries and now supported a population of over thirty thousand. They lived in what was virtually a whole new town that surrounded the much older middle, like a halved avocado cradling its stone. The skyline was dominated by three of the most stunning buildings James and Lauren had ever seen. The tiled parapets of the cathedral of Santa María de Mediavilla were like emeralds and sapphires in the waning sun. This was the one building in modern Teruel that Diego and Isabel would have seen, even though they had never set eyes on the glorious Moorish tower. It was no wonder that much of Teruel was now recognised as a world heritage site, thought James. The spectacular Torre de el Salvador rose from the streets below, it's style another reminder of the Moorish magic of this part of Spain. Even from a distance the stonework was intricate. There were mosaics of vivid green and white glazed ceramics nestled between golden sandstone. It was incredible to think this tower had been built in the fourteenth century. What a testament to the architectural prowess of those Moors who had been allowed to stay in Aragon after the Reconquista.

Lauren thought about the streets below it. They were where Diego and Isabel had lived. Where their families had been friends and neighbours before the Marcilla had lost everything to the locusts. Lauren savoured the image for a moment. Visions of Diego banging triumphantly on the door of Rafael de Segura's house popped into her head. She felt such kinship with the lovers.

James felt it too, though he couldn't shake the image of Don Pedro de Azagra mutilating poor Diego's corpse. It reminded him that the question of Don Pedro's presence at Austerlitz was still unanswered. His concern tainted what he knew should have been a special moment. All that changed when he saw the Church of San Pedro for the first time. Its sandcastle turrets sat atop many-sided walls in Moorish majesty, like candles on a cake. It was like no church he had ever seen. It could have been a castle. Perhaps even the accidental genius of a child's Lego construction, constant tinkering and adjustments that had in the end given birth to something spectacular. It was impossible to tell just how many sides those walls had, they were multifaceted and cut like gemstones. Four cigar-like turrets rose from the ramparts towards the heaven and one sat atop the church like the cherry on a Bakewell Tart. It was jaw-dropping. That was the only way to describe it. There could not have been a better place for the tombs of Isabel and Diego.

James and Lauren stepped off the train as night fell. Immediately, they felt the power and magic of the place under their feet for the first time. Even though everything that surrounded them was new and unfamiliar, alien even, it felt intimate and familial. There was no question in James' mind that they belonged here.

Once out of the station they crossed the road and went through the line of trees and past the two empty playgrounds. Any children would have long since been under curfew. In anywhere other than Spain this would have been a mere park, but here they were botanical gardens, all part of the nation's desire to incorporate flora into day-to-day life. At the end of the park, in Calle San Francisco, they found a hotel. It looked a reasonable size and was modestly priced. James purchased a room for the night, still mindful of the trail he might be leaving, and he would have given a false name if they hadn't asked for a passport. The truth was that by now the two lovers were so tired they were beyond caring about whoever might pursue them. It had been Lauren's idea to stay at a hotel for at least the first night. She knew they would be tired from the long journey and in need of some comfort. It would also be the moment they finally began to explore each other, having suppressed their desire for so long. It would have been terrible to lie on filthy sheets or huddled on a floor somewhere. In a hotel, they were guaranteed at least a minimum standard of cleanliness.

The friendly receptionist assigned James a room and he and Lauren caught the elevator to the fifth floor, where they entered their room. Thick golden curtains stood guard on either side of both windows in the room and net curtains protected them from any light assault from the rear. The beige walls blended seamlessly into the beige carpet and the only worthy feature in the room was the delicious curve of the mahogany headboard that sat atop a bed that was camouflaged in similar blandness.

James threw open the curtains. It needed a little more strength than he had expected. The glow of streetlamps streamed into the room like air into a vacuum. After moments of adjustment while he blinked against the infantry of light, he was disappointed at the view. He had hoped to catch a glimpse of the majestic Torre de el Salvador in the street behind but the room appeared to be on the other side of the hotel. He must have been disoriented by the twists and turns of the corridor, he reasoned. Instead, the view was across the north-east of the town and to the hills beyond. James knew that from their raised position on the Calle de San Francisco they would have a good view of them when they made an appearance in the daylight, and that would be ample consolation.

'I can't wait to explore the town tomorrow,' he said.

'Me too. I wonder if anything in this town has survived for eight hundred years.'

'Other than the cathedral, of course!' added James.

'Oh yes! Incredible, isn't it?'

'What?' he asked.

'To think that through Isabel and Diego, we actually heard the masons chipping away at the stones that built the cathedral.'

'I can't believe it either Lauren. And it's so beautiful! It must have taken about a hundred years to build!'

'Everything about this place is beautiful, James.'

'I know what you mean. It feels like we're meant to be here, doesn't it?'

'I've never felt more at home anywhere in my life,' Lauren replied.

James pulled her close. This was the moment. He wanted to make love to her more than he had ever wanted anything in his life. She wanted it to. He could feel her desire oozing into his conscious. But she pushed him away.

'Hold that thought!'

'But …'

'No buts! We've been travelling for the best part of two days. If you think I'm letting you anywhere near me until we've both had a shower, you've got another thing coming!'

'We could shower together?' said James in hope.

'We could, but we're not going to.' Lauren asserted. 'You go first.' With that, she thrust James a towel and he wandered to the bathroom. He showered and groomed himself, ready for the special moment. Then he stepped back into the bedroom with a towel hiding his modesty. It was too early in their relationship to be wandering around the room naked. He slipped under the cotton sheets and they felt welcoming and cosy. As he nestled into the pillow, he strained in vain to catch any glimpse at all of Lauren's naked frame as she stepped, under expert cover, into the shower.

The thought of her standing naked under the shower was tantalising. He could feel the passion trying to burst out of him. He longed to caress that pearly skin, to feel himself inside her. He knew it would be special. They would be making love with their bodies and minds and the thought drove him wild. In the moments when he wasn't imagining the love they would make all night, his mind was full of hope. He felt like destiny was within his grasp. The excitement of being in Teruel had pushed any sense of foreboding into the background. Right then, he couldn't have been happier.

He fought sleep bravely for several minutes before surrendering to a dreamy vision of future life in Teruel. It was a dream in which there was nothing other than their rapturous togetherness. So deep was James' slumber, that he didn't even notice Lauren return from the shower, didn't feel her climb onto the bed and spoon against his radiating body. He had no sense of her nestling her face into the back of his neck as she too welcomed sleep. Exhausted from the journey, they both lay there, sculpted together. Even the thumping water hammer from distant showers, couldn't wake them.

★

The staccato rip of a snare drum filled the air. Its beat spat incessantly across the town of Plymouth, carried on the fierce and perennial south-westerly wind. It was Drake's drum. Warning the English of the first sighting of the Armada. Edward Cooper rushed to the cliff top and stared out to sea. He gasped at the sight before him. Hundreds of Spanish galleons lined the horizon in full sail, their broad, white sails seeming to rise from the channel like icebergs in the distance.

The town responded to the snare with total panic. A fleet of that size had never been seen before, and the English sailors weren't ready. Most of them were still drunk from the night before and lay sprawled across the long wooden benches of the Minerva Inn, where Edward had left them. Luckily, the town, the country, had Sir Francis Drake, though at first he had seemed more interested in his game of bowls than in facing the Spanish. Eventually, after pocketing his victory purse, he roused the intoxicated rabble and launched the English fleet. All the while, the booms of Spanish cannon echoed across the channel like distant thunder. Those first few volleys were a challenge, a call to arms. The Armada was still out of range but Edward and the townsfolk watched on from their elevated positions on the seafront Hoe. They were euphoric as the first response smashed from the side of the *Golden Hind* and ripped through the rigging of the closest galleon. That was the trigger for the rest of the fleet to open fire and, from then on, the deafening clump of cannon shook the buildings of Plymouth to their very timbers. One by one, the Spanish ships were battered. They were like lambs to the slaughter, helplessly within range of the pride of England, but out of range themselves. They couldn't land a blow. Instead they slunk away to Calais, leaving death and debris floating side by side on the swollen surface of the sea.

That night there were celebrations across Plymouth, the like of which had never been seen. The revellers consumed barrels of weaker malty ale, which they nicknamed Range-Finder. Then they graduated to the stronger double-double, which became known as

Spaniard's Demise. Edward was in his element. He was
the ale-conner and never had he been so important. His
job was to make sure the ale was fresh. Unlike continental
beer, ale wasn't made with hops and that meant that
barrels had to be drunk quickly, before their contents
turned. As soon as each was opened it had to be sampled
to make sure it was fit to serve to customers. Innkeepers
had been known to be murdered for serving bad ale, so the
testing was sometimes a matter of life and death. Edward
was experienced and had been doing it since he was ten.
He could usually tell when it was off by sight and smell
alone, but he was still expected to check it the traditional
way. Patrons wouldn't just accept his word, they wanted
to see for themselves that the ale was good to drink. He
put on his leather britches and opened a barrel. Then he
poured some across an empty bench as a group of thirsty
patrons began to harangue him.

'Sit on it boy!'

'Come on, you lazy toad, we want to know if it's
good!'

As he had done a thousand times before, Edward
lowered his backside onto the bench and felt the moisture
seep into his leather britches. He had learned enough
about his role to know that, when he was checking the
beer, he was the centre of attention. Everyone in the
tavern was watching him and he began to play to the
crowd, spurred on by the Spaniard's Demise he had

sampled throughout the day. He began to raise his arms in the air, encouraging the chants of the eager crowd, who were enjoying his antics. This was his favourite part of the job. He loved having all eyes on him. There was an art to his work. To prolong the excitement, to milk the crowd, took skill. Each time he sat, he knew he had the entire tavern in the palm of his hand.

Finally, when the frenzied mob was fit to burst, he stood. Euphoria erupted across the tavern. The fact that he was able to stand meant the ale could be drunk. Had his britches stuck to the bench, it would have meant the ale was past its best and needed to be tipped into the streets. Stools and benches flew over as merry drinkers rose to their feet excitedly. Several of them purchased drinks for Edward and he consumed them steadily through the day in between his regular performances. He was in his element. It was the time of his life.

The party continued long into the night. Edward's britches became so wet that they stuck to the back of his thighs and chaffed his skin painfully. But he didn't care. The sweet smell of victory hung in the air. He felt full of vitality. His celebrity that evening had filled him with confidence, and he felt he could do anything. Achieve anything. It was a new feeling for him. Up until then he'd been riddled with self-doubt. It was difficult for most sixteen-year-olds in 1588; they were considered adults and had to make their own way among older, stronger rivals.

They were expected to grow up fast, indeed sixteen was a good age to make it to, and almost half the population died before they reached that particular landmark. That didn't make it any easier to break into a harsh and violent world though, one in which men dominated through wealth and strength. Through birth, Edward lacked the first, and he had yet to be old enough to achieve the second.

Edward determined that he would seize the moment. It didn't matter that it was the middle of the night. For him, the time was right. He needed to act. Molly. It was time to tell her how he felt. Mary Baker, or Molly, as everyone knew her, was the most astonishing girl he had ever met. She had hair as black as the timbers of the Minerva and eyes as green as the shallow seas that swirled across the volcanic rocks at the foot of Drake's Island in the Plymouth Sound. Molly and her father had moved to Plymouth recently and had set up a bakery at the other end of Looe Street, just down the road from the Minerva. That meant that Edward set eyes on her every day on his way to work. It was his favourite part of each morning. He would pause very deliberately outside, hoping desperately for a glimpse of her through the window. Even the sight of the back of her head was to be treasured, such was his desire for her. Then one day she had smiled at him and from then on, he was hopelessly lost. He would never forget the way that smile had made him feel. The glorious green of her eyes had glistened in the morning light as she flashed them in his direction. They seemed to be beckoning him to kiss her. It was truly magical. From then on Edward loitered even longer as he passed the bakery each day, waiting, hoping for a repeat. It was always forthcoming. He felt an air of expectance, of anticipation, whenever he approached. It made his heart skip with excitement at the thought of what was about to happen.

He had never spoken to Molly though. The timing had just never been right. They both worked long hours. In the mornings as he walked past, she was working tirelessly under her father's instruction, and it was always late in the evenings when he returned, through the black and festering streets that were filled with rotting vegetables, vagabonds and vermin. He thought of her asleep behind that small ebony door, and he dreamed that one day he would enter as her husband and lie next to her, waking her from her slumber with a kiss before making love. But that was all it was, a dream. Until tonight. It was different tonight. The air was purposeful and confidence oozed through his being. He would walk right up to that door. He would knock and holler until it opened, and then he would demand to see Molly.

That was the plan, but the reality was different. He walked along Looe Street, doing his best to avoid puddles and the slop that accumulated in the unmade street. All the while he prepared himself mentally for what he was about to do, rehearsing his assertive demand in his head.

He would not be denied this opportunity to unlock everything he desired in the world. When he reached the Baker's house his eyes widened with surprise. The door was ajar. All manner of thoughts jumped into his mind. His nerves were on edge. It wasn't normal to leave an outside door open like that. There were too many thieves, too many who were desperate and destitute, to trust they would leave you alone. Of all nights, tonight was the worst to do it. Every possible protector in the town was inebriated. There would never be a better opportunity for someone to take advantage of an open door.

Edward nudged the door gently and it creaked open far enough that he could peer through the gap and into the shop. There, lying face down on the floor was George Baker, Molly's dad. The room reeked of ale and he was snoring like a creaking rope on a speeding Spanish galleon. Edward relaxed a little and tried to sit George up. He was a large man and moving him was a challenge.

Help! Edward! Help me! Please!

He dropped George immediately and threw his hands to the sides of his temples in shock. A woman's voice was speaking directly into his head. Fear was his initial response. It was unnatural, unearthly. Shivers shuddered through his body at the thought of what had happened. He felt like fleeing.

Help! Edward! I need you!

There it was again. He had never heard her voice but

he knew this was Molly. He didn't understand how he knew that, but he had no doubt. There was an urgency to her words too. In that split second, he decided it didn't matter that this might be the devil's work. He needed to help her. He could feel danger and he could smell fear. He glanced quickly around the bakery and grabbed a rolling pin. It felt weighty in his hand as he headed for the stairs. This was a modern house where the open hall at the front had been covered over to create a room above. That was the perfect layout for a shop. It meant the family could live upstairs.

Edward crept upwards. The voice in his head continued.

Hurry! Hurry! Edward!

He began to run. He leapt the stairs two at a time. As he ascended, he began to hear a woman's muffled cry and the creaking of a struggle. He launched himself into the room. At that moment, he was terrified of what lay behind the door. He knew that whatever was happening meant danger for him too but it didn't matter. If anything happened to Molly, he would never be able to live with himself. That thought filled him with courage.

On the bed in front of him, Molly was struggling with a balding, drunken assailant. He held her mouth closed with his left hand and tugged at her skirts with his right. Molly was pummelling him with all her limbs, protecting herself as fiercely as she could, but it was a battle she was losing. Edward acted instantly. He bolted into the room. The floor complained as he placed his weight on it and the subsequent groan alerted Molly's assailant. Startled, he looked at Edward but couldn't avoid the swinging rolling pin as it smashed across his face. With a squeal of pain, he fell backwards and slumped to the floor. Edward recognised him. It was Benedict Maycott, a walrus of a man. The Justice of the Peace.

Edward approached Molly. She flung her arms around him and her touch felt magical. Her skin seemed to tingle against his. He held her tight. He could feel her body shudder with tears as relief and the sense of safety sank in. He embraced her until her heart slowed and her tears ebbed. All the while, he reassured in whispering tones that she was okay. That she was safe. Eventually she spoke.

'Thank you, Edward. You saved my life.'

'And I would do it again Molly. I will never let anything happen to you.'

'You mean that?'

'With all my heart. I have loved you since the moment I first saw you. I would die for you.' With that, Molly kissed him. It was the greatest moment of Edward's life. He wanted to hold her forever. To kiss her for an eternity. He could die quite happily there. It was blissful ignorance. Love without questions. But there were questions that he needed to ask. Needed to understand. He tore himself away reluctantly.

'How …'

'… I was waiting for this.'

'How did you do that? Speak into my head, I mean.' Edward didn't notice that Maycott had begun to stir behind him.

'I'm not sure I know how, Edward. All I know is that you and I are meant to …' She was interrupted by Benedict Maycott making a break for the door. Edward went to stop him but Maycott pushed him away and was off down the stairs before he could recover. There was nowhere to run, thought Edward. Plymouth was a town of no more than five thousand. And Maycott was well known.

'We're meant to what?' Edward prodded.

'We're meant to be together.'

'Now that's an idea that I love,' Edward smiled, 'but how do you know?'

'It's difficult to explain. Take my hand. Let me show you.' Edward took Molly's hand and instantly their connection fizzed like a gunpowder fuse. Memories of other lives began to flood into his mind. Not just glimpses, entire lifetimes. He was inundated by wave after wave of thoughts, smells, sounds. He felt he was going to explode. It was too much. He couldn't hold onto any piece of information for long enough to process it, so quick was the next. As his consciousness began to shut down, he focused on two names. Diego. Isabel. And then it all went black.

Edward woke to pounding footsteps on the stairs. So

many pairs of feet that they surely couldn't all be on the stairs at the same time.

'Molly! Wake Up! Something's happening!' Molly opened her eyes. The sound of stamping shoes echoed through the house.

'Well, what have we here?' It was Benedict Maycott. He had drummed up a lynch mob of twenty drunkards, who all streamed up the stairs behind him. 'Satan moves in mysterious ways indeed!'

'Satan? What are you talking about Maycott? I think we know who's closest to the devil here, don't we? You're the one who tried to rape Molly! What does that make you?' Edward was livid.

'I did not. You must be mistaken,' Maycott declared indignantly.

'Then how did you get that welt on your head? Are you denying that I had to knock you to the floor with this rolling pin?' Maycott looked at the group behind him.

'Do not believe what he says. He is protecting the girl.'

'He is telling the truth!' declared Molly.

'Beware the voice of Satan! Remember the word of our Lord! 2 Corinthians, 11-14. *And no wonder, for even Satan disguises himself as an angel of the light.*'

'What are you saying?' said Edward.

'That I bore witness to Mary Baker performing an unnatural act. Do you deny that she spoke straight into your mind? I heard you declare that myself!'

'And when would that be, Maycott? When you weren't here trying to rape Molly?'

'The circumstances are not important and I will not discuss them with an ale-conner. She is a witch. Seize her!' He looked at the men behind him and they rushed forward as one. The first two had to overpower Edward and the third and fourth dragged a kicking and screaming Molly out of the bedroom by her hair. Her knuckles scraped against the rough daub walls on the way down. All the way she screamed and protested her innocence, and the shrill sound of her terror burned Edward's ears as he struggled against the burly men who held him down.

As Molly's screams faded, the men released him. Edward shot past them like a cannonball and flew down the stairs. George Baker still lay unconscious on the floor, oblivious to the fate of his daughter. Edward doubted whether the man would ever drink again when he found out what had happened. It was hard enough for Edward and he had been actively trying to save Molly. He couldn't imagine what it would be like waking up to find that your daughter had been taken in the night, while you were comatose.

The streets were unusually busy. Houses were empty, and their occupants lined what was usually a street reserved for the rats at this hour. Most held rush-lights, and the flickering flames spluttered against the prevailing wind. The hum of the murmuring multitude was like a chant in the chill of the night. They were talking about Molly, Edward knew. The word had spread like wildfire. Not one of them mentioned the accusation against Benedict Maycott. It sickened Edward that a man like that could abuse his position. That he could be so trusted by the townsfolk that even an allegation of rape washed over him. Maycott had been clever, Edward realised. The mere mention of a witch was enough to trigger ancient fears that had been indoctrinated into every church-goer in the land. Quoting the scriptures had been an act of genius. It was evidence that God approved of his actions and that he should not be questioned. Molly was in a great deal of trouble.

She was held in the prison at the castle overnight, awaiting trial the following morning. Edward spent the night on the steps outside, steps that in thirty-two years' time would see the departure of the Pilgrim Fathers aboard the *Mayflower*. From there, he could feel Molly's quivering presence. He reached out to her with his mind and they connected through those thick prison walls.

I don't know how to save you Molly.

Neither do I Edward. Do you know what they're planning?

No. They haven't said. Whatever it is, it will be in the morning.

Then stay with me tonight. Let me feel your presence. Let me share what little time I may have left with you.

Of course, Molly. I wouldn't leave you to face this alone.

Whatever happens to you, I will be with you.

The sun's rise the following morning was thwarted by cloud. Dawn brought only a half-light that reflected the darkness in Edward's heart. He hadn't slept a wink and he was glad not to have, he wanted to make the most of every moment with Molly.

They came for her just after dawn. A similar, unruly mob to the one from the previous night. Edward recognised the two thugs who had sat on him while Molly was wrenched from his grasp. He wanted to harm them, to make them pay. They had rendered him helpless while his future was ripped away from him, but that wouldn't help him, he knew. Besides, he had a higher purpose now. Molly had passed on everything that she knew and it was now his role to make sure the power, the love, continued. He had no idea how he would do that, or where he needed to go. Right now, his main concern was for her.

She was taken in procession to the tidal banks of the River Plym, where she was paraded mercilessly before the masses. The townsfolk had gathered once more and were jostling for prime position. They wanted to hear, to see. It wasn't every day someone in Plymouth was accused of witchcraft. A ducking stool had been set up at the river bank. It was like a giant seesaw. One end, the part that hung over the mighty river, had a crude chair fashioned to it, the other was weighed down with sandbags. A hooded custodian stood around it. Clearly his role was to operate it.

Edward had seen one used before for punishment, usually for theft or other crimes. It was a tool for humiliation and its presence brought him hope. Neither he nor Molly cared about the thoughts of the people. The most important thing was that she stayed alive.

'Men and women of Plymouth. As your Justice of the Peace it is my role to ensure that perpetrators of crimes are tried and punished according to English law.' Maycott strutted pompously on the river bank. He jutted his head forward like a prized rooster. He was overweight and bald. An odious man, full of his own importance. He clearly relished his role in the judiciary. He had power over life and death and, to him, that made him a god. He could do what he liked, was feared and respected. Untouchable. This was his opportunity to rid himself of a mistake that otherwise might come back to haunt him. He continued, 'Before you, stands Mary Baker. She is accused of witchcraft. With my own eyes, I saw her talk straight into the mind of Edward Cooper. There can be no doubt over what I witnessed.'

'Enough of this lunacy!' George Baker had made an appearance. He looked as though he was still in state of shock from the events that had unfolded while he was incapacitated. 'Molly is no more a witch than I am.'

'You should be a little more careful with your words, Baker. Did you not hear me say that it was I who witnessed this act? Do you doubt me? If she is no more a witch than you are and I can prove that she is a witch, what does that make you? Seize him!' Baker made as if to run, but was rapidly engulfed by the crowd. They had no tolerance for witchcraft in the fine town of Plymouth. Baker had to be tried, just as his daughter would be.

'Based on the evidence I have presented,' Maycott continued, 'I have decided that Mary Baker should be tried by the ducking stool.' gasps slowly made their way through the watching horde. Few of them understood what trial by ducking stool meant. They had seen it used for petty crime but not for witchcraft. As word spread, so the murmuring increased.

'This is the test for witchcraft,' Maycott went on. 'It has been proven that a witch cannot be drowned. Mary Baker will be strapped to the stool and held underwater until the candle burns to this notch that has been scratched upon it. If she survives, then she is a witch and will be burned at the stake. If, on the other hand, she drowns, her name will be cleared and she will be buried in sacred ground.'

Edward was horrified. If he had understood correctly, it meant that, either way, Molly would be dead. He went to step forward. He had to stop this farce. Maycott couldn't be allowed to get away with this.

No Edward! You mustn't go against him. Your duty is to keep the line alive. You must forget about me. Promise me.

I can't! I won't give up on you like that!

You must. What we have is more important than either of us. It needs to outlast us both!

After Molly was strapped to the ducking stool, at Maycott's command the hooded operator removed the weights and her mass thrust the chair end under the water with an almighty splash. Cheers rang out around the crowd as the candle began to burn down. All Edward could think of was Molly. He would never be with her. He would never again kiss those lips.

Every flicker of that faltering flame seemed a lifetime. Edward felt helpless thinking about Molly, who he knew would be drowning. He needed to do something, anything. He knew he couldn't save her, but he couldn't abide the idea that he would let anyone wrench her from him without a fight.

Instinctively he sprinted past the flabbergasted Maycott and threw himself into the river. At first, he could feel Molly urging him to return, but when she realised what he was doing she beckoned him towards her. As he reached her, he could see her straining for air below the murky water.

He took a deep breath and forced himself below the surface. He gazed once more into those awesome eyes that seemed to light up the river. He could see and feel the love that she felt for him. He clasped his hands around her cheeks to steady himself, and put his lips to hers. Molly smiled as she breathed her last breath into his heartbroken mouth. With that, Edward felt Molly's life ebb away. His instant misery was deeper than the mighty Plym around him. He felt he had nothing more to live for. He knew he couldn't return to shore. He'd been seen cavorting with a witch, even if her death proved her innocence. He had only one choice. He gave a parting look at Molly's sallow and lifeless face and let go, allowing the river to sweep him away to the sea.

*

James woke with a jolt and gasped for air. His eyes were filled with Edward's tears. Tears that had combined with the waters of the salty estuary and formed a cocktail of grief. He had heard the screams of Benedict Maycott in the distance, demanding that someone jump in and capture the witch cavorter. Once again, James had felt the deep sorrow of tragedy. In those waking moments, he knew the odds were stacked against him and Lauren.

He looked over at the clock. He knew it was accurate because, like all hotel rooms, the clock had been wrong and he'd had to set it himself when they arrived. It was just after eleven. As he gathered his waking thoughts and tried to shake off the doom that swept through his dreams, James revelled in the glorious clinch in which the sleeping Lauren held him. He could feel her gentle breath on his neck and he relished the shower-fresh scent of her skin. He was cold yet warm at the same time. The front of him had been licked by the icy tongue of the Aragonian night that had crept through the open window, but his back sweated gently from the warmth he shared with Lauren. He turned towards her and held her close, caressing her dark and still-damp hair as it cooled the pillow on which she lay. This was the scene that James had dreamed of so often in the year since he had met Lauren. Of course, he had hoped the surroundings would be finer and he'd always factored in a romantic dinner before they returned to their room to make love, though their spoiled lunch in Barcelona was the closest they would get to that.

For a few moments, James just enjoyed the anticipation. It was electric. The thought of touching Lauren for the first time. Of seeing that beautiful petite frame in all its glory. The excited frenzy they would build to as they explored each other. He had thought about this so often since that day he'd first set eyes on Lauren, in his mind he had rehearsed it a thousand times. James knew his lines well and his fingers began their dialogue as they danced across her body's stage and started to cue her choreographed stirring.

Her skin was velvet to his touch, softer, warmer than James had ever imagined. He could feel Lauren's quickening pulse as his fingertips woke her senses. Once more he watched as sleep cleared from her eyes, which glistened a deeper, browner green in the light from the streets below. James leaned forward and kissed her receptive lips. They parted instantly.

Seconds later, Lauren pulled away abruptly.

'What was that?' she seemed fully awake and alert. She pushed James away and sat up.

'What? I didn't hear anything?' he leaned in to kiss Lauren once more.

'Not a sound, a feeling. Can you not sense something?' Lauren resisted him once more and was reaching for her clothes.

James could feel a number of senses coursing through his body and right now frustration was screaming the loudest. He quelled it as best he could and tried to tune into what Lauren was feeling but it was difficult to feel anything other than desire. He concentrated harder. Sure enough, there was something there, something out of place. This was supposed to be a scene of joy, laughter, pleasure and love. It was his time with Lauren. The time they would seal eight hundred years of love. There was no place in that room for anything else, yet he sensed doom. And it was growing. Steadily. Whispering a message of death. Within minutes he could feel it above everything else. It had conquered his passion to the point where he couldn't shut it out. Now that he'd felt it, it was eating away at him like a tapered candle burning slowly to its base. He wanted to concentrate on Lauren, to return to the expectant embrace that she had broken off. But he couldn't.

'I can feel it. It's awful. Whatever it is, I don't like it.' All the dread that James had been suppressing since Paris, dread that had been grinding away at him, now threatened to break through. 'I feel like we're in danger.'

'Me too, James.' Lauren was now dressed and motioned to James to do the same.

'What are you thinking?' James asked, hopping from leg to leg as he hurriedly pulled on his jeans.

'That we need to get out of here! Now!' she demanded.

James knew she was right. There was no question about it at all. Something terrible was about to happen. He could feel it. They had to get out of there. His sixth sense was screaming at him to flee. It was a case of leave and survive or stay and die.

They crept across the room. All the time the portent was becoming stronger. It was vengeful. Vile. Furious. They could feel a presence. Closing in on them. They knew it was now or never. They sneaked out of the room, mindful not to allow the door to slam. James was sure that whatever was after them could feel their presence too, but he wasn't going to make it easy for anyone to follow them.

They made for the emergency exit at the end of the corridor. Panic began to constrict their airways. The walls seemed to narrow as they passed, closing in on them like encircling raiders. Lauren rattled the bar on the fire door.

It wouldn't budge. Her rattling become more and more frantic as she began to panic. It was wedged shut. God help the guests in this place if there was ever a fire, James thought.

'Stand back!' he breathed assertively.

Crunch!

He brought his foot down onto the bar with all his weight and the door flung wide open. The crash of the yielding bar echoed through the empty corridors. The smash of the door on the metal railings outside filled the silent streets. The midnight wind thrust the dark air inside. It splayed the wispy net coverings inwards, and they danced like spectres.

James stepped out onto the iron staircase, five storeys up. Lauren followed quickly behind. The wind whipped across the rooftops and battered their exposed bodies. They crouched against its onslaught, fighting to retain their balance.

Mindful that he might glimpse a pursuer, James looked back. He thought that perhaps he would feel more comfortable if he could confirm what he was facing, though deep down he felt he knew already. As he turned, to his horror the illuminated corridor went black. Whatever was there was shielded by shadow. He turned back to Lauren. The steps were no longer visible.

Lauren led the way down the clanging steps, heading down towards the street lights below. Each glared with gloomy halos that blinded her advance. Her pace increased as her eyes grew accustomed to the lack of light. She began to take the stairs two at a time, stumbling occasionally. Each time she felt herself slip, she reached back to James. His supportive touch steadied her. She could feel fear flowing through his fingertips but she also sensed his resolve and determination. An unwavering courage, born from his love for her. At that moment, James seemed so strong. She knew he would do anything for her. That thought seemed to dissolve her own fear.

At the end of each staircase was a platform. At those landings, they basked briefly in the dim, golden, sodium lights that glowed through the fire-exit windows. Then those lights went out too. Floor by floor, as they descended, the hotel became shrouded in darkness. By the time they reached the pavement below, it was in complete shadow.

At the bottom of the fire escape they stood in momentary indecision. They were on an unfamiliar pavement in a town they barely knew. Where was best to go? Which way would be safe? Simultaneously they reached the same conclusion. Light. Head for the light. They sprinted to the brightest street, following their instincts. Occasionally James glanced over his shoulder and could see nothing but black. His heart was raging inside him. It was commanding his lungs to give it more oxygen, like a steam-train driver to an exhausted coalman.

James stopped for breath but Lauren dragged him forward. They pressed on urgently.

As they passed each light it flickered and died as a wave of obscurity seemed to follow them. Before long it overtook them and swamped the town into complete darkness. Alarms began to ring, accusing false burglars.

They could see nothing. The moon had forgotten them that night. It was so black that, at first, they ran with their arms stretched out in front of them to protect against any objects. In a short while their eyes began to register shapes and images. They were at least able to see the road.

In a town they knew well, they would have still been able to navigate, but Teruel was hardly that. If it hadn't changed since the thirteenth century they would have been fine, but in the modern world their ancient knowledge was more misleading than useful. They turned this way and that. Still mindful that something was on their tail. Something powerful. Something violent. They couldn't see or hear anything chasing them. But they could feel it. It was an enemy that brought with it a forgotten fear.

In their frenzied flight, they hit several dead ends. Each time they did so, James and Lauren doubled back, mindful that every wrong turn would lessen the gap to their pursuer. It was hopeless. They knew they'd never be able to outrun anyone; they had no idea where they were going. There was only one option. Hide.

James began to test every door they passed. If there were two close together, Lauren did the same. All the time they felt death closing in on them. Invading their minds. Laughing at their fear.

Most doors were blocked by ornate iron security doors. The windows were heavily shuttered; it was the Spanish way, but it couldn't have been less helpful. Both of them began to pray they would find safety soon. They surged onwards, surfing the giant waves of fear that were barrelling over them.

SLAP!

There was a noise ahead of them.

SLAP!

There it was again.

SLAP!

It grew louder as they closed in.

SLAP!

James recognised it for what it was. A door, banging in the wind! It was what he had prayed for. They might be safe after all. He ran towards it and blocked its next slam. He pushed at it, but it only opened wide enough for a leg or an arm. Something was restricting it. He'd have to force it. He lowered his shoulder and charged at the door with all his weight.

CRACK! It flew open and the noise startled a poor vagrant on the pavement, who screamed from her mountain of blankets.

'In here!' James commanded Lauren, mindful that this represented their only option.

They threw themselves inside the building and barricaded the door shut with whatever objects they could find nearby. Some wood. A tool box. Whatever this place was supposed to be, right now it seemed to be a building site.

They gasped for air in the darkness and were rewarded with a sawdusty concoction that would have to do the job. Their startled eyes began to gently make out shapes in a room that was even darker than the passageways outside. As they stumbled through the room, James lost count of the number of times he tripped on something unseen. It was no good. They needed light. And they needed something to defend themselves with.

They searched with their fingers, looking for torches, weapons, even candles. Anything that could be useful. Their hands fluttered across dusty surfaces and their mouths spluttered at the ensuing result. Shelved sentinels slammed to the floor as blundering hands disturbed their peaceful sleep. Each time something fell, James and Lauren flinched with fear. All the time, they felt their silent pursuer closing in.

James' frantic fingers felt a cloth and his hands burrowed inside. He hoped desperately that something useful lay underneath. His fingers jumped back as they touched something cold. No, moist. No, cold and moist.

Cold like stone. He returned them to their task and they ran over a smooth and icy surface that had been carefully carved. A more trained finger probably could have developed a mental picture but his panicked fumbling gave little insight. He threw off what he assumed was a dust sheet.

'James. I've found some candles. Lots of them!' Lauren whispered in relief.

'Please tell me you've found a match too?'

'Wait.' The pause was interminable. 'Yes!'

The phosphorescent sparkle snapped into the chilly air and blinded James' darkened eyes. Lauren reached forward to the candles and began to light them one by one. As she did so, she turned to face James and gasped, pointing down to where he knew his hands had been exploring. Uneasily James' eyes followed the path of her outstretched hand and there, beneath his fingers, reaching out to each other in eternity, were the tombs of the lovers of Teruel.

16

THEY WATCHED AS the shadows danced a mischievous ballet across the muted marble stage. With each flicker, the flames teased Lauren with the details of what lay in front of her. It was a place she had dreamed of. One she had expected to inspire her. To engage her. Ever since she had read about the tombs, she had longed to lay eyes on these representations of Diego and Isabel, and, since she had shared the story with James, he'd been the same. But neither of them had wanted it to be like this.

The eternity of the lovers' togetherness filled them both with awe. At the same time, the desperation with which the figures reached to each other riddled them with a deep and inherited sadness. The tomb, the lovers. They were the reason James and Lauren had chosen to make Teruel their home. It had been as though coming together in the place where it had all started would right an ancient miscarriage of fate. Now, in that darkened mausoleum, there was an aptness to the lovers' tragic end. It wrenched away what little hope James still held on to.

Deep in her heart, Lauren knew it was no coincidence they were there. Of all the places for her and James to confront fate, there could be none more appropriate. Something far greater than either of them could have imagined was at work here. It was distinctly unnerving. They each felt like pawns who had advanced in a game full of promises and were now being sacrificed in order to allow a grander piece to succeed.

A sense of the supernatural was everywhere. It did nothing to calm their already rampaging hearts. They had thought that they were fleeing from Lauren's husband. How wrong they had been. In fact, a psychic fear had been tracking their thoughts like a spy satellite. It had driven them to a predetermined destination. The only question that remained was whether it was good or bad that they were in their current location. Neither James nor Lauren were sure they knew the answer. They were scared. Very scared.

There was little time to absorb the freakish coincidence either. The air began to reek of impending death. Evil began to seep into the stale air. It sneaked its gnarly fingers into the cavorting shadows and toyed with the light. It sucked the oxygen from the room and left them breathless. It was a constricting doom that seized their throats and screamed in their faces. Whatever it was, it was approaching. Fast.

They knew they were about to face a ferocious fear, and they would do it together. They felt stronger as a team. Lauren gave James something to fight for. He knew he would stand in front of Lauren against whatever foe they faced. She was his courage. Protecting her was his single focus.

Destiny brought a certain calmness to Lauren. She felt there was a reason they were there. Whatever happened, she would accept it. Something far greater than her was at work here. It had kept the love of Diego and Isabel alive for centuries. Despite the tragedy of Ilse and Joachim, Sabine and Karsten, Molly and Edward, it had survived. Fate was pulling the strings. It would decide what happened next, she was sure of it.

In the flickering light, they scrabbled once more for weapons but found little more than candlesticks. James discarded the deformed stub of a burnt-out candle and gripped its iron holder. Its weight was reassuring. He whirled it in a wide arc, in aimless practice. It whistled through the air. His body quivered with adrenalin's peculiar flutter. Whatever was out there, he needed to face it. He was ready. As ready as he would ever be. He ignored the way his hand trembled as he swished those practice swings. A thought made him smirk. Here was he, James Jordan, in the mausoleum with a candlestick. It sounded like a game of Cluedo.

There was an imminence to the musty air. The candles shrank expectantly. The lovers knew that in just moments everything they feared would be upon them.

SMACK!

The door smashed against the makeshift barricade James had placed in front of it and bounced awkwardly back into place. It had thwarted a first attack but he knew it would yield to the next.

THWACK!

It crashed inwards and obliterated the barrier. Instantly, the darkened breeze extinguished the frolicking flames that were closest to it. The room descended further into gloom. James heard the familiar scream of the shivering vagrant as the splintering door disturbed her icy dream once more.

'I love you Lauren,' James muttered, half-declaring his affection and half-fuelling his own valour.

'I love you too, James.' Lauren sounded confident. Prepared to defend herself.

'I am sick of your fucking love!' boomed a throaty Spanish malevolence.

'Wh-who are you? Wh-what do you want?' James stuttered. His courage was trying to desert him but he clung manfully to its billowing cloak.

'You know who I am. I showed you my face in Paris. And in Barcelona.' He looked towards Lauren. 'Did you not recognise the smile of your husband? I am Don Pedro de Azagra, the first Lord of Albarracín.' With that he stepped forward into what was left of the shimmering light. His black Iberian eyes seemed to stay in the shadow and he oozed a menace that James had never before encountered, or wished to experience again.

'No. You look like him, but you are not him. You can't be. You're no older than my mum,' Lauren countered with a confidence that belied how she was feeling. At that moment, James couldn't have loved Lauren more. She was so strong. Heroic. He could have sworn that the floor shook with the Spaniard's maniacal laughter as he spat his retort.

'You know nothing, woman. You have your empty memories but you have not lived these years as I have. Every waking day these past eight hundred years I have fought to end the infernal lineage that these two adulterers handed down. Today is the day I will forever rest.'

'They weren't adulterers. They'd loved each other since they were children. It was just poor fortune that kept them apart!' James had found his voice again. He was surprised that his words didn't shake as he spoke them.

'Don't speak to me about the sickening love my wife shared with the Marcilla boy. I had lusted after her for years and each time her damned father refused to marry her to me.'

'That's because he promised Diego the chance to prove himself. He knew how much they loved each other.' James was feeling bolder by the minute. He was starting to become convinced that fate was presenting him and Lauren a chance to end this. To break free from centuries of tragedy.

'His word meant nothing to me. I told him to fuck the

promise he had made to a pauper. Still he wouldn't bend. I made life hard for him. I destroyed his business. In the end, I held a knife to his throat.'

'I only wish he'd given Diego longer. I saw the way you treated Isabel in that one night you were married. You didn't deserve her. She should have been with Diego!' James could hear the fight in Lauren's voice.

'I do not care for the opinion of a harlot.'

'If they hadn't somehow confused their dates you'd never have even married her!' she continued.

'You think that's what happened do you?' he laughed with total hostility.

'Well what did happen then? You seem to know everything. Tell us,' James challenged.

'There was no mix-up. I knew he was coming back. So did Isabel. I could feel him. I could smell him. When they were together they stank, just like the two of you.'

'If she knew he was coming back, why did she marry you?' James probed.

'Her promise was her word. She had promised to marry me after five years, and she had to stick to it. She knew what I would do to her father if she didn't.'

'But it wasn't five years, was it?' James was becoming indignant now. This man had cheated people that James had never met, yet were now very important to him.

'No! It wasn't! But that was easy to fix. There were no watches or calendars. The only person who knew the date was the village priest. You'd be surprised at what they'll do for a couple of willing whores.'

'You had the dates changed! That's why Diego arrived a day late?'

'He wasn't late at all!' Don Pedro sneered. 'But she didn't know that and it gave me great pleasure to see her misery when he failed to show. I made sure we were married at dawn the next morning. Finally, she was mine.'

'You bastard. They had a right to be together,' Lauren spat.

'They had no rights. I am the Lord of Albarracín and I get what I want. Then that infernal boy had the cheek to turn up at my house and beg my wife for a kiss. I'd already told her what I would do to her, him and her family if she so much as touched him and the clever girl chose to listen. It was a shame he collapsed at her feet. If I'd got to him earlier I would have rammed my steel into his throat.'

'You did that anyway, you coward.' Don Pedro chose to ignore Lauren's insult.

'She was going to kill you that night,' added James.

'A wimp of a girl against a mighty lord? I think not. No. What my damned wife did was far, far worse than killing me.'

'How could her dying be worse for you?' James was angry at Don Pedro's complete disregard for Isabel's life.

'I'll tell you what she did that was worse, boy!' Don Pedro roared. 'It was bad enough that she never looked at me the way she did him. I could have lived with that. I vowed to make her love me. I had hoped that when he was dead we could at last be together. But even his death couldn't separate them. At least when she died too I thought I'd get some relief from their infernal coupling, but I didn't. The bitch passed on that sickening love to someone else.'

'Beatriz,' Lauren added.

'The moment she died, I felt a darkness enter me. I didn't know straight away but over time I began to sense their love was repeating. Beatriz stank of it. She was the very image of Isabel. She too refused my advances, despite her father's wishes. Wherever she went I was reminded of the two adulterers. It was then that I swore I would rid the world of their love. I followed Beatriz across Europe. Hunting her was easy, her stench was rotten to my nose. I knew she would find one like Diego, it was clear to me there were other forces at work. The day before they were to be married, I killed them as they slept in their separate rooms. I drank myself silly that night, celebrating that I had snuffed out this fucking love.'

'But you hadn't,' said Lauren triumphantly.

'No, I hadn't. She had passed it on somewhere along the road from Barcelona to Paris. I could smell it once more. The air was rotten with it. And so it went on. I have killed every one of them but it seems I have been cursed with eight hundred years of misery. Not a day goes past when I don't pray for release from this hell. Today, it must end.'

'Wait,' James felt he needed answers before he was prepared to die. 'I have more questions.'

'And why should I answer them, boy?'

'Because you're going to kill us anyway? What difference does it make to you? I want to know about the others.'

'Who?'

'You said you'd killed them all. How did you kill Joachim and Ilse? They were shot by police!'

'I shot them as they tried to cross the border. It was easy. Everyone thought it was the government's work.'

'And Sabine?' asked Lauren.

'I knew she was coming. I threatened all of the French fishermen that if they let her on board I'd kill their families. She had to go with Alvarado. She had no choice. I was waiting for her.'

'And Molly?'

'Molly Baker? Ha! Now that was a long time ago indeed. She was so stupid I didn't even have to kill her! She did it for me. At least I had the joy of being there to see her drown.'

'And how did you find us?' Lauren wanted to know.

'I've followed you since you were contaminated on the beach.'

'Sabine!' James exclaimed.

'She should have been dead. Even after I threw her unconscious into the sea, the whore was still able to pass on the love disease. I'll give your kind one thing. You keep coming.'

'And you're too late,' said James, seizing on an opportunity. 'We've already passed it on to the next generation.'

'Don't lie to me boy! I know you have not passed on your little precious. Today is the day of reckoning. Today the damned lineage will die. Then I will rest in peace. Finally!'

James was overwhelmed by sadness at the vitriolic story of how each of his forebears had been cheated of their destiny. They hadn't lost out to ill-fate as he had assumed, or to a conspiring universe that refused to allow them to be together. No, it was the spiteful revenge of an ancient foe that had murdered each and every one of them. The wonder of it all was that nature kept finding more foot soldiers to throw at this vengeful villain. James was beginning to see he really was part of an ancient tide.

Don Pedro was right about one thing though, thought James. They *were* the last, because they *had* failed to pass the story on to anyone else. They'd been so absorbed by their desire to be together, that at no stage had it occurred to them they needed to find their successors. Right now, if he killed both of them as he surely would, then the legacy they had been entrusted with would be no more. The fact that it would evolve in front of the tombs of Diego and Isabel made it even worse. Being a part of an irrepressible and ancient tide was comforting, but being responsible for its end was a terrible burden.

Don Pedro moved towards them with a psychopathic swagger. The confidence of a hundred slaughters made his stride so much more purposeful. He had no fear of James or Lauren, even though this encounter was so different to those that had come before. Never had he had the opportunity to kill the two descendants together. He looked like he was going to go about his business with enormous relish.

As he approached, James readied the candlestick in his right hand and considered his defence with an adrenalin fuelled clarity. He decided he would swing for Don Pedro's temple and implored Lauren to attack his legs. James felt that a two-pronged attack would either kill or seriously weaken their assailant. Don Pedro thudded forward and James drew back his weapon. He seemed to be approaching unarmed and that gave them an advantage.

Don Pedro was excited as he made a sneering move forward. He was relishing the fear he could feel in his prey. He was thirsty for finality. As he approached, he reached behind his back and with a slicing clatter, he withdrew a long-sword from behind his back. The same sword he had sliced into Diego's throat that dreaded day at Albarracín.

The hate that burned in his eyes glinted with the swinging blade as he ran it through James' midriff. James doubled with the scorching pain and, as he did so, Don Pedro thrust his knee into James' face and smashed his nose to smithereens. With a foot to his chest, he pushed James backwards between the two tombs. As he fell, he crashed into the almost-clasping hands and severed Isabel's from the wrist. It fell to the floor with a poignant clatter.

Don Pedro laughed at the destruction and stood over James with his sword raised. A hundred lives flashed before James in a collage of disparate stories. He knew this was the end. He was too young to die, but that made no difference. Time stood still as he waited for that final, agonising blow. But it never came. While Don Pedro stood there, Lauren swung her candlestick and smashed it into his head. He fell to the already-bloodied floor and grimaced as Lauren prepared for a further assault. James could see the fury on her face. All those times when she had been a helpless victim. She was determined that would never happen to her again. She marched forward. Kill or be killed. At the last minute, Don Pedro saw her impending attack. He thrust his sword towards her. It went straight into her chest and Lauren fell backwards, impaled on the sword.

Instantly James felt Lauren die. Her death fired like lightning through his body as she fell lifeless to the floor. Despair and hatred took over James' body in alternating currents. Don Pedro cackled in pained triumph as he slumped to his knees, nursing a gaping head wound.

James was lost. Everything he had wanted for this last year had been taken from him. He had nothing. For the first time, he really understood the despair that had flooded Isabel when Diego had died. He knew that life was no longer worth living. There could be nothing without Lauren.

He reached a distraught and shaky hand behind him, desperately searching for a weapon. He knocked over one of the candles and felt a lick of flame as it ignited the dust sheet. His fingers touched a familiar cool, wet stone. He clasped the heavy hand that had fallen, dragged himself to his feet and staggered towards Don Pedro. The Spaniard was clearly still in severe pain from the blow that Lauren had dealt him and was trying to get back to his feet. With one swing, James rammed the marble hand down onto the back of his despicable head and he slumped to the floor. Dead.

With his death, the fear in the room subsided but the shadow of death remained. James knew it was waiting for him too. He crawled towards his beloved Lauren and wept his last tears as he felt life ebbing away. He felt such agony, though the pain of what he had lost was far greater even than the physical distress. His ailing body screamed from the blow it had been dealt. But the emptiness in his mind was worse. He had lost Lauren. They had so fleetingly been together and now, not only would they never be together again, they had failed to keep the legend alive.

As darkness began to shroud James' body he remembered the vagrant. It seemed perverse that he should try to crawl towards her rather than stay and die with Lauren, but something inside him was insisting he do it. He crawled to the door, sliding across the bloodied tiles like a snake through a swamp. All the while, fire began to take hold. The smoke had James gasping and gurgling through his final breaths as he reached the door.

To his surprise, the vagrant was no longer huddled in her doorway. She was approaching the entrance. As she did so, James notice a familiar sway of her hair and glimpsed a flash of emerald as a brief gap in the clouds allowed the moonlight to photograph her. She was just a girl. No more than fifteen. But she could have been Lauren. She reached out a hand to him. As their hands clasped, James' life drained away through their connection.

17

THE HIGHS WERE unrivalled, the depths as profound. In a sea of such knowledge, understanding was drowned. Love battled sorrow for every breath, and fate endured tragedy, conquering death.

So it was, every day, thought Carmen Borrega, as she sipped her *café con leche*, which the Australians rather blandly referred to as a flat white. The ghosts of history haunted her very existence. They seized any unoccupied second and burst from their archive into her consciousness, distracting her from even the most menial of tasks. At night time, they ran riot as their vivid tales commandeered her subconscious and transported her through centuries, though whatever the age and irrespective of the setting, the outcome was always the same. What she carried was a burden of love and loss, hope and despair. But it was the love that made that millstone worth carrying, one that she had witnessed in those frightening yet precious moments at the mausoleum, thirteen years earlier. Back then, Carmen had felt the absolute love that James and Lauren had for each other. It was unwavering and fierce. Tender and explosive.

Since then, she learned that all those who had come before her shared the same intense infatuation with each other. The thought that it was now her turn to unlock that raw passion, to love another person with such ferocity, filled her with excitement.

Teruel was never far from her thoughts. It was the seismic epicentre of all that had happened, and its shockwaves kept coming and coming. It was an important location in fate's master plan, that much was clear, but for her it was more than that. It had been her home, one in which she had been happy too. When her thoughts weren't ripped away from her control, she often thought of her parents and the cramped apartment in the Calle Rio Jiloca, the dark and narrow street she knew so well. Whenever she pictured them, they were always sitting on their balcony, in the warmth of the evening, cursing the positioning of the flats on the other side of the road that blocked what would have been a stunning view of distant Albarracín. Carmen knew they were waiting for her, desperate to see her once more, frantic to find out what had become of their daughter in the decade since she had left. It was a shame she could never go back.

Even now, the tragedy that had unfolded in front of her at the mausoleum sent shivers down her short and slender spine. Time had not healed the scars that the deaths of James and Lauren had branded her with. With every breath, she still sucked in the despair that had filled the air at the moment James realised Lauren had been taken from him. The agonised scream with which it took form resounded in her eardrums like a tragic tinnitus, and his vengeful rage still scorched behind her eyes as she recalled him crashing the marble hand down onto Don Pedro's head. In that moment, she had been filled by an insistence that compelled her to the scene. With every cell in her body she remembered what had happened next. With his last breath, James had grasped her hand and a monstrous tidal wave of memory inundated her senses, rendering her unconscious.

When Carmen had stirred, her body was cold. Bitterly cold. Even though inside the tomb the flames were cavorting unchecked around the bodies, she couldn't feel any heat. Coldest of all had been her hand. When she looked down, she saw she was still clutching James' lifeless fingers. They were icy and grey. Stiff from death. Instinctively, she had dropped the hand and sprinted for home, gathering her blankets from the pavement as she hurtled past. Adrenalin and fear whipped her those few blocks home, helping her cover ten minutes of distance in half that time. When she reached the sanctity of the apartment, she scaled the balcony and sneaked inside. The house was freezing and the tiled floor, so useful in summer yet so cruel in the winter, reminded her of those frozen fingers with every step.

When she reached her room, Carmen dived under her

duvet and pulled it over her head, hopeful that by doing so she would finally find some warmth again. Deep down, she also hoped it would ward off the shadows she felt had followed her home. Within minutes, she began to thaw, but sleep eluded her.

In the morning, she had stirred, unrefreshed from the sleepless night and dehydrated from the rivers of tears that had flowed bountifully. She had hoped that the daylight would bring a comforting distance from the events of the night before, but the whole experience refused to leave her. Instead she was forced to go about her daily routines in spite of the way she felt, and under the watchful eye of the ghosts of her predecessors, who stalked her relentlessly.

Carmen was still troubled by how she came to be at the mausoleum that night. She recalled that it had been one of those days where a dark cloud had hung heavy over her head, refusing to shift. Its gloom had sucked all the colours out of her life. The soft, pink carnations that were in translucent bloom on the balcony had seemed to shrivel into shadow. The delight at just being alive that Carmen had felt every morning disappeared, replaced by a feeling she could only describe as dread, one that hung around her neck like a festering albatross.

Despite the oppressive haze, that day had followed a normal path, though it was one she trod with increasing trepidation. As the day wore on, the darkness surrounding her assumed an ever-growing air of inevitability. She could feel the manipulation of the fingers of fate as they furled around her. Throughout the day, she spurned their attempts to coerce and compel, until at bedtime she could bear it no longer. By that time, fate was screaming at her with an urgency that would not be ignored. It had worn her down progressively and was now demanding action. Knowing she had little choice, Carmen had thrown some belongings into a backpack, grabbed a blanket and sneaked out of the house.

Her parents, Maria-Carmen and Miguel, never knew what had happened that night. They noticed that, as the subsequent days passed, their eldest daughter became steadily more withdrawn and distracted, but attributed it to the natural distancing that the arrival of womanhood was bringing to her. Until the events at the mausoleum, Carmen had been a model student, but afterwards she was just too distracted to work. The truth was that everybody else became perfunctory and unnecessary. There were just too many thoughts, too many experiences, too many tragedies for her to explore. With her head full of such vivid experiences, there was no room for physics or chemistry, Spanish or maths. In the wider scheme of things, they just didn't seem important any more. Nothing she could learn at school could possibly change the past, or influence the future. What fate had promised her could not be improved by homework, could not be improved through knowledge. The incendiary love she now knew was out there, was perfect in every sense.

As a result, Carmen's schoolwork suffered, and she lost count of the number of times her parents were summoned for emergency meetings with the principal. Her younger sister Maria's antics meant that the three of them were unfortunately already on first-name terms— she had been expelled from the school a year earlier for taking money at knifepoint from a final-year student, and the whole school had been shocked by the thirteen-year-old's behaviour.

Maria of course delighted in her sister's downfall. She had lived in Carmen's shadow for years and had grown jealous of her achievements. The praise and reinforcement her sister had received throughout her lifetime were complemented only by the punishments that were sent her own way. She had been secretly plotting revenge on her goody-goody sister for well over a year, and couldn't believe her luck when Carmen's star began to dim. The trouble was that, despite Carmen's fall from grace, the love that Maria-Carmen in particular showed towards her was unwavering. Her faith in her eldest daughter was unshakeable. Such blatant favouritism rankled Maria. She had never felt loved by her parents, and only in her misdemeanours did they seem to notice her.

For three long years, Carmen wrestled with her responsibility. The ever-present memories from eight centuries weighed heavily on her shoulders, and the terror that one day she would be confronted and questioned about the events of the night at the mausoleum triggered frequent panic attacks. Whenever the radio or the television mentioned the police investigation into what had happened, she broke out into sweats and made herself scarce. All the time, she felt the pressure increasing, building up and up, until inevitably it detonated.

That happened one day in 1995. The police were following up a new lead about a girl who had been seen running from the mausoleum that night. Carmen had long since begun to dread unexpected visitors, and the deep, assertive rap on the door that morning she remembered as being like the boom of a shotgun. She cowered inside her bedroom at the end of the corridor, while her father opened the door.

'Senor Borrega? Detective Ortiz. We are investigating a murder. May we come in?'

From her discreet vantage point, Carmen could feel panic storming through her body. She wanted to scream, to run. She felt her heart rate rocket. She dared not move, dared not breathe. They had come for her, she knew.

'Of course, come in detective,' said Miguel Borrega. He led the detective and his uniformed companion into the kitchen-diner, where the family entertained all their guests, and where Maria-Carmen was busy preparing lunch, the main meal of the day.

'The police? What has happened? What has Maria

done now?' she shrieked, dropping the carving knife with which she had been shaving jamón.

'It's okay, *Mi Tesoro,*' said Miguel, using his pet name for his wife. 'Let's hear what they have to say. Detective Ortiz?'

'There is no reason for alarm, Señora Borrega. We are making routine enquiries about a murder that took place three years ago. You remember the murder at the mausoleum?'

Carmen could hear every word. For a few brief seconds, the phrase 'routine enquiries' brought total and utter relief, though her dread returned immediately at the mention of that unforgettable night.

'The whole town remembers it, detective. And how exactly can we help?' said Miguel.

'We have a witness who claims to have seen a teenage girl fleeing the scene that night. Unfortunately, the description could apply to half the girls in the city.'

'And?' Maria-Carmen's tone was a little more acerbic than necessary, betraying her irritation at the suggestion one of her girls might have been involved. Even Maria wouldn't have done something so terrible, she thought.

'We are merely making enquiries Señora Borrega.' replied Ortiz forcefully, responding to her irritation in like manner. 'May we speak to your daughter Carmen?'

'Carmen?' laughed Miguel, both amused and relieved. Deep down, a part of him had been concerned that his rogue daughter Maria might have had something to do with it but, now he knew they wanted to talk to Carmen, it was clear there was nothing to worry about. 'Carmen? Of course you can Ortiz, but you're barking up the wrong tree!'

'Carmen!' called Miguel, 'come into the kitchen, *Florecita*. The police would like to ask you some questions. Nothing to worry about.'

In her room, Carmen was frozen with shock. Even if she had wanted to go, she doubted whether her wobbly legs would obey. She was terrified. What on earth was she going to say? In her whole life, she had never lied to anyone, yet there was no way she could tell the truth about that night; they simply would not believe her. With all her courage, and the knowledge that to a very great extent she was a puppet of fate, Carmen determined that she must face the detective. It was no more than thirty paces from her room to the kitchen, yet the distance seemed beyond her.

'I'm coming!' she shouted down the hallway, her voice as shaky in that instant as her legs.

When she entered the kitchen, the two policemen were sitting around the table. The one in uniform was fresh-faced and straight out of school, though Carmen didn't recognise him. Ortiz was older, perhaps thirty, and obviously took pride in his appearance. His short hair was expensively groomed and his designer stubble neatly trimmed. At first glance he seemed warm and friendly. In fact, there was nothing intimidating about him at all, yet unintentionally he terrorised her subconscious.

By this time, her mother seemed to be regaining her composure, at least enough that she was replacing the tea towel on the jamón, in order to keep the flies away. Her father was sitting at the table, opposite the two officers. He patted the seat of the chair next to him, beckoning Carmen to join him.

'It's okay, *Florecita*. The men are just making enquiries. If you know anything at all, you must tell them.' He placed a reassuring arm on her shoulder, and Carmen could swear that she could see it being moved up and down by the pounding of her heart.

'Carmen, I want to ask you some questions,' Ortiz began. 'Do you remember where you were the night of the murders in the mausoleum?'

Here it was. The moment of truth. Whatever she said now, there was no going back. Against her every instinct, and with guilt searing through her words, she lied.

'I remember that night well, Detective Ortiz. Who wouldn't?' she began, surprised by the confidence in her tone, which masked the terror she felt inside. 'I was at home in bed. I woke up to the news on the radio, just like everyone else. What on earth happened?'

'That's what we are trying to find out too, señorita. And your parents can back up your story?'

'Of course,' Maria-Carmen chimed in immediately. 'I said goodnight to Carmen that night, just as I do every night. I remember all of us listening to the terrible news on the radio the next morning.'

'Okay, well thank you all for your time. We will continue our investigation and, if we need to ask anything further, we will be in touch.' Ortiz stood to go, and the scrape of the metal chair leg on the tiled floor sliced through Carmen's fragile state of mind like a roaring chainsaw, making her flinch. Although Ortiz was busy shaking hands with her father and missed it, she caught the quizzical look from the young officer. In that moment, all the fear returned. Her palms began to sweat. Her skin started to tighten. Her heart threatened to burst free.

The next few moments were agonising, as the police made their way out of the apartment. Somehow, Carmen held herself together for long enough to exchange a few pleasantries with her parents, before making a beeline for her room. There, with the warm summer sun streaking through the window and spotlighting her performance, she succumbed to her distress.

When her sobbing subsided, Carmen knew it was time to leave Teruel. While there was no indication that the police knew she had been there that night, there was no guarantee they wouldn't return. And, when they did, who knew what they were going to ask her? It was much safer to leave and take her chances. Besides, now that she was eighteen, Carmen had begun to feel the oppression of her home town and had an overwhelming need to leave her past behind, and more importantly to locate that scorching love she knew was waiting for her somewhere out in the wider world.

She began to plan for her departure and made a list of all the things she would need. The truth was she didn't need much. The more she carried, the more restricted she would be on her journey, and so she was ruthless in the way she discarded items that had previously been important to her. If something had no purpose, it was forever left behind.

Atop the list were a passport and money. The latter was not a problem. Since she was fourteen, Carmen had worked part-time as a waitress at La Taparía del Sur, one of those typical, small tapas bars in town, the ones with no menu that always confused foreign visitors who didn't know they were supposed to ask what was available. The owner, Hernando, appeared to be very generous, though that was mostly to hide the guilt of his attempt to abuse her. The first time his hands had wandered in her direction, Carmen had put him in his place very quickly. Fearing his fondling would be discovered, he had taken to paying her over the odds and, as long as he stayed away from her, she was happy to take his money. Over the years since, she had religiously paid her weekly wages into the bank until they formed a tidy sum.

The passport, or lack of one, held her back temporarily. Carmen's family were not international travellers. They felt there were so many joys to be found in the great country of Spain that they had no need to travel anywhere else. After some research, Carmen discovered it was possible to obtain a passport in three weeks if she paid a premium, and so she set the wheels in motion.

The day it arrived, she was off without hesitation. Her bag had been packed for well over a week and she announced to her family that she was off to travel the world that very afternoon. She had little idea where she was headed, though she knew from the experience of all those who had gone before her that fate would somehow bring her together with the man she was meant to meet.

As Carmen's thoughts returned to the present, she sipped her coffee and recoiled as the now tepid liquid brushed her lips. It was no surprise that her drink had gone cold; these days it was impossible for her to maintain her concentration in the here and now. There were just too many distractions. Even though ten years had passed, and Teruel and her family seemed so distant, the events at the mausoleum still echoed in a weird stereo in her head. The memories from James had mingled with hers and her mind perpetually retold the story from both perspectives.

A sense of anxious excitement returned as she remembered there had been something about the coffee shop that day. She had been drawn—no beckoned—to it. It was odd, because coffee wasn't her drink of choice. Her caffeine fix came from regular doses of Pepsi-Max throughout the day, and coffee shops were an alien environment to her, even though it was hard to avoid them in Melbourne, where they were ubiquitous. All she knew was that she needed to be in this particular one, The League of Honest Coffee, on Little Lonsdale, at the head of one of the many small laneways between Exhibition and Russell Streets. It was crowded, full of early-morning coffee meetings between executives of varying levels of importance.

Carmen watched them, knowing that none of them were meant for her. She knew she was in the right place, but she couldn't feel him, whoever he was. Of course, she knew what he looked like, they all looked the same. He would be the spitting image of James, of Diego. More importantly, the destiny they shared would mean that the room would light up the instant he walked in. She hoped it would be soon. Hers had been a long journey across many continents, and she wanted it to be over.

She had played this moment over in her head many times, and had considered what she would do. It was time to set her plan in motion. Her aim was to lure him in, just like Lauren had lured in James. Then she could share the story with him and talk about their destiny. That was how she would play it. It seemed to have worked well for Lauren.

Her heart leapt every time the door opened, sending bursts of anticipation throughout her body, then it would sink again as she failed to recognise one entrant after another. Then, finally, it happened. Before the door even opened, she knew it was him. She felt his presence, just as she knew she would. A wind of excitement blasted through her body, whipping the soft fluff on her arms into a frenzy. The air was electric and cracked with endless possibilities. Above all, she could feel him, closer and closer, her heart pounding feverishly. And then in he stepped.

He was the vision of everything she had dreamed of. Her very own Diego, his blue-green eyes like the shimmering wall of water at the crest of a wave. The colour of the tide, the ancient tide, at the head of which she roared to shore. It was her time. It was her turn. She felt the world begin to sing with rapturous possibilities. After eight hundred years, there was finally nothing to stand in their way, nothing to keep them apart. It was time for Carmen to seize the moment.

Printed in Australia
AUOC02n0829120417
284721AU00003B/3/P

9 781925 595673